His Heart's Queen

Mrs. Georgie Sheldon

His Heart's Queen

by

Mrs. Georgie Sheldon

HIS HEART'S QUEEN

By

MRS. GEORGIE SHELDON

AUTHOR OF

"Dorothy's Jewels," "Earl Wayne's Nobility," "The False and the True,"
"Helen's Victory," "Tina," "Trixy," etc.

1903

Popular Books
By MRS. GEORGIE SHELDON
In Handsome Cloth Binding

Audrey's RecompenseMagic Cameo, The

Brownie's TriumphMarguerite's Heritage

Churchyard Betrothal, TheMasked Bridal, The

Dorothy Arnold's EscapeMax, A Cradle Mystery

Dorothy's JewelsMona

Earl Wayne's NobilityMysterious Wedding Ring, A

Edrie's LegacyNora

Faithful ShirleyQueen Bess

False and The True, TheRuby's Reward

For Love and HonorShadowed Happiness, A

Sequel to Geoffrey's Victory Sequel to Wild Oats

Forsaken Bride, TheSibyl's Influence

Geoffrey's VictoryStella Roosevelt

Girl in a Thousand, AThorn Among Roses, A

Golden Key, The Sequel to a Girl in a Thousand

Heatherford Fortune, TheThreads Gathered Up

Sequel to The Magic Cameo Sequel to Virgie's Inheritance

He Loves Me For MyselfThrice Wedded

Sequel to the Lily of MordauntTina

Helen's VictoryTrixy

Her Faith RewardedTrue Aristocrat, A

Sequel to Faithful ShirleyTrue Love Endures

Her Heart's Victory Sequel to Dorothy Arnold's Escape

Sequel to MaxTrue Love's Reward

Heritage of Love, A Sequel to Mona

Sequel to The Golden KeyTrue to Herself

His Heart's Queen Sequel to Witch Hazel

Hoiden's Conquest, ATwo Keys

How Will It EndVirgie's Inheritance

Sequel to Marguerite's HeritageWedded By Fate

Lily of Mordaunt, TheWelfleet Mystery, The

Little Marplot, TheWild Oats

Little Miss WhirlwindWinifred's Sacrifice

Lost, A PearleWitch Hazel

Love's ConquestWith Heart so True

Sequel to Helen's Victory Sequel to His Heart's Queen

Love Victorious, A

CONTENTS

CHAPTER I. A FRIGHTFUL ACCIDENT.

CHAPTER II. V. D. H. IS CLAIMED BY HER FRIENDS.

CHAPTER III. WILLFUL VIOLET HAS HER OWN WAY.

CHAPTER IV. A PARTING SOUVENIR.

CHAPTER V. VIOLET ASSERTS HERSELF.

CHAPTER VI. A CONFESSION AND ITS REPLY.

CHAPTER VII. "HE IS MY AFFIANCED HUSBAND."

CHAPTER VIII. "I'LL BREAK HER WILL!"

CHAPTER IX. VIOLET BECOMES A PRISONER.

CHAPTER X. "YOU WILL BE TRUE THOUGH THE OCEAN DIVIDES US."

CHAPTER XI. "DEATH HAS RELEASED YOU FROM YOUR PROMISE."

CHAPTER XII. "YOU HAVE GIVEN YOUR PROMISE AND YOU MUST STAND BY IT."

CHAPTER XIII. THE DAY IS SET FOR VIOLET'S MARRIAGE.

CHAPTER XIV. "THERE WILL BE NO WEDDING TO-DAY"

CHAPTER XV. "SHE IS MY WIFE."

CHAPTER XVI. "I MUST FIND HER—I MUST FOLLOW HER."

CHAPTER XVII .LORD CAMERON AND WALLACE BECOME FIRM FRIENDS.

CHAPTER XVIII. THE FACE AT THE WINDOW.

CHAPTER XIX. A RETROSPECTIVE GLANCE.

CHAPTER XX. VIOLET RETURNS TO AMERICA.

CHAPTER XXI. VIOLET MAKES AN ENGAGEMENT.

CHAPTER XXII. VIOLET AND HER UNRULY PUPIL.

CHAPTER XXIII. VIOLET GAINS A SIGNAL VICTORY.

CHAPTER XXIV. VIOLET MEETS WITH AN ACCIDENT.

CHAPTER I.
A FRIGHTFUL ACCIDENT.

Just at sunset, one bright spring day, the car that plies up and down the inclined plane leading from the foot of Main street up the hills to the Zoological Gardens, of Cincinnati, started to make the ascent with its load of precious human freight.

The car was full of passengers, though not crowded, while among the occupants there were several young people, whose bright faces and animated manner bespoke how light of heart and free from care they were—what a gladsome, delightful place the world seemed to them.

One young lady, who was seated about midway upon one side of the car, attracted especial attention.

She was, perhaps, seventeen years of age, slight and graceful in form, with a lovely, piquant face, merry blue eyes, and a wealth of curling golden hair, that clustered about her white forehead in bewitching little rings.

She was richly dressed in a charming costume of tan-brown, trimmed with a darker shade of the same color. Upon her head she wore a jaunty hat of fine brown straw, with a wreath of pink apple-blossoms partially encircling it, and fastened on one side with a pretty bow of glossy satin ribbon, also of brown. A dainty pair of bronze boots incased her small feet, and her hands were faultlessly gloved in long suede gauntlets. A small, brown velvet bag, with silver clasps, hung at her side, and in her lap lay an elegant music-roll of Russian leather.

Everything about her indicated that she was the petted child of fortune and luxury. Her beautiful eyes were like limpid pools of water reflecting the azure sky; her lips were wreathed with smiles; there was not a shadow of care upon her delicate, clear-cut face.

Directly opposite her sat a young man whose appearance indicated that his circumstances were just the reverse, although no one could ever look into his noble face without feeling impelled to take a second glance at him.

He was tall and stalwart of form, broad-shouldered, full-chested, straight of limb, with a massive head set with a proud poise above a well-shaped neck. He looked the personification of manly beauty, strength, and health.

His face was one that, once seen, could never be forgotten. It was grave and sweet, yet having a certain resolute expression about the mouth which might have marred its expression somewhat had it not been for the mirthful gleam which now and then leaped into his clear, dark-brown eyes, and which betrayed that, beneath the gravity and dignity which a life of care and the burden of poverty had chiseled upon his features and imparted to his bearing, there lurked a spirit of quiet drollery and healthy humor.

His features were strong and regular; the brow full and shapely, the nose aquiline, the mouth firm, the chin somewhat massive. It was a powerful face—a good face; one to be trusted and relied on.

The young man was, perhaps, twenty-three or twenty-four years of age, though at first his dignified bearing might lead one to imagine him to be even older than that.

He was clad in a very common suit, which betrayed his poverty, while at his feet, in a basket, lay a plane and saw, which indicated that he belonged to the carpenters' guild.

The pretty girl opposite stole more than one curious and admiring look at this poor young Apollo, only to encounter a similar, though wholly respectful glance from his genial and expressive eyes, whereupon the lovely color would come and go on her fair, round cheek, and her eyes droop shyly beneath their white lids.

When the car left its station at the base of the plane and began to make its ascent, not one among all its passengers had a thought of the terrible experience awaiting them—of the tragedy following so closely in their wake.

It had nearly reached the top; another minute, and it would have rolled safely into the upper station and have been made fast at the terminus.

But, suddenly, something underneath seemed to let go; there was an instant's pause, which sent a thrill of terror through every heart; then there began a slow retrograde movement, which rapidly increased, until, with a feeling of terror that is utterly indescribable the ill-fated people in that doomed car realized that they were being hurried swiftly toward a sure and frightful destruction.

Cries and shrieks and groans filled the place. There was a frantic rush for the door, the doomed victims seeking to force their way out of the car to leap recklessly from the flying vehicle, and trust thus to the faint hope of saving their lives.

But both doors were securely fastened—they were all locked within their prison; there was no hope of escape from it and the terrible crash awaiting them.

When the beautiful girl whom we have described realized the hopeless situation, she gave one cry of horror, then seemed to grow suddenly and strangely calm, though a pallor like that of death settled over her face, and a look of wild despair leaped into her eyes.

Involuntarily she glanced at the young man opposite her, and she found his gaze riveted upon her with a look of intense yearning, which betrayed that he had no thought for himself; that all his fear was for her; that the idea of seeing her, in all her bright young beauty, dashed in pieces, crushed and mangled, had overpowered all sense of his own personal doom.

She seemed to read his thoughts, and, like one in a dream or nightmare, she almost unconsciously stretched forth her hands to him with a gesture which seemed to appeal to him to save her.

Instantly he arose to his feet, calm, strong, resolute.

His face was as pale as hers, but there was a gleam in his eyes which told her that he would not spare himself in the effort to save her.

"Will you trust me?" he murmured hoarsely in her ear, as he caught her trembling hands in his.

Her fingers closed over his with a frantic clutch; her eyes sought his in desperate appeal.

"Yes! yes!" Her white lips framed the words, but no sound issued from them.

The car had now attained a frightful velocity; a moment or two more and all would be over, and there was not an instant to lose.

The young man reached up and grasped with his strong, sinewy hands the straps which hung from the supports above his head.

"Quick now!" he said to his almost paralyzed companion; "stand up, put your arms about my neck, and cling to me for your life."

She looked helplessly up into his face; it seemed as if she had not the power to move—to obey him.

With a despairing glance from the window and a groan of anguish, he released his hold upon the straps, seized her hands again, and locked them behind his neck.

"Cling! Cling!" he cried, in a voice of agony.

The tone aroused her; strength came to her, and she clasped him close—close as a person drowning might have done.

He straightened himself thus, lifting her several inches from the floor of the car, seized again the straps above, and swung himself also clear, hoping thus to evade somewhat the terrible force of the shock which he knew was so near.

He was not a second too soon; the crash came, and with it one frightful volume of agonizing shrieks and groans; then all was still.

The car had been dashed into thousands of pieces, burying beneath the *debris* twenty human beings.

A group of horrified spectators had gathered in the street at the base of the plane when it was rumored that the car had lost its grip upon the cable, and had watched, with quaking hearts and bated breath, the awful descent.

When all was over, kind and reverent hands began the sad work of exhuming the unfortunate victims of the accident.

It was thought at first that all were dead—that not one had escaped; that every soul had been hurled, with scarcely a moment's warning, into eternity.

The brave young carpenter was found lying beneath two mangled bodies, with the beautiful girl whom he had tried to save clasped close in one of his arms; the other lay crushed beneath him.

"Brother and sister," some one had said, as, bending over them, he had tried to disengage the lovely girl from his embrace.

He had only been stunned, however, by the shock, when the car struck, and he now opened his great brown eyes, drawing in a deep, deep breath, as if thus taking hold anew of the life that had so nearly been dashed out of him.

This was followed by a groan of pain, and he became conscious that he had not escaped altogether unscathed.

"Is she safe?" he gasped, his first thought, in spite of his own sufferings, being for the girl for whom he had braved so much, while he tried to look into the white, still face hidden upon his breast.

They tried to lift her from him, but her little hands were so tightly locked at the back of his neck that it was no easy task to unclasp them.

"She is dead," a voice said, when at last she was removed, and some one tried to ascertain if her heart was still beating; "the shock has killed her."

"No, no!" sobbed the now completely unnerved young carpenter; "do not tell me that she is—dead."

"Who are you, my poor fellow? Where do you live? Shall we take you to the hospital, or do you want to go home?" they asked him.

"Oh, no, not to the hospital—home to my mother," the young man returned, with difficulty, for his sufferings seemed to increase as he came to himself more fully.

"No. —— Hughes street," the poor fellow gasped, and then fainted dead away.

They had not thought to inquire if the young girl was his sister, but they took it for granted that she was, so they laid them side by side and bore them away to Hughes street.

They found, upon inquiry, that the house referred to was occupied by a Mrs. Richardson.

The woman was away when the sad cortege arrived at her home, but a latch-key was found in the pocket of the young man, by which an entrance was effected, and they deposited him upon a bed in a small room leading from the sitting-room, while the young girl was laid upon a lounge in the neat and cozy parlor. Then they hastened away to procure a physician to examine the injuries of the two sufferers.

Mrs. Richardson returned, just about the time that the surgeon arrived, to find that her only son had been one of the victims of the horrible tragedy, a rumor of which had reached her while she was out, and that a strange but lovely girl had also been brought, through mistake, to her home.

The surgeon turned his attention at once to this beautiful stranger, who, to all appearance, seemed beyond all human aid; but during his examination his face suddenly lighted.

"She is not dead," he said; "the shock has only caused suspension of animation. Her heart beats, her pulse is faint, but regular, and I cannot find a bruise or a scratch anywhere about her."

He gave her into the hands of some women, who had come in to offer their services, with directions how to apply the restoratives he prescribed, and then turned his attention to the son of the house, who by this time had recovered consciousness and was suffering intense pain from his injuries.

His mother was bending over him in an agony of anxiety and suspense, while she strove, in various ways, to relieve his sufferings.

"Wallace—Wallace!" she cried; "how did it happen that you were going up in that car at this time of the day?"

"I cannot tell you now—some other time," he returned.

Then turning to the surgeon, who entered at that moment, while he strove to stifle his groans in his anxiety to learn how it fared with the girl whom he had so bravely tried to save, he asked, eagerly.

"How is she?"

"She is not injured; there is not a bone broken that I can discover, and she will do well enough unless the shock to her nerves should throw her into a fever or bring on prostration," the doctor replied.

"Thank Heaven!" murmured the carpenter, and then fainted away again.

A thorough examination of his condition revealed the fact that two ribs had been fractured and his left arm broken in two places, while it was feared that there might be other internal injuries.

All that could be done for him was done at once, and, though weak and exhausted, he was otherwise comparatively comfortable when the surgeon got through with him.

He then turned his attention once more to the fair girl in the other room.

"You will have your hands more than full, Mrs. Richardson, with your son and daughter ill at once," he remarked. "You must have an experienced nurse to assist you."

"The poor girl is not my daughter; I do not even know who she is," the woman replied, as she bent over the beautiful stranger with a tender, motherly face.

"Not your child! Who can she be, then?" her companion inquired, in surprise.

They searched in her pretty velvet bag, hoping to find her card or some address; but nothing was found save some car tickets and a generous sum of money.

The inscription upon her music-roll revealed scarcely more—only the initials "V. D. H." being engraven upon its silver clasp.

She had recovered consciousness, but still lay so weak and faint that the surgeon did not think it best to question her just then, and, after taking one more look at his other patient, he went away to other duties, but promised to look in upon them again in a couple of hours.

When he did return he found Wallace comfortable and sleeping; but the young girl was in a high fever and raving with delirium.

"Shall I have her taken to the hospital?" Doctor Norton asked of Mrs. Richardson. "The care of both patients will be far too much for you, and her friends will probably find her there before long."

"I cannot bear to let her go," Mrs. Richardson replied, with staring tears. "She is so young, and has been so delicately reared. I know that she would have the best of care; still I recoil from the thought of having her moved. Leave her here for a day or two, and, if my son is comfortable, perhaps I can take care of her without neglecting him."

Thus it was arranged, and the physician went away thinking that women like Mrs. Richardson were rare.

Two days later the following advertisement appeared in the Cincinnati papers:

Wanted, information regarding Miss Violet Draper Huntington, who left her home, No. —— Auburn avenue, on Tuesday afternoon, to take a music lesson in the city. Fears have been entertained that she might have been one of the victims of the Main street accident, but though her friends have thoroughly searched the morgue and hospitals, no tidings of her have as yet been obtained.

Doctor Morton read the above while on his way to visit his two patients in Hughes street, and instantly his mind reverted to the initials engraved upon the unknown girl's music-roll.

"V. D. H.," he said, musingly, as his eyes rested upon the name Violet Draper Huntington in the advertisement. "That is my pretty patient, poor child! and now we will have your friends looking after you and relieving that poor overworked woman before another twelve hours pass."

He showed the advertisement to Mrs. Richardson upon his arrival at the house, and she agreed with him that her lovely charge must be the Miss Huntington referred to in the paper.

The girl continued to be in a very critical state. She was burning with fever, was unconscious of her surroundings, was constantly calling upon "Belle" and "Wilhelm" to "help her—to save her."

"She is not so well," the physician said, gravely, as he felt the bounding pulse, "her fever is increasing. I shall go at once to Auburn avenue and inform her relatives of her condition."

CHAPTER II.
V. D. H. IS CLAIMED BY HER FRIENDS.

Doctor Norton easily found the residence of Violet Huntington's friends on Auburn avenue, and as he mounted the massive granite steps and rang the bell of the handsome house he read the name of Mencke on the silver door-plate.

"Aha! Germans," mused the physician, "wealthy people, too, I judge."

A trim servant in white cap and apron answered his summons, and, upon inquiring for Mrs. Mencke, he was invited to enter.

He was ushered into a handsome drawing-room, where, upon every hand, evidence of wealth met his eye, and after giving his card to the girl, he sat down to await the appearance of the lady of the house.

She did not tax his patience long; the "M. D." upon his card had evidently impressed Mrs. Mencke with the belief that the physician had come to bring her some tidings of the beautiful girl who had so strangely disappeared from her home a few days previous. She came into the room presently, followed by a man whom Doctor Norton surmised to be her husband.

Mrs. Mencke was a large, rather fine-looking woman of perhaps thirty years. Her bearing was proud and self-possessed, and, while there was a somewhat anxious expression on her face, she nevertheless impressed the kind-hearted doctor as a person of selfish nature, and lacking in womanly sympathy.

Her husband was a portly man, dark-complexioned, and German in appearance. There was a cunning, rather sinister expression on his face; he had small, black eyes, and a full, shaggy beard, while a pompous swagger in his bearing betrayed an arrogant disposition and excessive pride of purse.

"Doctor Norton," Mrs. Mencke began, without waiting for him to state the errand that had brought him there, "have you come to bring me news of my sister? Was she in that fatal car—is she injured—dead?"

"If my surmises are correct, and Miss Violet Huntington is your sister, I can give you tidings of her," Doctor Norton returned.

"Yes, yes; that is her name," Mrs. Mencke interposed.

"Then I am happy to tell you that a young lady of perhaps seventeen or eighteen years was rescued."

"Rescued!" cried Mrs. Mencke, eagerly. "William," turning to her husband, "do you hear? How was she rescued?"

"Perhaps I should not have spoken with quite so much confidence," corrected the doctor. "But the young lady to whom I refer had with her a music-roll upon the clasp of which the letters 'V. D. H.' were engraved."

"That must have been Violet," said Mrs. Mencke. "She went to the city that afternoon to take her music lesson at four o'clock."

"Then she was saved by a young man—a Mr. Wallace Richardson—in the recent accident on the inclined plane. Mr. Richardson was severely injured, but he has been able to give an account of how he prevented the young lady from being dashed to pieces like many of the other victims," Doctor Norton returned.

He then proceeded to relate what Wallace had told him had occurred during those few horrible moments when that ill-fated car was plunging at such a fearful rate toward its doom.

Mrs. Mencke appeared to be greatly affected by the thrilling account; but her phlegmatic husband listened to the recital with a stolidity which betrayed either a strange indifference or a wonderful control over his nerves and sympathies.

"Oh! it is the most wonderful thing in the world that she was not killed outright," Mrs. Mencke remarked, with a shiver of horror, "and we have been very anxious. You say that she is seriously ill?" she questioned, in conclusion.

"Yes; the shock to her system has been a serious one, madame," the physician replied, "and, although there is not a scratch nor a bruise upon her, she is very ill and delirious at the home of this brave young carpenter to whom she owes so much."

"Young!" repeated Mrs. Mencke, remarking the adjective for the first time, and looking somewhat annoyed. "How old is he?"

"About twenty-three or twenty-four, I should judge," was the reply.

A frown settled upon the woman's brow; but after a moment she asked:

"Do you consider her dangerously ill, Doctor Norton?"

"Yes, madame, she is. Your sister is delicately organized, and her system has had a terrible shock; the horror and fright alone, of those few dreadful moments, were sufficient to unhinge the strongest nerves," the physician gravely replied.

As he said this he happened to glance at Mr. Mencke, and was astonished, amazed, to observe a look of unmistakable satisfaction, if not of absolute triumph, flash from his eyes.

What could it mean?

Was it possible that the man, for any secret reason, could desire the death of this young and beautiful girl?

He had not once spoken as yet, having simply nodded to the doctor, with a half-suppressed grunt, in answer to his courteous salutation.

"William, do you hear?" his wife now said, turning to him. "Violet is dangerously ill down on Hughes street. I must go to her at once."

"Certainly, of course," responded her better half, with a shrug of his corpulent shoulders.

"She is my sister, though much younger than myself, and I have had the care of her ever since the death of our parents," Mrs. Mencke explained. "What can I do? Will it be possible to bring her home?"

"I fear not at present," Doctor Norton returned, "but it would be well to provide a competent nurse for her where she is, as Mrs. Richardson has her hands more than full with the care of both patients and her domestic duties also."

"Certainly, Violet shall have every attention," the woman responded, somewhat haughtily, while the frown deepened upon her brow at the mention of the people upon whose care her sister had been so strangely thrown.

Doctor Norton was inwardly indignant that neither of his listeners should express the slightest gratitude or appreciation for what brave Wallace Richardson had done to save the young girl's life. Evidently they were not pleased that she should owe so great a debt to so plebeian a source.

Mrs. Mencke now arose and excused herself, saying that she would make ready to accompany the physician to Hughes street to attend to her sister's needs.

"That was a horrible affair," Doctor Norton observed to Mr. Mencke, as she left the room, determined to draw out his reticent companion if that were possible.

"It was beastly," grunted the man, with another shrug; "and the corporation will have a pretty sum to pay for damages. Will—do you think the girl—Violet—will die?" and the man leaned eagerly forward, a greedy sparkle in his small, black eyes.

A flush of anger and disgust mounted to the good doctor's brow at this question, and like a flash the man's character was revealed to him.

He saw that he was a shrewd, grasping, money-making man, who measured everything and everybody by dollars and cents; that already, instead of feeling gratitude, he was computing the chances of making something out of the "corporation" in the event of the death of his wife's sister, if, indeed, the girl herself did not possess a fortune which would also fall into his hands should she die.

"I shall do my best to save her, sir; that is, if I am allowed to retain the case—and I see no reason why, with proper care, she should not recover," he forced himself to reply, as courteously as possible.

"Humph!" grunted Mr. Mencke, and then he fell to musing again, doubtless computing the chances upon some other money-making scheme.

Presently Mrs. Mencke returned, dressed to go out and bearing a well-filled satchell in her hands. She had hastily gathered a few articles of comfort for her sister's use.

Doctor Norton and his companion proceeded directly to Hughes street, where Mrs. Richardson welcomed Mrs. Mencke with motherly kindness and interest, and then conducted her at once to the bedside of the unconscious Violet, who was still calling piteously upon Belle and Wilhelm to save her.

"Belle is here, Violet," said her sister, bending over the sufferer; "you are safe, and nothing can hurt you now."

At the sound of her familiar voice the sick girl glanced up at her, and a flash of recognition and consciousness returned for a moment.

"Oh, Belle!" she cried, with a sigh of relief, as she seemed to realize for the first time that she was safe. "It was so horrible—horrible! But he was so brave—a hero, and so handsome——"

"Hush, dear; you must not talk about it," interrupted the proud woman, her brow contracting instantly at this mention of the young carpenter, while she glanced about the humble though pretty room with an air of disdain that brought the sensitive color into Mrs. Richardson's cheeks, and made the physician glare angrily at her for her rudeness.

"Will you remove your hat and wrap, Mrs. Mencke? You will probably like to remain with your sister for a while," her hostess remarked, with a lady-like courtesy which betrayed that, whatever her present circumstances might be, she had at some time moved in cultured society.

"Yes, I shall remain until a suitable nurse can be obtained," the woman said, coldly, as she gave her hat and mantle into her hands.

Then she turned to Doctor Norton and remarked:

"Doubtless you know of some one who would be competent to take charge of Miss Huntington?"

"Yes, I know of just the person—she is a trained hospital nurse; but her compensation is fifteen dollars a week besides her living," Doctor Norton responded.

"I do not care what her compensation is," replied Mrs. Mencke, with a slightly curling lip; "I wish Violet to have the best of care. Are you sure it will not do to have her taken home?" she concluded, with an anxious glance toward the room, where she had caught a glimpse of the other patient as she entered.

"Very sure, madame," returned the physician, decidedly. "I would not be answerable for the consequences if she were removed. With an efficient nurse, the young lady can be made very comfortable here. Mrs. Richardson has kindly resigned this room—the best she had—for her use. It is cool and airy, and you do not need to have any anxiety about her on the score of her accommodations. If you insist upon removing her, however, it must be upon your own responsibility."

Mrs. Mencke thought a moment, then she said:

"Very well; it shall be as you advise, and I will come every day to spend as much time as possible with her. Mrs. Richardson shall be well paid, too, for her room and all inconvenience."

Mrs. Richardson's delicate face flushed again at this coarse reference to their obligation to her. There had not been one word of thanks or appreciation for what she had already done; it seemed as if the haughty woman considered that her money would cancel everything.

"The dear child is welcome to the room and any other comfort that I can give her," she said, quietly; then added: "It is time now for her fever drops."

She leaned over the sufferer, who had again relapsed into her delirious state, and gently put the spoon to her lips.

Violet unclosed her eyes and looked up into the kind, motherly face, hesitated a moment, then swallowed the drops, while she murmured, as her glance lingered on her countenance:

"You are good—I love you," then, with a sigh, she turned her head upon the pillow and dropped into a sleep, while her companions stole from the room to complete their arrangements for her future comfort.

"Your son—how is he?" Mrs. Mencke inquired, as they entered the sitting-room, and she felt that it devolved upon her to make the inquiry.

"Better, thank you. He has not so much pain, and Doctor Norton thinks his bones are going to knit nicely. He suffers more from his bruises and cuts than from the broken bones. I am very thankful that he has escaped with his life," Mrs. Richardson answered, tremulously, and with startling tears.

"Was he badly hurt?" inquired the lady, languidly.

"Well, he has a couple of protuberances upon his head, three serious bruises on one leg, and a deep cut on the other from broken window-glass. Our young hero—and he is a hero, Mrs. Mencke—is pretty well battered up; but, please God, we are going to save him, and he'll come out as good as new in time." Doctor Norton returned, with an energy that made Mrs. Richardson smile, though with tremulous lips.

"It was a frightful accident," murmured Mrs. Mencke, with a slight shiver.

"You may well say that, madame; and it was a happy inspiration on the part of Mr. Richardson to try to save Miss Huntington in the way that he did. By suspending himself from the straps and make her cling to him he broke the force of the crash for both of them; and, if she lives, there is not the slightest doubt in the world that she will owe her life to his thoughtfulness," said the worthy doctor.

"I am sure it was very good of him, and—we are very grateful to him," was the tardy admission of Violet's proud sister; but it lacked the ring of sincerity, and her patronizing manner plainly indicated that her pride rebelled against all feeling of obligation to an humble carpenter.

"You certainly have reason to be," Doctor Norton retorted; then, bowing coldly to her, he went into the small bedroom leading from the sitting-room, to see how his hero fared.

"How is she now, doctor?" Wallace eagerly asked, the moment he crossed the threshold.

It was always his first thought and inquiry whenever the physician made his appearance, and he would never allow him to pay the slightest attention to himself until he had first made an examination of Violet's condition.

"Pretty sick, my boy; but I hope she is going to pull through," he cheerfully replied.

"Thank heaven!" murmured the young man, fervently.

Doctor Norton observed him keenly for a moment, with a kindly yet somewhat anxious gleam in his eyes; then he said:

"Look here, my fine fellow, let me give you a little timely warning; don't you go to falling in love with this pretty Violet—you'll only make mischief for both yourself and her if you do, for her friends are rich, and proud as Lucifer—as hard-hearted, too, if I am not mistaken—and nothing but a fortune will ever tempt them to yield her to the best lover in the world."

The young man flushed a vivid crimson at this blunt speech, and the physician, noticing it, continued:

"No doubt you think I'm meddling with what is none of my business, but I've seen enough to-day to convince me that such a romantic result of this accident would be the worst thing that could possibly happen to you. But how do you find yourself to-day?" he concluded, abruptly changing the subject.

"I have some pain in this right leg, but not enough to fret over," Wallace replied, turning his now pale face away from the doctor's keen eyes.

There had suddenly come a sharper pain in his heart than any physical suffering that he had as yet endured, as, all at once, he became conscious that he had already been guilty of doing exactly what the good surgeon had warned him against.

Already he had begun to love Violet Huntington with all the strength and passion of his manly, honest heart. He had been instantly attracted by her lovely face and lady-like appearance, when he entered the car that bright spring afternoon. When his glance met hers a magnetic current had seemed to be established between them. When she had realized the horror of their situation, after the grip upon the cable had been lost, and thrown out her hands so appealingly to him, his heart had been suddenly thrilled with the desire to save her, even at the expense of his own life; in that one brief instant he had given himself to her, for life or death. When he had clasped her hands about his neck and lifted her upon his breast—when he had felt her head droop upon his shoulder, and the beating of her frightened heart against his own, a feeling almost of ecstasy had taken possession of him, and the strange thought had come to him that he was perhaps going into eternity with the woman who should have been his wife—with the one kindred soul designed for him by his Maker.

But now the doctor's words had given him a rude shock, and he resolved, rather than allow a suspicion of his affection to make trouble for the sweet girl who had become the one coveted object of his life, to bury it so deep in his heart that no other should ever mistrust it.

CHAPTER III.
WILLFUL VIOLET HAS HER OWN WAY.

That same evening a thoroughly competent nurse was installed by Violet's bedside, and Mrs. Mencke, having given certain directions regarding the care of her sister, returned to her home on Auburn avenue.

She came every day afterward, however, to ascertain how Violet was progressing, and though for a week her fever ran very high, and the doctor considered her alarmingly ill, yet at the end of that time she began slowly but surely to mend.

Consciousness returned, and with it the memory of all that had occurred on that never-to-be-forgotten day, while she talked continually of the brave young man who had saved her life.

When she was first told that she was in the same house with him, the rich color suffused her face, and an eager look of interest leaped into her eyes.

"In his home—am I? How strange!" she murmured; "how did it happen that I was brought here?"

"Those who found you thought that you were brother and sister," the nurse told her, thinking it no harm that she should know all the details, if she did not get excited. "They found you together, one of his arms clasping you close to him, and both your hands locked about his neck."

A burning blush shot up to the girl's golden hair at this information.

"He told me to—to cling to him," she said, in a low tone.

"Of course; and it showed his good sense, too, for it was the only thing that saved your life, dear child," replied the nurse; "and it seemed as if he had not one thought for himself, then nor since, for his first question, when the doctor goes to him, is about you."

"How good—how noble of him! and he is so badly hurt, too," Violet said, tremulously.

"Oh, but he is coming out of it finely," the nurse said, reassuringly. "There isn't a scratch on his face, and his broken bones are mending nicely. He is already up and about, though he looks rather peaked, as if he were still a good deal shaken up over the dreadful tragedy—for I suppose you know that you and he are the only ones who came out of it alive."

"Oh! was every one else killed?" said Violet, with a shiver of horror. "How dreadful!"

She lay there, very quiet and thoughtful, for some time after that, but by and by she asked:

"Nurse, when may I get up?"

"In a few days, dear, if you continue to improve as you have done during the last week," the woman replied.

"Then may I see him—Mr. Richardson? I must see him and thank him for what he has done. Just think—he saved me from getting even a scratch or a bruise."

"Um!" returned the nurse, pursing up her lips; "your sister, Mrs. Mencke, has given orders that you are not to receive any visitors while you are here?"

"Well, of course, and I do not care to see company much until I go home; but you must let me see Mr. Richardson," Violet said, with some show of spirit.

"Well, maybe Mrs. Mencke wouldn't object; you can ask her when she comes," said the nurse, doubtfully.

"I shall do no such thing, and I am going to see Mr. Richardson!" retorted Violet, wilfully, and flushing hotly. "The idea of her objecting, when he saved my life, and when dear Mrs. Richardson has been so kind! They would think me very ungrateful not to tell them how very, very thankful I am."

"But Mrs. Mencke said——" began the nurse, objectingly, for Violet's sister had given very strict orders upon this very point.

"I don't care what Belle said—Belle is too fresh sometimes!" Violet cried, spiritedly, and relapsing a trifle into slang, in her irritation over her sister's interference.

The nurse changed the subject, and nothing more was said about the matter.

Three days later Violet was allowed to get up for the first time, and after that she sat up every day.

One morning she seemed to feel much stronger than usual, and the nurse allowed her to be regularly dressed in a pretty pale-blue cashmere wrapper, which Mrs. Mencke had sent the previous day; then she drew her chair beside one of the windows, where she could look out upon the street.

She seemed very bright, and told the woman that she began to feel quite like herself again. She certainly looked very pretty, though somewhat pale and thin, showing that she had lost a little flesh during her illness.

"Now, nurse," Violet said, when the woman had tidied up the room, and there seemed to be nothing more to be done just then, "don't you want to go out and get the air for a little while? You have not been out once since you came, and I am so well and comfortable to-day, you might go just as well as not."

"Thank you, miss; it would be a pleasant change," the woman returned, with a longing look out of the window.

"Then go, by all means, Mrs. Dean," Violet said, eagerly, "and stay an hour if you like. I know Mrs. Richardson would wait upon me if I should need anything, which I am sure I shall not," she concluded, with a furtive glance toward the sitting-room, where, during the last half-hour, she had heard, now and then, the rattle of a newspaper, and surmised that her young hero was engaged in perusing the morning news there.

The temptation proved too strong to be resisted, and Mrs. Dean, taking Violet at her word, yielded, and soon after went forth into the glorious sunshine, to enjoy the privilege so kindly given.

Violet sat and watched her until she was well down the street, a queer little smile on her pretty lips; but her attention was presently attracted by the entrance of Mrs. Richardson, who came to see if she wanted anything, and to bring her a little silver bell, to ring in case she should need her.

"How well you are looking to-day, dear," she said, as she noticed her bright eyes and the faint flush which was just beginning to tinge her cheek, "I am really surprised at your rapid improvement during the last few days."

"I feel almost well. I believe I could do an hour's practice if there was only a piano here," Violet answered, as she glanced wistfully at her music-roll, which lay on the table near her.

"I am sorry that we have none," Mrs. Richardson replied, "but perhaps it is just as well, after all, for the effort might be too much for your strength. Can I do anything for you?"

"Thank you, no," Violet answered, with an appreciative smile.

"Then I am going down into the laundry for a while, but I will leave this bell with you; if you need me, ring, and I will come instantly."

"You are very good," the young girl said, then, with a rising flush and downcast eyes, she asked: "How is Mr. Richardson this morning?"

"Doing finely, dear, thank you, only he gets a trifle impatient, now and then, because his arm is useless, and he cannot go back to work."

"It must be very tedious for him, and I am very sorry," Violet said, with a regretful sigh. Then with a timid, appealing glance: "May I not see him, Mrs. Richardson, and tell him how I appreciate his heroism and the service he rendered me?"

Mrs. Richardson colored at this request, for she had overheard Mrs. Mencke telling the nurse to be sure and not allow any one to see Violet, save those who had the care of her, and she well understood what that injunction meant; consequently her pride and sense of what was right would not allow her to take advantage of the nurse's absence to bring about a meeting between the young people. So she replied, with quiet gravity:

"I would not like to assume the responsibility of granting your request to-day, dear; we must not tax your strength too much at first; some other time, perhaps."

She put the bell where Violet could reach it, telling her to be sure to ring if she needed anything, then she went out, leaving the door slightly ajar.

As she disappeared Violet nodded her sunny head mischievously, and shot a wicked little smile after her.

"You are the dearest darling in the world," she murmured, "and I know you are resolved not to be guilty of doing anything to offend my proud sister. You will not 'assume the responsibility,' but I will. Mrs. Belle just isn't going to have her way, all the same, and I am going to have mine if I can manage it. I wonder if I could walk into the other room."

She glanced toward the door and seemed to be measuring the distance with her eye.

"I am going to try it anyway," said this willful little lady, as she deliberately slipped out of her chair and stood upon her feet.

She found herself still very weak, and for a moment it seemed as if her trembling limbs would not support her, but the determination to outwit her haughty sister had taken possession of her, and she was bound to accomplish her purpose.

She managed to get to a common cane-seat chair, and pushing this before her as a support, sitting down once or twice to rest, she at length reached the door leading into the other room.

Wallace Richardson was sitting by a window, his back toward the parlor where Violet had been ill. He had been reading the morning paper, but it had dropped upon his knees and he had fallen into a fit of musing, his thoughts turning, as they did involuntarily, to that fearful ride down the inclined plane, while he always saw in imagination that wild look of appeal upon the lovely face of Violet Huntington, as she instinctively turned to him for help.

Suddenly he was startled by a slight movement near him, and, glancing up, he beheld the object of his thoughts standing in the door-way just behind him.

"Miss Huntington!" he cried, starting to his feet in amazement and consternation, "I am afraid you are very imprudent. Do you want something? Can I do anything for you?"

"Yes, if you will please help me to that chair I will be much obliged; I am not quite so strong as I thought I was, and find myself a little tired," Violet replied, looking very pale after her unusual exertion.

"I should think so, indeed! Here, take this chair," said Wallace as he gently helped her, with his well hand, to the chair that he had just vacated.

"Thank you," Violet said, as she sank panting into it; then, glancing up at him with a roguish smile, she continued: "Don't look so shocked, Mr. Richardson; I suppose I am a trifle pale, but I am not going to faint, as I see you fear. I was lonely in there by myself and imagined that you were also, so I took a sudden notion that I would pay you a little visit. I—I thought it was about time that we made each other's acquaintance and compared notes upon our injuries."

Wallace thought that he had never seen any one so pretty as she was at that moment. Her golden hair had been carelessly knotted at the back of her head, while a few short locks lay in charming confusion upon her white forehead. Her delicate blue wrapper, with its filmy lace ruffles at the neck and waists, was exceedingly becoming, while the laughing, roguish light in her lovely azure eyes thrilled him with a strange sensation. Then, too, the thought that she had made all this exertion just for the purpose of seeing him made his heart leap with delight.

"I had no idea that you were able to make such an effort," he managed to say in reply, though he could never remember afterward what answer he did make.

Her strength and color were coming back now that she was seated, and she laughed out mischievously.

"It was an experiment," she said, "perhaps a hazardous one, and I must make my visit and get back before nurse returns, or I fear I shall get a vigorous scolding; but I just had to come to see you—I couldn't wait any longer. When I think of how much I owe you, it seems perfectly heartless that I have not told you how thankful I am for the life that you have saved; but for you I might have shared the fate of the others," and tears were in the beautiful eyes uplifted to his face.

"Do not think of it, Miss Huntington," Wallace said, growing pale as his own thoughts went back to those moments of horror.

"Why not?" she cried, impulsively. "Why should I not think of it and speak of it, too, when I see this poor arm"—and she touched it almost reverently with her dainty fingers—"when I realize how thoughtless of self you were in trying to save me? Ah! and that poor hand, too," she added, as she caught sight of his right hand, which had been badly cut by broken glass, and on which she saw a broad strip of court-plaster, "how much you have suffered!"

And carried away by her feelings, forgetful of all but the gratitude that filled her warm, young heart, she suddenly bent forward and impulsively touched her lips to the wounded hand that hung by his side.

Wallace caught his breath. That touch was like electricity to him, and the rich color surged up to his brow.

"Miss Huntington, don't!" he cried; "you overestimate what I did."

"No, indeed I do not," Violet returned, earnestly, and then, overcome by the sudden realization of what she had done—that he was almost a stranger and she had been guilty of a rash and perhaps unmaidenly act—a burning blush leaped to the roots of her hair, and for the moment she was speechless from shame and embarrassment.

"Pardon me," she said, after an awkward silence. "I forgot myself—I forgot everything but that I owe you my life."

Then tossing back her head and shooting a half appealing, half defiant look at him, to cover her confusion, she said, with a bewitching little pout:

"But now that I have come to call upon you, Mr. Richardson, aren't you going to entertain me?"

The change from embarrassment to this pretty piquancy was so instantaneous and so charming that Wallace's face grew luminous with admiration and delight. A smile wreathed his lips, and there came a look into his eyes that made her flush consciously again.

"Certainly; I shall only be too happy. What can I do to amuse you? Shall I read to you?"

Violet shrugged her shoulders.

"No, talk to me," she said, with pretty imperiousness. "I have been shut up so long that I am pining for entertaining society."

Wallace flushed at this. He was not used to talking to fine young ladies; he had been very little in society, and had met but very few people in fashionable life. His days were occupied by work, for he had to support himself and his mother, while his evenings were devoted to study.

But he really desired to amuse his lovely visitor, and so, going to a book-case, he took down a large, square book and brought it to her.

"Have you ever seen any agricultural drawings, Miss Huntington?" he inquired.

"No," Violet said.

"Do you think it would interest you to examine some?"

"Oh, yes," she answered, eagerly.

She would have been interested in anything which he chose to talk about.

"I am glad of that," he returned, "for architecture is to be the business of my life, and I can talk more fluently upon that subject that upon any other."

Then he opened the book and began to show her his drawings.

"Since a little boy I have desired to be an architect," he told her, "and while my father lived I had every advantage which I chose to improve; but after his death misfortune obliged me to give up school and to go to work. I chose the carpenter's trade—my father was a contractor and builder—for I reasoned that a practical knowledge of the construction of buildings would help me in the profession which I hope, even yet, to perfect myself in. All my evenings during the past four years have been spent in the drawing-school, and where, during the last two years I have, a portion of each night, served as a teacher."

He pointed out to Violet several of his own designs, all of which, she could readily see, were very fine, and some exceedingly beautiful.

While discussing some point, Violet casually compared it with something that she had seen in ancient structures abroad, and this led them to enlarge upon the architecture of the old country, until they grew very free and friendly in their conversation.

Neither was aware how rapidly time was passing, until the clock struck the hour of eleven; then, with a sudden start, the young girl exclaimed that she must get back to her own room at once, or run the risk of being scolded should the nurse find her there.

"I can get back to my chair much more quickly, Mr. Richardson, if you will help me," she said, with an arch look, as she arose from her seat by the window; and Wallace, with another thrill of delight, gave her his well arm and assisted her to cross the room, a feat which she accomplished much more easily than before.

When he had seated her comfortably, she gave him a roughish glance, and remarked, playfully:

"I suppose it is polite for people to return calls, isn't it, Mr. Richardson?"

He laughed out heartily, and thought her the most bewitching little piece of humanity he had ever seen.

"I suppose it is," he answered; then growing grave, he added, "but I understand that your sister does not think it advisable for you to have visitors."

"Nonsense!" began Violet, impatiently, then espying the nurse just mounting the steps, she continued, "but there is Mrs. Dean. I will discuss the calling question with you some other time. Good-by."

Wallace took the hint implied in this farewell, returned to the sitting-room, where he was apparently deeply absorbed in the contents of his paper when the refreshed and smiling nurse entered.

CHAPTER IV.
A PARTING SOUVENIR.

A week went by, and both patients continued to improve, but the weather being unfavorable—a cold wind prevailing—the physician would not consent to have Violet removed to Auburn avenue until it was milder.

Every pleasant morning, however, Violet insisted upon having the nurse go out for an airing, telling her to remain as long as she liked, and just as often the young girl succeeded in securing an interview with Wallace.

She saw that both he and Mrs. Richardson were averse to his returning her call, and she did not urge it; but in her pretty, imperious way she insisted that he must help her out into the sitting-room or she should get "awfully homesick" staying in the parlor all the time.

They could not well refuse her request, and every morning as soon as the nurse disappeared she went out to them.

Sometimes Mrs. Richardson would remain and join in their conversation, but this could not always be, for her household duties must be attended to, and so they were often left by themselves.

Occasionally Wallace read to her from the daily paper, or from some interesting book; but more frequently they spent the time conversing, growing every day more friendly, and falling more and more under the spell of each other's society.

Wallace realized his danger—knew that every hour spent in the fair girl's presence was serving to make him more wholly her slave.

That first meeting, when she had come upon him so unexpectedly, had assured him that he could not see her often without riveting the chains of his love more hopelessly about him. Her exquisite beauty, her artless, impulsive manner, the glance of her beautiful eyes, all moved him as he had never been moved before, and warned him that danger to both lay in indulging himself in the delight of her society.

Danger! Yes, for he well knew that he—a poor carpenter who had to toil with his hands for his daily bread—ought never to speak words of love to the delicate girl who had been reared amid the luxuries of wealth; knew that her haughty relatives would scorn such an alliance with one in his humble circumstances.

But he seemed powerless to prevent it—powerless to save either himself or her; for Violet, all unconscious of the precipice toward which they were drifting, thinking only of the enjoyment of the moment, persisted in seeing him, day after day, and thus, before she was aware of the fact, becoming entangled in coils from which she was never to escape.

Mrs. Mencke came every afternoon, but never remained long, for she was a woman of many social obligations, and thought if she simply came to inquire regarding Violet's welfare, she was doing her whole duty by her.

She always found her alone with the nurse, or with Mrs. Richardson, if the former was busy, and fondly imagined that everything was all right; never suspecting the mischief—as she would be likely to regard it—that was being brewed by that artful little god of love—Cupid.

Doctor Norton finally gave his consent to having Violet removed, and on the same day, when Mrs. Mencke paid her usual visit, she was told that to-morrow she would be taken home.

The young girl received this unwelcome news in silence, but a great darkness seemed suddenly to have fallen around her.

After her sister's departure she turned to Mrs. Richardson, and the woman saw that her eyes were full of tears.

"Dear Mrs. Richardson," she said, "I am so sorry to leave you! I have been so happy here—it is such a quiet, peaceful place, and you have been so kind to me, I really feel homesick at the thought of going home—and that sounds like a paradox, doesn't it?"

Mrs. Richardson smiled fondly into the fair face lifted to hers, though an expression of pain flitted over her brow at the same time.

"I shall be just as sorry to give you up as you can be to go," she replied. "You have been a very patient invalid, and it has been simply a pleasure to have you here. Still, your home is so delightful, and you have so many kind friends, you will soon forget your quiet sojourn on Hughes street."

"No, indeed—never!" Violet returned, flushing. Then she added, impulsively, while a great longing seemed to sweep over her: "I know that my home is beautiful with everything that money can buy, but—there is no soul in it."

"My dear child! I am sure you do not mean that," said Mrs. Richardson, reprovingly. "That is a very sad thing to say about one's own home."

"Yes, I do mean it," Violet answered, with quivering lips. "Belle is good enough in certain ways, and I suppose she is fond of me, after a fashion; but she is a society woman, and always full of engagements, while Wilhelm cares for nothing but his horses and his business. I wish I had a mother," and a pathetic little sob concluded the sentence.

During the weeks of her illness, the young girl had found a long-felt void filled by the care and tenderness of this motherly woman.

Mrs. Richardson laid her hand caressingly upon the golden head, and her heart yearned over the fair invalid. She also had longed for a loving daughter, to brighten and soothe her declining years, even as Violet longed for a mother.

Violet reached up and clasped the tender hand, and brought it round to her lips. She was naturally an affectionate little thing, and much given to acting upon the impulse of the moment.

"I shall always love you, dear Mrs. Richardson, and you will let me come to see you, will you not?" she asked, appealingly.

"Certainly, dear. I shall be very glad to see you at any time," she answered, heartily, and deeply touched by the young girl's evident affection for her; but she changed the subject, and began to chat entertainingly upon other topics, for she saw that she was really depressed by the thought of going back to her "soulless" home.

The next morning an elegant carriage, drawn by a pair of coal-black horses in silver-mounted harness, drove to the humble home of the Richardsons in Hughes street, and the colored driver presented a note from Mrs. Mencke, saying that Violet was to return home at once; that she had an important engagement and could not come for her herself, but wished that the nurse should attend her instead.

Violet was very pale and quiet as they dressed her for the drive, while her heavy eyes often turned to the door leading into the sitting-room with a wistful, regretful glance.

"I shall miss you so much, Mrs. Richardson. You will come to see me, will you not?" she said, as she put up her lips for her good-by kiss.

"Yes, I will come within a few days. I shall want to know how you are getting on. There, you are all ready now, I believe," she concluded, as she folded a light shawl about her shoulders, for though the day was warm, they wished to guard against all danger of her taking cold.

But Violet stood irresolute a moment, then she said:

"I want—may I go to say good-by to all—to Mr. Richardson?" and a burning flush mounted to her brow as she made the request.

Mrs. Richardson looked grave as she remarked the blush, but she gave the desired permission; and while she went to assist the nurse to put Violet's things in the carriage, the young girl moved slowly toward the sitting-room, where she found Wallace, looking pale and depressed, his fine lips drawn into a firm, white line.

"I have come to say good-by," Violet remarked, as she approached him with downcast eyes. "I—I hope you will soon be quite well again; but, oh! Mr. Richardson, if I could only do something to show you how— —"

"Please, Miss Huntington, never refer to the accident in that way again," Wallace returned, speaking almost coldly, because of the restraint he was imposing upon himself.

He had not realized until that morning how very desolate he should feel when Violet was gone, for she might as well be going out of the world altogether, as far as he was concerned, he thought, as back to Auburn avenue.

How could he let her go—resign her to another sphere, as it were, for some favorite of fortune to win? He was suffering torture, and it seemed almost impossible for him to bid her a formal good-by.

Violet lifted a pained, startled look to his face at his cold, reserved tone.

"Forgive me. I did not mean to offend you," she said; "but you must understand something of how I feel. I know that you have saved my life. I shall never forget it as long as I live, and you must let me unburden my heart in some way. At least, I may give you a little keepsake, if nothing more," she pleaded, earnestly.

He smiled into her upturned face. She was so fair, so eager, he had not the heart to repulse her.

"Yes, I should be very glad of some souvenir—you are very good to think of it," he said, with a thrill in his tones which brought the color back to her pale cheeks.

"Thank you for conceding even that much," she returned, brightening; "and now I wonder what it shall be."

"The simplest thing you can think of," Wallace said, hastily; "something that you have worn would be most precious——"

He cut himself short, for he felt that he was betraying too much of what was in his heart.

Violet flashed a sly look at him, and her pulses leaped at his words, and the glance that accompanied them.

"Something that I have worn," she murmured, musingly.

She glanced at her hands, where, upon her white fingers, gleamed several valuable rings, but she instinctively felt that none of these would be a suitable offering.

He certainly would not care for a bracelet—he would not accept her watch.

Then suddenly one dainty hand went up to her throat, where her collar was fastened with a beautiful brooch to which there was attached a pendant as unique as it was lovely.

"Will you have this?" she asked, touching it. "Mamma gave it to me one birthday—you shall have the pendant to wear on your chain, and I will keep the brooch always."

She unfastened the ornament and held it out to him.

The pendant was a small golden medallion with richly enameled pansy, a tiny diamond in its centre, on one side, while upon the other was engraved the name "Violet."

Wallace flushed with pleasure; he could have thought of nothing that would afford him so much gratification. Still he hesitated to take it.

"I do not like to rob you of your mother's gift," he said, gently.

"Please take it; I want you to have it—that is, if you would like it," Violet said, eagerly, and looking so lovely in her earnestness that he longed to take her in his arms and claim her for his own, then and there.

"You are sure you will not regret it?" he asked.

"No—no, indeed; and you can easily detach it, for it is only fastened by this slender ring."

"I think you will have to do that for me," he returned, smiling, and glancing down at his bandaged arm, "for I have only one hand at my disposal."

"True; how thoughtless I am," Violet answered, flushing, and, taking a pair of scissors that lay upon the table, she easily pried the ring apart, detached the pendant and laid it in his hand.

"Thank you," Wallace said, but he was very pale as his fingers closed over the precious gift, and he felt that fate was very cruel to force him to keep silent when his heart was so full of a deathless love. "It is a beautiful little souvenir, and I shall prize it more than I can tell you, Miss Huntington."

Violet tapped her foot impatiently upon the floor and frowned.

"Miss Huntington," she repeated, sarcastically; "how formal! Call me Violet—I do not like to be held at arm's length by my friends. But Mrs. Dean is calling me, and I suppose I must go. I have been very happy here in your home in spite of my illness; I have learned to love your mother dearly, and she has promised to come to see me; will you come with her?"

How sweet and gracious she was! how she tempted him with her beauty and her artless, impulsive ways, and it required all his moral strength to resist her and preserve the secret of his love.

"I am afraid I cannot," he replied.

"Why not?" Violet questioned, in a surprised, hurt tone.

"You forget that I am but a laborer—I have little time for social pleasures."

"But you cannot work now—it will be several weeks yet before your arm will be strong enough to allow you to go back to your duties," Violet returned, searching his face intently.

Wallace flushed hotly; he knew that was a lame excuse to give her; he knew, too, that he must not put himself in the way of temptation; and, believing a straightforward course the wisest, he frankly said:

"Miss—Violet," faltering a little over the name, but not wishing to wound her again by the more formal mode of address, "I do not need to tell you, I am sure, how much pleasure it would give me to meet you now and then, but you well know that poor young men, like myself, are not often welcome in the home of the rich; indeed, I should feel myself out of place among the fashionable people with whom you mingle."

"You need not!" Violet exclaimed, earnestly. "I should feel proud to introduce you to any, or all, of my friends, and I promise that you shall receive a most cordial welcome in my home if you ever honor me by entering it. Now, good-by, Wal—Mr. Richardson, for I must go."

She held out her hand to him, and he took it in a strong, fond clasp—the first time he had ever held it thus, and the last, he told himself—with almost a feeling of despair, for he believed that henceforth they would go their separate ways and have nothing in common.

He accompanied her out and helped her into the carriage, but with a keen pain in his heart, as he saw two diamond-like drops fall upon the velvet cushions as she took her seat, and knew that they were tears of regret over this parting.

The nurse followed her charge, the coachman sprang upon his box, and with one wave of a white hand, one lingering look from a pair of azure eyes, Violet was gone, and that humble home in Hughes street seemed, to one person at least, like a house in which there had been a death, and from which peace and contentment had forever flown.

There was no one but the servants to welcome Violet home, for Mrs. Mencke had not returned, and the poor girl felt forlorn and desolate enough.

After bidding the nurse good-by, for the woman had only been commissioned to see her safely home, she went wearily up to her own room, where, after removing her wraps and dismissing her maid, she threw herself upon her bed in a passion of tears, and longing for the caressing touch of Mrs. Richardson's tender hand and the sound of her affectionate, motherly voice.

When Mrs. Mencke finally returned and went to her she found her sleeping, but looking feverish, the tears still upon her cheeks, and with a mournful droop to her sweet lips that was really pathetic.

She awoke with a start and found herself gazing up into the handsome face of her sister.

"Well, Violet, I suppose you are glad to be at home again," Mrs. Mencke remarked, cheerfully, but regarding her searchingly.

Violet gave utterance to a deep sigh, but hesitated before replying.

"It is very comfortable here," she at last said, glancing around the luxurious apartment.

"I should think so, indeed, after the close quarters you have inhabited of late," said Mrs. Mencke, with a contemptuous laugh. "Why, the servants' rooms here are better than any portion of that house."

"Ye-s, but it was very quiet and peaceful and home-like there, and everything was very neat and clean," said Violet, with another sigh.

"Well, everything is neat and clean here also, isn't it?" demanded her sister, sharply, for cleanliness was one of her especial hobbies.

"Of course; but where have you been, Belle?" Violet asked, anxious to change the subject, and glancing over her sister's richly clad figure.

"Oh, to a grand luncheon given by the Lincoln Club," Mrs. Mencke replied, all animation; "and if you had only been well I certainly should have taken you; I don't know when I have attended so brilliant an affair. But, never mind, you will come out next season, and then we will have plenty of amusement."

Violet did not appear to share her sister's eager anticipation of this event and Mrs. Mencke was secretly much irritated by her languid indifference.

"I sincerely hope that beggarly carpenter hasn't had an opportunity to put any nonsense in her head," she mused. "What a piece of luck!—that she happened to be in that car that day. Of course, the fact that he saved her life has cast a glamour of romance around him—Violet is very impressionable—and it may take time to disenchant her. I hope that nurse was vigilant and did not allow her to see much of him; however, one thing is sure, she won't get a chance to see him henceforth."

Mrs. Mencke was very confident of her ability to put an end to the acquaintance, but she had yet to learn that there were certain events in life which she was powerless to control.

CHAPTER V.
VIOLET ASSERTS HERSELF.

Mrs. Richardson never paid Violet her promised visit, for Mrs. Mencke realized almost immediately that something was very wrong about her young sister, who appeared strangely listless and unhappy, and she often found her in tears.

"This will never do," the worldly woman said, with an energy and decision that governed all her movements. "I'm not going to have Violet moping about like a silly, love-sick damsel."

And after a hasty consultation with the family physician, with scarcely a day's warning, she whisked her off to Saratoga, where she engaged rooms at the Grand Union for two months, and when Mrs. Richardson called to see her recent patient, she found the elegant mansion on Auburn avenue closed and could not ascertain whither the Menckes had gone.

The change proved to be very beneficial. Saratoga was, of course, very gay; there was a constant round of pleasure into which Violet was at once drawn, for Mrs. Mencke was a great lover of society, and she soon became interested as any young girl naturally would under the same circumstances. There was no more moping—there were no more tears; Violet gave herself up, with true girlish abandon, to the allurements that presented themselves on every side, became a great favorite among the guests of the large hotel, grew round, rosy, happy, and more beautiful than ever, much to the satisfaction of her sister, who congratulated herself that the "beggarly young carpenter" was entirely forgotten.

Two months were spent at this fashionable resort, then six weeks more were occupied in visiting other places of interest, and when they returned to Cincinnati, about the middle of September, Violet seemed entirely herself once more; she was full of life and spirits, the old light of mischief and happiness danced in her beautiful eyes, while she was planning for and looking forward to the coming season with all the zeal and enthusiasm of a young debutante.

The day following their arrival at home Violet came in from a round of calls that she had been making, and, feeling too weary to go up to her room just then, she threw herself into a comfortable chair in the library, and took up a paper that lay on the table.

Almost the first words that caught her eye, and sent a thrill of horror through her, were these:

"DIED—On the 12th instant, at her home, No. —— Hughes street, Mary Ida Richardson, aged 48 years and 9 months. Funeral from her late residence, the 14th, at 2 o'clock P. M."

A cry of pain broke from Violet as she read this.

Her dear, kind friend dead! Gone away out of the world into eternity, and she would never see her again!

It did not seem possible; she could not believe it. Poor Wallace, too! how desolate he would be! And, bowing her face upon her hands, the young girl sobbed as if her heart was broken.

All at once, however, she started to her feet.

The fact that this was the 14th had suddenly forced itself upon her. The paper was two days old.

Glancing at the clock she saw that it was half-past twelve; but she might be in time for the last sad services for the dead if she should hasten.

Mrs. Mencke was out, as usual, and Violet was glad of it, for she knew that she would oppose and might even flatly forbid her going.

Hastening to her room, she exchanged her elaborate visiting costume for a simple black cashmere, tore a bright feather from a black hat, drew on a pair of black gloves, and thirty minutes later was in the street again.

She hailed the first car that came in sight, and even though she was obliged to take a second car, she reached Hughes street about twenty minutes of two.

As she entered the home of the Richardsons she was met by a kind-looking woman, a neighbor, whom she had seen once or twice during her illness, and with a quivering lip she begged that she might go into the parlor herself and take a look at her friend before the people began to gather.

Permission was readily given to her, the woman herself leading the way, and considerately shutting the door so that she might be by herself, as she took her last look at the dear friend who had been so kind to her.

Mrs. Richardson must have died suddenly, she thought, for she was not changed in the least, and lay as if calmly asleep. There was nothing ghastly or unpleasant about her. A look of peace and rest was on the sweet face. Her hair had been dressed just as she was in the habit of wearing it, and a mass of soft lace had been filled into the front of her dress, while some one had placed a few sprays of mignonette and lilies of the valley in her still hands.

"Oh, dear Mrs. Richardson, you cannot be dead!" Violet breathed, as she bent over her with streaming eyes. "It is too, too sad; you were so kind, and I had learned to love you so dearly. What will Wallace do? How can he bear it?"

She smoothed her soft hair with her trembling fingers, never thinking of shrinking from the still, cold form, for it was so life-like. She drew the lace a little closer about the neck, and arranged the flowers less stiffly in her hands, murmuring fond words and tender regrets while thus engaged.

But, after a few moments, overcome with her grief, she seated herself upon a low ottoman behind the casket, and leaned her head against it, weeping silently.

She was so absorbed by her sorrow that she did not hear the door as it was softly opened and closed again, and was not conscious that any one else was in the room, until she heard a deep, heart-broken sob, and a familiar voice break forth in the agonized cry:

"Mother! oh, mother!"

Then she realized that Wallace was there, and her heart went forth to him in loving sympathy, for she knew that he had lost the only near friend that he had in the world.

She did not move for a few moments, however, for she felt that his grief was too deep and sacred to be disturbed; but after a little he grew more calm, and then she said, in a low, tremulous tone:

"Wallace, I am so grieved."

He started, and turned his pale face toward her.

"Violet!" he exclaimed, astonished.

"Yes," she said. "I only came home yesterday, and by the merest chance read the news of this to-day. Oh, Wallace, she was a dear, dear woman!"

"She was, indeed," he replied, clasping the hand she extended to him, and feeling inexpressibly comforted by this fair girl's tribute to his loved one.

He noticed, and was touched also by the fact, that Violet was all in black, and he knew that she had robed herself thus out of grief for his dead.

"I loved her," the young girl said, with touching simplicity. Then she added: "I know I cannot say anything to comfort you, but, believe me, my heart is full of sorrow for her loss, and of sympathy for you."

How lovely she was, standing there beside him, her fair face and sunny hair in such striking contrast with her black dress, and with her azure eyes raised in such heartfelt sympathy to his.

Her hand still lay in his, for both had unconsciously retained their clasp after their first greeting, and he knew by her clinging fingers how sincere her sorrow and sympathy were.

"My darling, I know it; and your presence is inexpressibly comforting to me."

"My darling!"—he had said it without thinking.

During all the long weeks that they had been separated he had called her thus to himself, and now the word had slipped from him unawares, and he would have given worlds to have been able to recall them.

Violet's white lids fluttered and then drooped consciously, while a vivid flush arose to her brow.

This brought Wallace to his senses. He also colored hotly, and a feeling of dismay took possession of him. There was a dead silence for a moment; then he added, humbly:

"Forgive me; I did not know what I was saying."

He would have released her hand, but her small fingers closed more firmly over his; she shot one dazzling gleam of light up at him from her lovely eyes and whispered, shyly:

"I am glad!"

And he knew that she was all his own—that she loved him even as he loved her.

A great wave of thankfulness, of sacred joy, swept over his soul, only to be followed by a feeling of despair, darker and deeper than any he had yet experienced, for he knew that he should not, must not accept the priceless boon of her love which she had so freely and so artlessly yielded to him.

But there was no time for explanations, for at that moment the door was opened again, and the woman, Mrs. Keen, whom Violet had met when she first came, entered, to make some inquiry of Wallace, and to tell him that the clergyman had arrived.

Presently others, neighbors and acquaintances, began to gather, and then it was time for the service.

Violet never forgot that simple ceremony, for the clergyman, who knew Mrs. Richardson intimately, seemed to glorify the death of the beautiful woman.

"She had simply stepped," he said, "from darkness into light—from toil and care into rest and peace. The vail betwixt her and the Master, whom she had loved, was lifted; her hitherto fettered soul was free, and in the light of an eternal day no earthly sorrow, doubt, or trial could reach her."

Death, after that, never seemed the cruel enemy that it had previously seemed to Violet.

After it was all over, and Wallace had passed out to his carriage, Mrs. Keen came to the young girl and asked her if she would like to follow her friend to the cemetery.

"If I may," Violet replied. "She was not a relative, but I loved her very much."

"Then come with me," the woman said, and, as she led the way out, she explained that there were no relatives save Mr. Richardson, and it seemed too bad that there should be no one but himself to follow his mother to the grave, and that was why she had asked Violet to go with her.

The next moment Violet found herself in the carriage with, and seated opposite to, Wallace.

A feeling of dismay took possession of her, for she knew that the world would criticise her severely for taking such a step.

She had not dreamed that she would have to ride in the same carriage with Wallace, and she wondered if he would understand how it had happened.

The matter could not be helped now, however, and for herself she did not care; her motives had been good and pure; why then need she care for the criticisms of people?

The ride to Spring Grove Cemetery was a long and sad one, for scarcely a word was spoken either going or returning. Wallace seemed absorbed in his own sorrowful reflections, Mrs. Keen preserved a prim and gloomy silence, and Violet was thus left to her own thoughts.

She could not keep from thinking of those few sad yet sweet moments when she had stood alone with Wallace by the casket of his mother, and heard him speak those words which had changed, in one instant, her whole life.

"My darling, your presence is inexpressibly comforting to me!"

She knew that he had not meant to speak thus, that only a sense of his own desolation and her unexpected sympathy, had made him forget himself, break down all barriers, and betray the secret of his love.

It had been an unexpected revelation to her, however; she had not suspected the nature of his feelings toward her, nor of hers toward him, until then; but now she knew that she loved him—that all the world, with every other blessing and luxury at her command, would be worthless to her without him to share it.

When they reached Hughes street again Violet held out her hand to Wallace, saying it was so late she must go directly home.

Then he suddenly came to himself and realized how very tedious the long, silent ride must have been for her.

"Let me send you home in the carriage," he said, eagerly.

"Thank you, no; I will take a car," Violet replied, so decidedly that he did not press the matter further.

It was very late when she reached home, and she found her sister quite anxious over her prolonged absence.

"Where have you been, Violet?" she demanded, somewhat impatiently; "it is not the proper thing at all for you to be out so late alone. Mercy! and you are all in black, too; I should think you had been at a funeral."

"I have; I have been to Mrs. Richardson's funeral," Violet replied, hot tears rushing to her eyes.

Mrs. Mencke looked startled.

"Mrs. Richardson!" she repeated. "When did she die?"

"Day before yesterday; and it was all by chance that I saw the notice of her death in a paper. She died very suddenly of heart disease."

"I wish I had known it, I would have gone with you," said Mrs. Mencke, looking disturbed.

"Would you?" Violet exclaimed, surprised.

"Yes; it was not proper for you to go alone."

The young girl's face fell; she had hoped her sister wanted to show this tribute of respect to one who had been so kind to her.

"Where was she buried?" Mrs. Mencke inquired.

"At Spring Grove Cemetery."

"Did you go out there?"

"Yes," and Violet flushed slightly.

"With whom did you ride?" demanded her sister, suspiciously.

"With—Mr. Richardson and a Mrs. Keen."

"Violet Draper Huntington!" ejaculated Mrs. Mencke, with indignant astonishment, "you did not do such an unheard of thing?"

Violet bridled at this. She was naturally sweet and gentle, but could show spirit enough if occasion required.

"Yes, I did," she returned, flushing, but tossing her small head defiantly. "There were no friends excepting Mr. Richardson. Mrs. Keen invited me to go with her, and, as I wanted to show the dear woman this mark of respect, I went."

"Don't you know that it was a very questionable act to follow Mrs. Richardson to her grave in the company of her son?" demanded Mrs. Mencke sternly. "What do you suppose the people of our set would say to such a proceeding?"

"I presume the people of 'our set' might consider it a questionable act," Violet returned, with sarcastic emphasis. "Polite society is not supposed to have much heart, anyway. But, to tell the truth, I thought I was to ride in a separate carriage with Mrs. Keen, until I went out and found Mr. Richardson in it. I was not going to wound him then by refusing to go; and 'our set,' if it find it out, can say what it pleases."

"I most earnestly hope that none of our acquaintances will learn of your escapade; they would be sure to couple your name very unpleasantly with that of that low-born carpenter, especially if they should find out that you put on mourning," returned Mrs. Mencke, with an expression of intense disgust.

"'Low-born carpenter,' indeed!" retorted Violet indignantly, and flushing hotly. "Aren't you ashamed of yourself, Belle Mencke, after what he has done for me? Wallace Richardson is a gentleman in every sense of the word, and I am proud to call him my friend."

"Perhaps you would be proud to accord him a more familiar title, even. Our friends would be likely to suspect that he was thus favored if they should discover what you have done to-day," sneered the haughty woman.

Violet blushed vividly at this thrust, and for a moment looked so conscious that her sister became suspicious and secretly alarmed.

"I don't care, Belle," Violet said, hotly, after a moment of awkward silence, "it would have been very ungrateful in me to stay away and I would do the same thing over again to show my regard for dear Mrs. Richardson. Now, if you please, you may let me alone upon the subject."

"Look here, Miss Violet, you are trying me beyond all bounds," Mrs. Mencke returned, losing control of her temper; "and now there is just one thing that I want to say to you, and that is that you are to drop this fellow at once and for all time. I won't have any nonsense or sentiment just because he happened to do what any other man with a germ of humanity would have done to save you from a violent death. It is all very well to feel properly grateful to him, and I intend to pay him handsomely for it, only I don't want to hear anything more about him from you."

Violet had grown very pale during the latter portion of this speech, and her sister, who was observing her closely, could see that she was trembling with suppressed emotions.

"Belle Mencke," she said, in a husky tone, "do you mean to say that you intend to offer Mr. Richardson money in return for my life?"

"Of course. What else can I do? We must make him some acknowledgment, and people in his station think more of money that of anything else," was the coarse response.

"That is false!" cried Violet, with blazing eyes. "Reverse your statement, and say that people in your position think more of money than of anything else, and you would come nearer the truth. Don't you dare to insult that noble fellow by offering him money; if you do, I will never forgive you while I live. Make him all the verbal acknowledgments you please, as will be just and right, but don't forget that he is a gentleman."

Mrs. Mencke saw that she had gone too far, and made an effort to control herself. She knew, from experience, that when Violet was once thoroughly aroused it was not an easy matter to tame her.

"There, Violet, you have said enough," she remarked, with forced calmness. "You are only making yourself ridiculous, and I think we had best drop the subject; only one thing I must insist upon, that you will cut this young man's acquaintance at once."

She arose as she spoke to meet her husband, who entered at that moment, and Violet flew to her own room to remove her black attire, and to ease her aching heart by shedding a few scalding tears, which would not be kept back.

It was very hard to hear Wallace spoken of so contemptuously when she had learned to love him with all the strength of her soul, and knew him to be, by nature and in character, far superior to the man whom her sister called husband.

She did not regret what she had done that day, and she had no idea of dropping Wallace Richardson's acquaintance. No, indeed! Life would be worth but very little to her now if he were taken out of it; and, though she knew she would have many a vigorous battle to fight with her proud sister if she defied her authority, she had no thought of yielding one inch of ground, and was prepared to acknowledge Wallace as her betrothed lover when the proper time to do so should come.

CHAPTER VI.
A CONFESSION AND ITS REPLY.

Wallace, in his lonely home, was of course very sad and almost stunned by the blow that had fallen upon him so suddenly.

For many years his mother had been the one object upon which he had lavished the deep, strong affection of his manly nature. He had lost his father when but a youth, but Mrs. Richardson had struggled bravely to keep him at school, and give him as good an education as possible, for he was a lad possessing more than ordinary capabilities and attainments. By the time, however, that he graduated from the high school in the city of Boston, Massachusetts, where they were living at that time, their slender means gave out, and Wallace found that he must relinquish, at least, for the present, his aspiration to perfect himself as an architect, and do something for his own and his mother's support.

He was but seventeen years of age at this time, but he was a strong, manly fellow, and he resolved to take up the carpenter's trade, much about which he already knew, for during his vacations he had often worked, from choice, under the direction of his father.

As he had told Violet, he felt that a practical and thorough knowledge of the construction of buildings would be of inestimable benefit in the future, for he had not by any means given up his intention of ultimately becoming an architect.

He applied to the builder and contractor who had grown up under and succeeded to the business of his father, and the man readily agreed to engage him, provided he would be willing to go to Cincinnati, where he had managed to obtain a very large contract, and, for a lad of Wallace's age, he offered him unusual inducements.

At first Wallace demurred, for he could not bear the thought of leaving his mother, and at that time they could not both afford to make the change.

But he finally concluded to make the trial, and at the end of six months he had made himself so valuable to his employer that the man had increased his wages, and promised him still further promotion if he continued to progress as he had done.

This change in his circumstances enabled Wallace to send for his mother and to provide a comfortable little home for her.

He was very ambitious; every spare moment was spent in study, while he also attended an evening school for drawing, where he could receive instruction in his beloved architecture.

Thus, step by step, he went steadily on, perfecting himself in both his trade and his profession until, at the opening of our story, six years after leaving his native city, Boston, we find him and his mother still residents of Cincinnati, and the young man in a fair way to realize the one grand object of his life.

Already he had executed a number of plans for buildings, which had been approved, accepted, and fairly well paid for, while he had applied for, and hoped to obtain, a lucrative position in the office of an eminent architect, at the beginning of the new year.

His accident had interrupted his business for several weeks, but he knew that he should lose nothing pecuniarily, for the company that controlled the incline-plane railway had agreed to meet all the expenses of his illness, and pay him a goodly sum besides; so his enforced idleness had not tried his patience as severely as it would have otherwise done.

Indeed, he had not been idle, for he had devoted a good deal of time, after he was able to be about, to the study of his beloved art. His right hand, being only slightly injured he could use quite freely, and he executed several designs which he was sure would be useful to him in the future.

His mother's sudden death, however, was a blow which almost crushed him. He had never thought that she could die at least for long years for she had apparently been in the enjoyment of perfect health.

They were sitting together one evening, and had been unusually social and merry, when Mrs. Richardson suddenly broke off in the middle of a sentence, leaned back in her chair as if faint, and before Wallace could reach her side, her spirit was gone.

Wallace would not believe that she was dead until the hastily summoned physician declared that life was entirely extinct and then the heavily afflicted son felt as if his burden were greater than he could bear.

He did not look upon that loved face again until the hour of the funeral, when he went alone into their pretty parlor to take his last farewell, and found Violet there before him.

Her presence there had been "inexpressibly comforting" to him as he had said, and in the sudden reaction and surprise of the moment he had betrayed the secret of his love for her.

He was shocked and filled with dismay when, after his return from the grave of his mother, he had an opportunity to quietly think over what he had done.

He felt that he had been very unwise—that he had no right to aspire to the hand of the beautiful heiress, for he could offer her nothing but his true heart, and this, he well knew, would be scorned by Violet's aristocratic relatives.

Yet, in spite of his remorse, his heart leaped with exultation over the knowledge that the lovely girl returned his affection. She had not spoken her love, but he had seen it in her shy, sweet glance of surprise and joy at his confession; he had felt it in the clinging clasp of her trembling fingers, that would not let him release her hand; he had heard it in every tone of her dear voice when she had told him, simply, but heartily, that she "was glad."

Was she glad to know that she was his "darling," or only glad because her presence was a comfort to him in his hour of trial?

Both, he felt very sure, and he kept repeating those three words over and over until they became sweetest music in his soul.

But he told himself that he must not accept the priceless gift of her love.

"What shall I do?" he cried, in deep distress. "I have compromised myself; I have gone too far to retract, and she would deem unmanly if I should keep silent and let the matter drop here."

He sat for hours trying to decide what course to pursue, and finally he exclaimed, with an air of resolution:

"There is no other way but to make a frank explanation—confess my sorrow for my presumption and ask her forgiveness; then I must take up the burden of my lonely life and bear it as well as I can."

The next morning, after he had partaken of his solitary breakfast, which a kind and sympathizing neighbor sent in to him, he sat down to his task of writing his confession to Violet.

That evening the fair young girl received the following epistle:

"MY DEAR MISS HUNTINGTON:—I am filled with conflicting emotions, which it would be vain for me to try to explain, in addressing you thus; but my mother taught me this motto in my youth—and I have endeavored to make it the rule of my life ever since—'If you do wrong confess it and make what reparation you can.' I realize that I was guilty of great presumption and wrong in addressing you so unguardedly as I did yesterday, when we stood alone by my mother's casket. Pray forgive me, for, while I am bound to confess that the words were forced from me by a true, strong love, which will always live in my heart—a love such as a man experiences but once in his life for a woman whom he would win for his wife, if he could do so honorably—I know that, situated as I am, with a life of labor before me and only my own efforts to help me build up a possible fortune, I should not have betrayed myself as I did. I was unnerved by my great sorrow, and your gentle sympathy, coming as it did like balm to my wounded heart, unsealed my lips before I was aware of it. Again I beg your forgiveness, and with it forgetfulness of aught that could serve to lower me in your esteem.

"Sincerely yours,

"WALLACE RICHARDSON."

Violet was greatly excited by the contents of this letter, and burst into a flood of tears the moment she had perused it.

She understood just how matters stood.

She comprehended how Wallace had grown to love her, even as she had, though at the time unconsciously, learned to love him while she was an invalid in his home; how, with his proud, manly sense of honor, he had determined never to reveal his secret, from a fear that he would be regarded as a fortune-hunter, and that her aristocratic relatives would scorn an alliance with him on account of his poverty.

But Violet felt that he was her peer, if not her superior, in every respect save that of wealth; that a grand future lay before him—grand because he would climb to the top-most round in the ladder of his profession, if energy, perseverance, and unswerving rectitude could attain it.

He might be poor in purse now, but what of that? Money was of little value compared with a nature so rich and noble as his; and, more than that—she loved him!

"Yes, I do!" she exclaimed, as she pressed to her lips the precious letter that told of his love for her. "I am not ashamed of it either, and—I am going to tell him of it."

A crimson flush mounted to her brow as she gave expression to this resolution, and, for a moment, a sense of maidenly reserve and timidity oppressed her. The next she tossed back her pretty head with a resolute air.

"Why should I not tell him?" she said. "Why should I conceal the fact when the knowledge will make two true, loving hearts happy? I have money enough for us both, for the present, and by and by I know he will have an abundance. I suppose Belle and Wilhelm will object and scold, but I don't care; it is the right thing to do, and I am going to do it," and she proceeded to put her resolution at once into action.

She drew her writing tablet before her, and, with the tears still glittering on her lashes and a crimson flush on her cheek, she penned the following reply to her lover's letter:

> "DEAR WALLACE:—Your letter has just come to me. I have nothing to 'forgive'—I do not wish to 'forget.' Perhaps I am guilty of what the world would call an unmaidenly act in writing thus, when your communication does not really call for a reply, but I know my happiness, and, I believe, yours also, depends upon perfect truthfulness and candor. Your unguarded words by your mother's casket told me that you love me; your letter to-day reaffirms it, and my own heart goes forth in happy response to all that you have told me.
>
> "You have made use of the expression, 'presumption and wrong.' Pardon me if I claim that you would have been guilty of a greater wrong by keeping silent. Heaven has ordained that somewhere on this earth each heart has its mate, and there would be much less of secret sorrow, much less of domestic misery, if people would be honest with each other and true to themselves. How many lives are ruined by the worship of mammon—by the bondage of position! Perhaps I might be accused of 'presumption'—of offending against all laws of so-called etiquette, in making this open confession. However it may seem, I am going to be true to myself, and my convictions of

what is right, and so I have opened my heart to you. Still, if in writing thus, I have done aught that can lower me in your esteem, I pray you to forgive and forget.

"VIOLET HUNTINGTON."

Violet would not allow herself to read over what she had written.

She had penned the note out of the honesty and fullness of her fond little heart; and, though she stood for a moment or two irresolute, debating whether to tear it into pieces and thus cast her happiness forever from her with the fragments, or to send it and trust to Wallace's good sense to interpret it aright, her good angel touched the balance in her favor, and she resolutely sealed and addressed the missive.

Then she stole softly down stairs and out to the street corner, where she posted it with her own hands, after which she sped back to her chamber and relieved her sensitive heart in another burst of tears.

She would not have been human if she had not regretted her act, now that it was past recall. She grew nervous and self-abusive, declared that she had been unmaidenly, and made herself as wretched as possible.

She dared not think what would be the result of her letter. Would Wallace despise her for unsexing herself and almost proposing to him? Would he, with his exaggerated ideas of honor still claim that it would be unmanly to accept the love which she had so freely offered him?

Thoughts such as these occupied her waking hours up to the following afternoon, when she expected a letter from Wallace, and was deeply disappointed when none came.

Mr. and Mrs. Mencke had gone out to make some social calls, and Violet was striving to divert her mind from the all-important theme, by going over her music lesson for to-morrow. It was useless, however; there was no music in her—everything was out of harmony, and her fingers refused to do their work.

She then tried to read, but her mind was in such a chaotic state that words had no meaning for her, and she finally grew so nervous that she could do nothing but pace up and down the room.

The hours slowly dragged on, evening came, and she was upon the point of going up stairs to bed, when a sudden ring at the door-bell made her start with a feeling of mingled shame and joy.

She listened breathlessly, while a servant went to answer the summons, and then heard her usher some one in the drawing-room.

A moment later the girl appeared in the library doorway, bearing a card on a silver salver.

"A caller for you, Miss Violet," she said, as she passed her the bit of pasteboard.

Violet grew dizzy, then the rich color surged over cheek and brow, as she read the name of Wallace Richardson, written upon the spotless surface in a beautiful, flowing hand.

CHAPTER VII.
"HE IS MY AFFIANCED HUSBAND."

Violet stood as if dazed for a moment, after reading her lover's name, and realized that he had come in person to reply to her letter, her cheeks fairly blazing with mingled joy and agitation, her heart fluttering like a frightened bird in its cage.

Then she grew pale with a sudden fear and dread.

What would be the outcome of this interview?

Would it bring her happiness or sorrow?

With trembling limbs, and a face that was as white as the delicate lace about her throat, she went slowly toward the drawing-room to learn her fate.

Wallace, no less nervous and perturbed than herself, was pacing the elegant apartment, but stopped and turned eagerly toward Violet as she entered, his face luminous in spite of the stern self-control which he had resolved to exercise.

All the light died out of it however as he saw how pale she was.

"Violet!—Miss Huntington! are you ill?" he cried, regarding her anxiously.

Again the rich color surged up to her brow at the sound of his dear voice, for the tremulous tenderness in it told her that his heart was all her own, and her elastic spirits rebounded at once.

She shot a shy, sweet glance up into his earnest face, a witching little smile began to quiver about her lovely lips, then she said, half-saucily, but with charming confusion:

"No—I am not ill; I—was only afraid that I had done something dreadful. Have I?"

All the worldly wisdom, with which the young man had tried to arm himself, in order to shield the girl whom he so fondly loved from rashly doing what she might regret later, gave way at that, and before he was aware of what he was doing he had gathered her close in his arms.

"My darling! no," he said; "you have done only what was true and noble, and I honor you with my whole soul. If all women were one-half as ingenuous there would be, as you have said, less misery in the world. But so many are simply worldly-wise—thinking more of wealth and position than they do of true affection, that their hearts starve, their lives are warped and ruined. Violet, my heart's dearest, how shall I tell you of my heart's great love? I cannot tell it—I shall have to let a life-time of devotion attest it, but you have glorified my whole future by assuring me of your affection."

"Oh, I was afraid you would think me very bold—that you would regard me with contempt," Violet sighed, tremulously. "After my letter had gone, and I tried to think over what I had written more calmly, and to wonder how you would regard it, I was almost sorry that I had sent it."

"'Almost,' but not really sorry?" questioned Wallace, with a fond smile.

"No, for I had to tell you the truth, if I told you anything, and no one can be sorry for being strictly candid," she returned, "and," with a resolute uplifting of her pretty head, while she looked him straight in the eyes, "why should I not tell you just what was in my heart? Why does the world think that a woman must never speak, no matter if she ruins two lives by her silence? You told me that you loved me, although you did not ask me if I returned your affection; but I knew that my life would be ruined if I did not make you understand it. I do love you, Wallace, and I will not be ashamed because I have told you of it."

The young man was deeply moved by this frank, artless confession. He knew there was not a grain of indelicacy or boldness in it; it was simply a truthful expression of a pure and noble nature, the spontaneous outburst of a holy affection responding to the sacred love of his own heart, and the avowal aroused a profound reverence for an ingenuousness that was as rare as it was perfect.

He bent down and touched his lips to her silken hair.

"There is no occasion," he said, earnestly, "and you have changed all my life, my dear one, by adopting such a straightforward course. Still," he added, with a slight smile, "I did not come here intending to tell you just this, or with the hope that our interview would result in such open confessions."

"Did you not?" Violet asked, quickly, and darting a startling look at him.

"No, love; nay, rest content just where you are," he said, as she would have withdrawn herself from his encircling arms, "for you may be very sure I shall never give you up after this; but your letter must be answered in some way; I knew that we must come to some final understanding, and though truth would not allow me to disavow my love for you, yet I wished you to realize fully that I would not presume to take advantage of anything which you might have written upon the impulse of the moment. I would not claim any promise of you which you might regret when you should come to think of it more calmly; while, too, I wished to assure myself that your friends would sanction your decision, and absolve me from any desire to take a dishonorable advantage of you. I would win you fairly, my Violet, or not at all."

Violet flushed at this.

"Did you expect to obtain the sanction of my sister or her husband to—to our engagement?" she asked.

"I did not come expecting to gain anything that I wanted," Wallace returned, smiling, "for I had resolved not to take you at your word until I had assured myself that you fully understood all that it would involve; then, of course, I knew that the proper thing for me to do would be to ask their consent to our betrothal."

"And you intend to do this now?" Violet questioned.

"Certainly. You are not of age, are you, dear?"

"No; but, Wallace, they will never sanction it," Violet said, with burning cheeks, but thinking it best to prepare him for the worst at the outset.

"Because of my present poverty and humble position?" he question, gravely.

"Yes, and money is their idol," the young girl frankly answered.

"Then, Violet, I do not think it will be right for me to bind you by any promise to become my wife, until I have earned a position and a competence that will meet their approval and warrant me in asking for your hand."

Violet put him a little from her, and stood erect and proud before him.

"You do not need to bind me by any promise," she said, in a low, thrilling tone, "for when I gave you my love, I gave you myself as well. I am yours while I live. In confessing my love for you, I have virtually bound myself to you, and even if I am never your wife in name, I shall be in soul until I die. You can ask the sanction of my sister and her husband, as a matter of form. I know they will not give it; but they have no moral right to come between us—they never shall! They are very proud and ambitious; they hope"—and Violet colored crimson at the confession—"to marry me to some rich man; but my heart and my hand are mine to bestow upon whom I will; and, Wallace, they are yours, now and forever."

Wallace regarded her with astonishment, while he wondered if there was ever so strange a betrothal before.

He had asked no promise, but he felt that she could not have been more surely bound to him if their marriage vows had already been pronounced—at least, as far as her fidelity to him was concerned.

"I am young, I know," Violet went on, after a moment—"I am not yet quite eighteen—and Wilhelm is my guardian. He can control my fortune until I am twenty-one; but that need make no difference with our relations. You will be true to me, I know, and I do not need to assure you of my own faithfulness, I am sure. Meantime you will be working up in your profession, and when I do reach my majority and come into possession of my money, I can do as I like, without asking the consent of any one."

"My faithful, true-hearted little woman, I had no idea there was such reserve force beneath your gay, laughing exterior," Wallace returned, tenderly. "What a royal gift you have bestowed upon me, my darling! I accept it reverently, gratefully, and pledge you my faith in return, while I do not need to assure you that I will not spare myself in striving to win a name and a position worthy to offer my heart's queen. You have changed the whole world for me," he continued, with emotion. "I am no longer alone, and you have armed me with a zeal and courage, to battle with the future, such as I should never have known under other circumstances. My darling, I take your promise with your love, and when the right time comes I shall claim my wife."

He drew her to his breast again, and lifting her sweet face to his, he touched her lips with a fond and reverent betrothal kiss.

"Humph! Pray, Miss Violet, allow me to inquire how long you have been posing for this interesting tableau?"

This question, in the gruff, sarcastic tones of Wilhelm Mencke, burst upon the lovers like an unexpected thunderclap, and, starting to her feet, Violet turned to find her sister's husband standing not six feet from her.

Mrs. Mencke seemed rooted just inside the doorway, apparently too paralyzed by the scene which she had just witnessed to utter a word, while there was an indescribable expression of anger and disgust upon her handsome face.

For a moment Violet was so astonished and confused she could not utter a word; then, with that slight uplifting of her fair head which those who knew her best understood to indicate a gathering of all the force of her will, she quietly remarked, though a burning flush mounted to her brow:

"Ah, Wilhelm! I thought you and Belle had gone out for the evening."

"No doubt; and you had planned to enjoy yourself in your own way, it seems," sneered the angry master of the house, as he glared savagely at Wallace, who now arose and advanced to Violet's side.

"Stop, if you please, Wilhelm," the young girl said, as he seemed about to go on, and her clear tones rang out warningly. "When you went out I had no thought of receiving visitors; but of that I will speak with you later. Allow me to introduce my friend, Mr. Richardson. Mr. Richardson, my brother-in-law, Mr. Mencke; my sister you have already met."

Wallace bowed courteously, while he marveled at Violet's remarkable self-possession; but neither Mr. Mencke nor his wife acknowledged the introduction otherwise than by bestowing a malignant look upon him, and this slight aroused all Violet's spirit to arms.

"Friend!" repeated Mr. Mencke; "one would naturally judge from the touching scene just enacted that the young man sustained a much nearer relation to you."

"He does!" flashed out Violet, as she boldly faced both the intruders, and reckless of the consequences of the avowal; "he is my affianced husband!"

"Violet!" almost screamed her sister, as she sprang forward and seized the young girl by the arm. "Are you crazy?"

"Pardon me, madame," said Wallace, courteously, as he advanced toward the group, "and pray give me your attention for a moment while I explain what may seem an unpardonable intrusion, and for which I am wholly to blame."

"No," interrupted Violet, releasing herself from her sister's grasp; "I alone am responsible for what has occurred this evening. Mr. Richardson, in an unguarded moment, revealed to me the fact that he entertained an affection for me such as I have long known, exists in my own heart for him. I responded to it— —"

"Shameless girl!" ejaculated Mrs. Mencke, in an angry tone.

"No, Belle, I am not a shameless girl. I simply gave truthful expression to an attachment in return for a confession that gave me great happiness, and notwithstanding that Mr. Richardson told me he would not bind me by any promise until, as he expressed it, he should be in a suitable position to warrant him in asking my hand of you, I told him outright that my acknowledgment of affection was as binding with me as any promise— —"

"Mr. and Mrs. Mencke," Wallace now interposed, "I cannot allow your sister to assume the responsibility of all this, for it is really my place to shield her. I love her with all the strength of my nature, and I now formally ask you, as her guardians, to sanction the compact we have made this evening."

"Never!" emphatically retorted Mrs. Mencke, in her haughtiest tone.

"It is not worth while to discuss such an impossible proposition, and you will best suit us, young man, by making yourself scarce without more ado," supplemented Mr. Mencke, with a menacing air.

"Belle! Wilhelm!—do you call yourself a lady, a gentleman, and dare to insult a friend of mine in your own house?" cried Violet, quivering with indignation, her eyes glittering like coals of fire.

Mrs. Mencke began to realize that they were arousing a spirit which might be difficult to manage; consequently she deemed it advisable to adopt a different course.

"We have no wish to insult any one, Violet," she began, with dignity, but in a more conciliatory tone; "but of course we are very much astonished by such a declaration as you have just made, and you a mere child yet——"

"I believe you were married at eighteen, Belle; I shall be eighteen in two months," Violet quietly interrupted, but with a roguish gleam in her blue eyes.

Mrs. Mencke colored.

She had by no means forgotten the circumstances connected with her own marriage, which had been an elopement, because of a stern parent's objections to the man of her choice; though this fact was not known in the circle where she now moved.

"Well, you will not marry at eighteen," she answered, tartly.

"Perhaps not; indeed, I have no desire to, but when I do, Mr. Richardson will be the man whom I shall marry, and I want the matter understood once for all," Violet returned, with a gravity which betrayed her unalterable determination.

"You had best put the child to bed, Belle, and I will show this young carpenter the way out," Mr. Mencke remarked, contemptuously, as if he really regarded Violet's assertion as simply the iteration of a willful child.

Violet shot him a look that made him wince; then turning, she laid her hand upon Wallace's arm.

"It is a shame!" she said, with quivering lips. "I blush that relatives of mine can stoop to offer any one such indignity. Forgive me that I am powerless to help it."

"I have nothing to forgive, and I have everything to honor you for, Violet; but it is best that I should go now, and we will settle this matter later," the young man replied, in a fond yet regretful tone.

It had been very hard to stand there and preserve his self-control; but for her sake he had borne all in silence.

"You will never give me up?" the young girl pleaded, her small fingers closing over his arm appealingly.

He took her hand in a strong yet gentle clasp.

"No, never, until you yourself ask it," he said, firmly.

"That I shall never do. Do you hear, Belle, Wilhelm?" she cried, turning defiantly to them. "I have given Wallace my promise that I will be his wife, and he has said that he will never give me up. Just so sure as I live, I shall fulfill that promise."

Mrs. Mencke lost control of herself entirely at this.

"Violet Huntington!" she cried, white to her lips "with rage, you will at once retract that rash vow or this house is no longer your home."

"Mrs. Mencke, let me entreat that the subject be dropped for the present," Wallace here interposed. "Believe me, I shrink from being the cause of any disturbance in your household, and since this union, which appears to cause you such uneasiness, cannot be consummated for some time yet, I beg that you will not distress your sister nor yourself by further threats."

"I will drop the subject when you both agree to cancel this foolish engagement. Give me your word of honor that you will never claim the fulfillment of Violet's rash promise to you, and I will drop the matter and be glad to do so."

"I cannot promise you that," Wallace firmly replied, though he had grown very pale as he realized how determined they were to separate them. "I love your sister, and if she is of the same mind in the future, when I can feel justified in claiming her, I shall certainly make her my wife."

"And you know me well enough, Belle, to be sure that I shall not change—that I shall not retract one word that I have said to-night," Violet added, with no less firmness than her lover had manifested.

"I know that you are a rash and obstinate girl, but you will find that I can be just as relentless as yourself, and you will make me the promise I demand or this house can no longer be your home," Mrs. Mencke sternly retorted.

"I shall never make it," Violet reiterated, with white lips, while she looked up into her lover's face with such an expression of affection and trust that he longed to take her to his heart and bear her away at once from such unnatural guardianship.

CHAPTER VIII.
"I'LL BREAK HER WILL!"

Mr. Mencke here interposed. When his wife's temper was aroused she was liable to be rash and unreasonable. He thought if they could but get rid of Wallace they could perhaps coax Violet into a more pliable frame of mind.

He turned to the young man, and said, sternly:

"We have had enough of this for to-night, but I will confer with you later about this matter."

Wallace bowed a courteous, but dignified, assent to this broad hint to take his departure.

He bade Violet good-night in a low tone, tenderly pressing her hand before releasing it, then, after a polite bow to Mrs. Mencke, which she did not deign to notice, he walked with a firm, manly bearing from the house, bidding its master a gentlemanly good-evening at the door.

In spite of her rage against Violet and her poverty-stricken lover, Mrs. Mencke could not help admiring the latter's self-possessed exit, while she secretly confessed that "the fellow was uncommonly good-looking."

When the door had closed after him, she turned again to her sister.

"Violet, I am scandalized——" she began, when that young lady interrupted her.

"There is no need, I assure you, Belle," she said, coldly. "I confess I would have preferred that you did not see us just as you did, but I have been guilty of nothing which should cause you to feel scandalized. We may as well understand each other first as last, and you may as well make up your mind to the inevitable, for, if I live, I shall marry Wallace Richardson. If I cannot do so legally until I am of age, I shall wait until then, and you know, Belle, when I take a stand like this, I mean it."

With this parting shaft Violet, with uplifted head and flashing eyes, walked deliberately from her sister's presence and up to her own room.

"The little vixen will do it, Belle, as sure as you live," remarked Wilhelm Mencke, who had returned to the drawing-room in season to catch the latter portion of Violet's remarks.

"She shall not!" cried his wife, angrily. "Marry that low-born carpenter who has to labor with his hands for daily bread! Never!"

"I do not see how you are going to help it; you know she has the grit of a dozen common women in that small body, and a will of iron," replied Mr. Mencke.

"Then I'll break her will! I came of a resolute stock, too, and it will be Roman against Roman, with the advantage on my side. She shall never compromise herself, nor us, by any such misalliance."

Mr. Mencke looked a trifle sheepish at this spirited speech. He could not forget, if his wife did, that some fourteen years previous he had been as badly off, if not worse, than this young carpenter. He had been a laborer in the employ of Miss Belle Huntington's father, and she had not felt that she was compromising herself or her parents by marrying him, and the wealthy pork-packer's daughter had run away with the man whom she loved.

"What will you do to prevent it?" he asked, after a few moments of awkward silence. "The girl can marry him any day if she takes a notion; the will says we are to be the guardians of the property 'until she is twenty-one or marries.' It would make it rather awkward for me if she should, for her husband would have the right to demand her fortune, and—Belle, the duse would be to pay if I should lose my hold on that money."

"What is the matter, Will?" demanded Mrs. Mencke looking startled.

"Hum—nothing much, only—it is so mixed up with my own affairs it would cripple me to have to fork it over on short notice," Mr. Mencke replied, looking exceedingly glum.

"You may rest satisfied upon one point; you will never have to surrender it to that fellow," his wife returned, decisively. "I will send Violet to a convent first, and she would be kept straight enough there."

"That is well thought of Belle," said her husband, eagerly, his usually stolid face lighting up greedily. "It would never do, though, to send her to one here; suppose we get her off to Montreal, where there will be no one to interfere; we can keep her there as long as we like, and meantime I will make Cincinnati too hot to hold that youngster."

"We will do it, Will, and she shall stay there until she promises to give up this silly love affair."

"You are a very conscientious and affectionate sister, Belle," said her husband, with a sarcastic laugh. "What do you suppose Eben Huntington would say to— —"

"Hush!" returned Mrs. Mencke, with an authoritative gesture, "that is a secret that must never be breathed aloud; but all things are fair in love and war, and to Montreal and into a convent Violet shall go without delay."

But if Mrs. Mencke could have caught a glimpse of the white, resolute face of her young sister, as she stood at that moment just outside the drawing-room door, she might not have felt quite so confident of her power to carry out her project.

Violet, after leaving Mrs. Mencke, intended to go at once to her room, but upon reaching the top of the stairs, she remembered that she had left upon the piano, in the library, Wallace's letter, in a book that she had been reading.

Not wishing other eyes than her own to peruse it, she stole quietly down again to get it, and happened to pass the drawing-room door just as her sister made her threat to send her to a convent.

She had always had a horror of convent life, and though Mrs. Mencke had been educated at one, Violet would never consent to go to one, and had attended the public schools of the city, until she graduated from the high school, after which she spent a year at a noted institution in Columbus, "to finish off."

She was greatly agitated as she listened to the conversation of her two guardians, and she wondered how they could scheme so against her. It was cruel, heartless. There had never been open warfare between them before, though Violet had not always been so happy as young girls usually are. There was much about her home-life that was not congenial, but she was naturally gentle and affectionate, and, where principle was not at stake, she would yield a point rather than create dissension. Occasionally, however, there would arise a question of conscience, and then she had shown the "grit" and "will of iron" of which Mr. Mencke had spoken.

Mrs. Mencke arose as she made her last remark, and Violet, fearing to be found eavesdropping, sped noiselessly on into the library, where she secured her book and letter; then fleeing by a door opposite the one she had entered, and up a back stair-way, she reached her own room without exciting the suspicion of any one that she had overheard the plot concerning her.

Locking herself in, she sat down at once and wrote all that she had overheard to Wallace, telling him that she should certainly grieve herself to death if she was immured in a convent, and asking him what she should do in this emergency.

She informed him that she should take a German lesson at three the next afternoon, and begged him to meet her in the pupils' reception-parlor of the institute at four o'clock.

She was so wrought up that she could not sleep, and tossed restlessly most of the night, while she wondered why Belle and Wilhelm were so cruel to her, and what the secret was to which Belle had referred; she had not, until then, been aware that there was anything mysterious connected with their family history.

She arose very early the next morning, and stole forth to post her letter, long before any of the household were astir, after which she crept back to bed and fell into a heavy, dreamless slumber, which lasted until late in the forenoon.

Wallace received Violet's letter by the morning post, and was greatly exercised over it.

At four o'clock precisely he entered the pupils' reception-room at the institute where Violet took German lessons, and was thankful to find no one there before him.

Presently Violet entered, looking pale and unhappy. She sprang toward her lover, and laid two small hot hands in his, while she lifted a pair of sad, appealing eyes to him.

"What shall I do, Wallace?" she cried, with quivering lips. "I will not go to Montreal, and yet I know they are determined to make me."

"Your sister or her husband has no right to insist upon your going into a convent, if you do not wish to do so," Wallace returned, gravely.

"But they are my guardians; I have no other home, no other friends; they have the care of my money and I have to go to them for everything I want. I do not expect they will tell me that they are going to take me to a convent unless I will submit to them—they are too wise for that; they will plan to go on a journey, say they are going to shut up the house, and I must of course go with them; then when they get to Montreal they will force me into a convent," Violet said, excitedly.

"I cannot believe that they would do anything so underhanded and dishonorable," said Wallace, greatly shocked.

"They will," Violet persisted, excitedly. "Belle said 'anything was fair in love and war,' and when she gets aroused, as she was last night, she stops at nothing. Then, too, she hinted at some secret, and I am greatly troubled over it."

"Violet," began Wallace, solemnly, as he bent to look into her face, while he held her hands in almost a painful clasp, "are you sure that you love me—that you will never regret the promise that you made me last night? You are very young, you have seen but little of the world, and a larger experience might cause you to change by and by."

Violet's delicate fingers closed over his spasmodically.

"Wallace! you are not sorry! Oh, do not tell me that you regret, and that I am to lose you," she pleaded, almost hysterically.

"My darling," he answered, with gentle fondness, "you are all the world to me, and if I should lose you, I should lose all that makes life desirable; but I wish you to count the cost of your choice and not make enemies of your only friends, to regret it later."

"No, Wallace—no! I shall not regret it. I love you with my whole heart, and—I shall die if we are separated," Violet concluded, with a pathetic little sob that went straight to her lover's heart.

His face grew luminous with a great joy; he knew then that she belonged to him for all time.

"Then listen, love," he said; and bending, he placed his lips close to her ear, and whispered for a minute or two.

Violet listened, while a strange, wondering expression grew on her fair face, and a burning blush mounted to her brow and lost itself among the rings of soft, golden hair that lay clustering there.

She was very grave, almost awe-stricken, when he concluded, and then she stood for a moment silently thinking.

"Yes," she said, softly, at last, and dropped her face upon the hands that were still clasping hers.

They stood thus for another moment, then Wallace led her to a seat, and sitting down beside her, they conversed in repressed tones for some time longer.

Violet reached home just as her sister returned from making calls.

"Where have you been, Violet?" Mrs. Mencke asked, suspiciously.

"To take my German lessons," the girl responded, with a sigh.

Her heart was heavy and sore, and she longed for love and sympathy instead of sour looks and words.

"Your term is nearly ended, isn't it?" Mrs. Mencke continued, as they entered the house together.

"I have one lesson more," said Violet.

"Come in here; I want to talk with you," her sister rejoined, as she led the way into the drawing-room.

Violet followed, with flushing cheeks and eyes that began to glitter ominously. Her spirit was leaping forth to meet the trial in store for her.

"I have been thinking," Mrs. Mencke began, throwing herself into a chair and trying to speak in an offhand way, "that another little trip would do us all good. Will has business that calls him to Canada, and he thinks he would like company on the journey; so we have decided to combine business and pleasure, and take in all the sights on the way. He is to start a week from Wednesday, and we can easily be ready to accompany him by that time. What do you say, Vio?"

Violet thought a moment, then meeting her sister's eye with a steady glance, she briefly replied:

"I do not wish to go."

Mrs. Mencke flushed. She did not like that quiet tone.

"I am sorry," she returned, "for we have decided to shut up the house during our absence, and I could not think of leaving you behind."

"Nevertheless, Belle, I shall not go with you to Montreal," Violet answered, steadily.

"Who said anything about Montreal?" quickly demanded Mrs. Mencke, and regarding her sharply.

"I may as well be straightforward with you, Belle," Violet continued, "and tell that I know just what you have planned to do, and I am not going to Montreal to be placed in a convent!"

"Violet!" ejaculated the startled woman, with a crimson face.

"You need not attempt to deny anything," the young girl continued, calmly, "for I overheard you and Will planning it last night. I came down to get something that I had left in the library, and as I was passing through the hall I heard you say you would send me to a convent. Of course, having learned that much, I was bound to hear all I could of the plan."

Mrs. Mencke looked blank over this information for a moment; then her temper getting the better of her, she burst forth into a torrent of reproaches and abuse.

Violet sat with quietly folded hands and did not attempt to interrupt her; but finally the woman grew ashamed of the sound of her angry voice and words and ceased.

"Are you through, Belle?" Violet then inquired, in a cold, strangely calm tone.

"Well, you have driven me nearly to distraction by the way you have carried on of late," Mrs. Mencke said, apologetically.

"I think I have had something to bear as well from you," the young girl returned; "but I am no longer a child to be taken hither and thither against my will. If you and Will wish to take a trip to Canada you can do so by yourselves. I shall not accompany you."

"What will you do—remain in Cincinnati and meet that vulgar carpenter on the sly, I suppose," retorted her sister, angrily.

"I can go to Mrs. Bailey's. Nellie has long been wishing me to spend a few weeks with her."

"And she will aid and abet you in your love-making, perhaps you imagine," sneered Mrs. Mencke. "No, miss; you will go with us, whether you want to or not, and you will also go into a convent, where you will remain until you give me your solemn promise to relinquish all thoughts of ever marrying that low-born Yankee."

Violet arose at this point and stood pale and erect before her sister.

"Belle, I shall not go to Montreal. I will not be forced to go anywhere against my inclination," she said, with a resoluteness that betrayed an unalterable purpose. "I know that you and Will were appointed my guardians, and that I shall not reach my majority for three years yet; but I know, too, that there is some redress for such abuse of authority as you are attempting to exercise, and if you persist in this course—much as I shall dislike the notoriety of such a proceeding—I shall appeal to the courts to set you aside and appoint some one in your place. You said last night that it would be 'Roman against

Roman' in this matter. You said truly; and hereafter, Belle, you will have to meet me in an entirely different spirit before you and I can ever be upon the old footing again. I hope, at least, that you now understand, once for all, that I shall not accompany you and Wilhelm upon any trip."

She turned and walked with quiet dignity from the room as she ceased speaking, leaving Mrs. Mencke looking both startled and confounded by the resolute and unexpected stand that she had taken regarding her guardianship.

"Where on earth can she have found out about that point of law?" she muttered, angrily. "Some more of that carpenter's doings, I suppose."

She sat for some time absorbed in thought; but finally her face cleared, and rising she rang the bell.

The housemaid answered it almost immediately.

"Tell James to put the horses back into the carriage as quickly as possible, as I have forgotten something and must go immediately to the city again," she commanded, as she rearranged her wrap.

In less than ten minutes she was on her way, not back to the city, but to call upon an intimate friend in Eden Park.

CHAPTER IX.
VIOLET BECOMES A PRISONER.

Mrs. Alexander Hartley Hawley, as she was always particular to write her name, was much the same type of a woman as Mrs. Mencke, but with the advantage of not possessing such an exceedingly high temper.

She was more suave and insinuating in her manner, and where she had a difficult object to attain she always strove to win by strategy rather than to antagonize her opponents by attempting to drive.

She also was intensely proud and tenacious of caste—a leader in society and a great stickler regarding outward appearance.

In the old days, when Mrs. Mencke had so offended against upper-tendom by eloping with the poor clerk in her father's employ, Mrs. Hawley had dropped her from her extensive list of acquaintances; but after Mr. Huntington's death, when the young couple came into possession of a handsome inheritance, the former friendship was renewed and their intimacy, if anything, had been closer than during their youthful days.

To this friend and ally, who resided among the glories of Eden Park, Mrs. Mencke now repaired to ask her advice regarding what course to pursue with Violet in her present unmanageable mood.

She frankly confided everything to her, and concluded her revelation by remarking, with an anxious brow:

"I am at my wits' end, Althea, and have come to ask your help in this emergency."

"Certainly, Belle, I will do all in my power to help you," Mrs. Hawley replied, eagerly, for she dearly loved to exercise her diplomatic talents, "but I fear that will not be much, for we have decided, quite suddenly, to sail for Europe the tenth of next month."

"Yes, I learned of your plans to-day through Mrs. Rider, and when Violet got upon her stilts, on my return from my calls, it suddenly occurred to me that perhaps if the matter was rightly managed and you would not mind the care for a while, she would accept an invitation from you to travel in Europe for a time. I would appear to oppose it at first, but gradually yield to your persuasions, and, later, I would myself join you abroad and relieve you of your charge. Once get her across the Atlantic, and it will be an easy matter to keep her there until she comes to our terms."

Mrs. Hawley readily lent herself to this scheme.

"It would be a great pity," she said, with a little intentional venom pointing her words, "to have Violet sacrifice herself and compromise her position by rashly marrying this low carpenter; and," she added, eagerly, "I should be delighted to have her with me—she is excellent company, while, as you know, I am quite fond of her, and it will be the easiest thing in the world to persuade her to go with us."

"Do you think so?" Mrs. Mencke asked, somewhat doubtfully, for she began to stand a little in awe of her young sister's rapidly developing decision of character.

"Yes; Violet and Nellie Bailey are quite intimate, are they not?" Mrs. Hawley asked.

"Yes; they were firm friends all through their high-school course, and have visited each other a good deal since," returned Mrs. Mencke.

"Well, then, Mrs. Bailey came to me yesterday, asking if I would act as chaperon to Nellie, who has long wanted to spend a year in Milan to study music, and, as I readily granted her request, Miss Nellie will be my companion during at least a portion of my tour."

"I do not believe Violet knows anything about it," Mrs. Mencke replied.

"Very likely not; for her mother told me she had said nothing to Nellie—that she did not wish to arouse hopes to disappoint them, until she could arrange for a proper escort for her," Mrs. Hawley explained. "But," she added, "she probably knows it by this time. However, I am going to call there this evening, to arrange our plans a little, and will come around to your house later. I will try to bring Nellie with me. She will be full of the trip, and doubtless express a wish that Violet could go with her; and I will second her wishes by at once inviting her to make one of our party. In this way we can bring it about without appearing to have thought of such a thing before."

Mrs. Mencke was greatly pleased with this plan, and after discussing it a while longer, she took leave of her friend, and returned home with a lightened heart.

She met Violet at dinner-time, as if nothing unpleasant had occurred, and did not once refer to the Canada expedition, or any other disagreeable subject.

About seven o'clock Mrs. Hawley made her appearance, and, greatly to Mrs. Mencke's delight, she was accompanied by Nellie Bailey.

"Oh, Vio!" exclaimed that elated young lady, after the first greetings were exchanged, "I have the most delightful piece of news to tell you."

Violet looked interested immediately.

"What is it?" she asked.

"I am going to Europe next month," Nellie replied, with a face all aglow.

"Going to Europe!" Violet repeated, with a look of dismay; for her heart sank at the thought that she was about to lose her only friend.

"Yes; mamma has finally consented to let me have a year of music at Milan, and Mrs. Hawley, who is also going broad, has consented to take me under her friendly wing.

"Going for a year!" sighed Violet. "What shall I do without you?"

"Oh, it will soon slip by," said the happy girl, to whom the coming twelve months would seem all too short. "Of course I shall miss you dreadfully. I only wish you were going too. Wouldn't it be just delightful?"

"Yes, indeed. And why not?" here interposed Mrs. Hawley, who appeared to have been suddenly arrested, by this remark, in the midst of an account of a brilliant reception, which she was giving to Mrs. Mencke. "You know I am fond of your company, and should like nothing better than to have two bright girls with me. Belle, let me take Violet, too. She ought to have a nice trip abroad, now that she is out of school."

Mrs. Mencke looked thoughtful, and not especially pleased by the proposition.

"You are very kind, Althea, to propose it, but Mr. Mencke and I had planned a trip to Canada for this month and next, and we intended to take Violet with us."

Violet turned a cold, steadfast look upon her sister.

"I told you that I should not go to Canada, Belle," she said, quietly, but decidedly.

"Then come with us, by all means. I am sure it cannot make much difference whether you go to Europe or Canada, and Nellie would be very happy to have you for a chum," interposed Mrs. Hawley.

"Indeed I should. Oh, Violet, it would be simply charming. Wouldn't you like it?" Nellie cried, enthusiastically.

"Ye-s," the unsuspicious girl replied, though somewhat doubtfully, as she thought of the thousands of miles that would separate her from Wallace, if she accepted this invitation. "How long do you intend to be absent?" she concluded, turning to Mrs. Hawley.

"Oh, I shall be gone a year, perhaps two, and should enjoy having you with me all the time; but Mr. Hawley and my sister, Mrs. Dwight, will return in about three months, so if you should get homesick you could come back with them."

Mrs. Hawley was very wise; she knew that Violet would be much more likely to go if she felt she could return at any time.

The young girl wondered what Wallace would say to this plan. She really felt attracted by it; at least, it would afford her a release for a time from her sister's irritating authority.

"Why not let her come then, Belle, if she does not wish to go with you to Canada?" urged Mrs. Hawley, insinuatingly, as she turned to her friend, with a sparkle of mischief in her eyes, as she saw that Violet was really inclined to go.

"Well, I do not know," said Mrs. Mencke, contemplatively. "I suppose I should have to consult my husband—then there is the trouble of getting her ready."

"Oh, she will not need anything for the voyage except some traveling rugs and wraps and a steamer chair. We can replenish her wardrobe in Paris for half what it would cost here, so you need not trouble yourself at all on that score. Will you come, Violet?" and Mrs. Hawley turned with a winning look to the fair girl.

"Say yes—do, Vio," pleaded Nellie; and then turning to Mrs. Mencke, she added: "You will let her, won't you?"

"I have half a mind to," mused the crafty woman.

"There, Vio," cried Nellie, triumphantly; "there is nothing to hinder now."

"It is very sudden—I will think of it and let you know," Violet began, reflectively.

"There will not be very much time to think of it," Mrs. Hawley remarked, pleasantly. "You had better decide the matter at once, and thus avoid all uncertainty."

"I will let you know by the day after to-morrow," Violet returned, but she lost color as she said it.

She wanted to go, to get away from her brother and sister, but she shrank from leaving Wallace.

"She is planning to consult that fellow," Mrs. Mencke said to herself, and reading Violet like a book; "but I will take care that she doesn't get an opportunity to do so."

Mrs. Hawley said no more, but arose to take her leave, feeling that she had done all that was wise, for that day, in the furtherance of her friend's schemes.

But Nellie lingered a little, and tried to coax her friend into yielding; she was very anxious to have her companionship upon the proposed trip.

Violet was firm, however, and said again that she would like very much to go, but could not decide at such short notice.

Mrs. Mencke did not renew the subject after their caller's departure, and wisely maintained a somewhat indifferent manner, as if she did not care very much whether Violet went or not.

Mr. Mencke came in a little later from his club, and she broached the plan to him before Violet. Of course it had all been talked over before between husband and wife.

He, also appeared to graciously favor the proposition.

"Why, yes," he said, "if Violet wants to go to Europe, let her; you say she does not like the idea of going to Canada with us, and as we are going to shut up the house, she must go somewhere."

"But she is not quite sure that she even wants to go with Althea," Mrs. Mencke remarked, while she watched her sister closely.

"Humph," responded Mr. Mencke, bluntly; "it must be either one thing or the other. Which shall it be, Violet—Europe or Canada? We can't leave you here while we are away."

"It is a somewhat important question to decide at such short notice," Violet returned, coldly, and determined that she would not commit herself until she could consult Wallace.

She was a little surprised that he should still talk of Canada, for she had imagined that the trip had been planned wholly on her account.

She could not know that this was a pretense, intended to blind her still further.

The next morning Mrs. Mencke went up to Violet's room about nine o'clock and found her apparently engaged in reading a magazine.

"I am going out shopping," she remarked. "I have a great deal to do; don't you want to come and help me?"

Violet looked up in surprise.

"Why, Belle, you know that I never suit your taste in shopping, and you always veto what I suggest," she said.

"But you will need a great many things yourself for your trip abroad, and you can at least purchase handkerchiefs, stockings, underwear, and so forth," her sister returned.

"But I have not yet decided to go," Violet replied, annoyed that her acquiescence should be thus taken for granted, "and in case I do not I have plenty of everything for my needs at present."

"Well, then, Vio, come to keep me company," Mrs. Mencke urged, trying to conceal her real purpose, to keep her sister under her surveillance, beneath an affectionate exterior.

"Thank you, Belle, but really I do not want to go, and you will be so absorbed in your shopping that you will not miss me," Violet responded.

"Very well, then; just as you choose," Mrs. Mencke returned, irritably, and suddenly swept from the room, locking the door after her.

As the bolt shot into its socket, Violet sprang to her feet.

"Belle, what do you mean?" she cried, a flood of angry crimson surging to her brow.

"I mean that if you will not go with me, you shall stay where you are until I return," Mrs. Mencke sharply answered, and then she swept down the stairs with a smile of triumph on her face, for she congratulated herself that she had done a very clever thing.

Violet stood, for a moment or two, speechless and white with anger over the indignity offered her.

"She has dared to lock me up like a naughty, five-year-old child!" she cried, passionately. "I will not submit to such treatment; and besides, I have promised to meet Wallace again at two o'clock. What am I to do? Belle evidently suspected that I meant to see him, and has taken this way to prevent it."

She sat down again and tried to think, though she was trembling with excitement and anger.

There was no other outlet to her suite of rooms, and it certainly appeared as if she must remain where she was until her sister's return.

Meantime Mrs. Mencke, upon going below, had called the housemaid and confided to her that, for good reasons, she had locked Violet in her room and she charged the maid not to let her out under any circumstances.

She ordered her to carry a nice luncheon to Violet at twelve, but to be sure to lock the door both going in and coming out, and on pain of instant dismissal to pay no heed to Violet's entreaties to be set at liberty.

Then, feeling that she had safely snared her bird, at least for a few hours, she went about her shopping with an easy mind.

Violet, after thinking her condition over for a while, resolved not to make any disturbance to attract the attention of the servants.

She reasoned that Sarah, the second girl, would bring her some luncheon at noon, and she determined to seize that opportunity to effect her release; just how that was to be accomplished she did not know, but get out and go to the city she must before two o'clock.

She dressed herself for the street, all save her hat and wrap, and then began to plan ways and means.

Suddenly her face lighted, and going into her dressing-room, she surveyed the large mirror which was suspended above the marble bowl.

Taking a penknife from her pocket, she deliberately severed the heavy cord by which it was held in place, and then exerting all her strength, she let it carefully down until the bottom of the frame rested upon the marble, while the top leaned against the wall.

Having accomplished this and assured herself that the glass was perfectly safe, she went quietly back to her reading and managed to amuse herself until the clock struck twelve.

Shortly afterward she heard a step on the stairs, accompanied by the rattle of dishes, and knew that Sarah was bringing her up some luncheon.

Darting into her dressing-room, Violet seized the mirror, drew it to the very edge of the marble and assuming a strained position, she had the appearance of having caught the glass just as it was falling and in time to save it from being dashed in pieces.

Sarah unlocked the chamber-door, and finding no one there, called out:

"Miss Violet, where are you?"

"Oh, Sarah, is that you? Come here quickly, for I am in trouble," the young girl cried, appealingly.

Sarah put down her tray, but took the precaution to change the key from the outside of the door to the inside and lock it before going to the other room.

Then she went to see what was the matter.

"Why, Miss Violet," she cried, with dismay, as she took in the situation, "how did that happen?"

"The cord has parted," panted Violet, as she glanced at the ragged ends where she had sawed it asunder with her dull knife. "You will have to help me," she added, "and I think we can manage to lift it to the floor without breaking it. I do not dare to leave it standing here; it might slip on the marble."

"No," said the girl, never suspecting any ruse to outwit her, "we must take it down."

She seized one side of it in her strong arms, and, with Violet's help, managed to get it safely down upon the floor.

"Hold it a moment, please, until I get my breath," Violet said, as if wearied out by the exertion.

"Have you had to hold it there long?" Sarah asked, innocently, as she allowed the heavy frame to rest against her.

"No, not very long; but I am so glad that you came just as you did, for if it had fallen it would have frightened me terribly," Violet answered, and she uttered no untruth, for she was glad that Sarah came just as she did, because she was getting very anxious to go to Wallace and she would have been frightened if the glass had been broken.

"Sure enough, miss," the girl replied, gravely, "and it's a sign of death in the house to have a looking-glass broken. And look! the moths must have been at this cord to make it give way, for it is like a rope and could not break," and she stooped to examine the frayed ends as she spoke.

Violet seized this opportunity and slipped quickly from the room, drawing the door to and locking it after her, thus making Sarah a prisoner and securing her own liberty.

But her kind little heart and tender conscience smote her for the strategy which she had employed to accomplish her purpose, and kneeling upon the floor, she put her lips to the key-hole and said:

"Forgive me, Sarah; but it was all a little plot of mine to get out. The cord did not break; I cut it."

"Oh, Miss Violet, let me out; please, let me out," the girl cried, in distress. "Mrs. Mencke said she'd send me off without a reference if I didn't keep you safe till she came back, and I never dreamed you were playing me such a trick."

"It is a little hard on you, I confess, Sarah," Violet responded, regretfully, "and I am very sorry; but I had to do it, for I have an important engagement down town. Belle had no business to treat me so like a child, and she shall not discharge you if I can help it. I will tell her just how I deceived you, and then, if she will not be reasonable, I will give you a month's wages and help you to another place."

Sarah continued to plead to be let out, but Violet remained unshaken in her purpose.

"No, you will have to stay here a little while," she said, "but when I go down I will send the cook up to release you. When Belle comes home you can tell her that she will find me at Nellie Bailey's and that I shall not come home until she apologizes for her shameful treatment."

She could not get over her indignation at being put under lock and key, with a servant set over her as jailer.

She hastily donned her hat and wrap, drew on her gloves, and quietly left the room.

Going to the top of the basement stairs, she rang a bell for the cook.

"Bridget, Sarah wants you to go up to my dressing-room to help her with a mirror that has come down," she said; and then, without waiting for a reply, Violet sped out of the house, and, hailing the first car that came along, was soon rolling toward the city to meet her betrothed.

CHAPTER X.
"YOU WILL BE TRUE THOUGH THE OCEAN DIVIDES US."

About four o'clock of that same day Violet entered the private parlor of her friend, Nellie Bailey, her face glowing, her eyes gleaming with excitement.

"Oh, you dear child!" cried that young lady, leaping to her feet and springing forward to meet her visitor, "you have come to tell me that you are going to Europe with me."

"I have come to stay all night with you if you will let me," Violet replied, returning the eager caress with which Nellie had greeted her.

"If I will 'let' you! You know I shall be only too glad to have you. But how happy you look! You surely have good news to tell me."

Violet flushed, and her eyes drooped for a moment.

"Yes, I believe I shall go to Europe with you," she answered, her face dimpling with smiles, and Nellie immediately went into ecstasies over the announcement.

"I am perfectly enchanted," she cried; "and will you remain the whole year?"

"I do not know about that," Violet thoughtfully replied. "I have not set any time for my return. I shall go for three months at any rate, and I may conclude to remain longer."

"I wish you could come to Milan to study music with me," Nellie remarked, wistfully.

"I imagine that Belle would not consent to that," Violet returned. "She would be afraid that we two girls would get into mischief if left to ourselves. I suppose I shall travel with Mrs. Hawley, but I will try to pay you a visit now and then if I remain any length of time."

The girls found much to talk about in anticipation of their journey, and the time passed quickly and pleasantly until the dinner hour, while during the meal the family were all so agreeable and entertaining—for Violet was a great favorite with them—that she forgot, for the time, the unpleasantness of the morning and her clear, happy laugh rang out with all her customary abandon.

She had not mentioned her misunderstanding with her sister, for her pride rebelled against having it known that she was not entirely happy in her home; and when, shortly after dinner, Mrs. Mencke called and asked to see Violet alone, she excused the circumstance by remarking that she supposed it was upon some matter of business.

Mrs. Mencke had been furious, upon her return home to find how she and Sarah had both been outwitted, and she had come to Mrs. Bailey's prepared, not to apologize, but to be very severe upon the offender for her defiance of all authority.

But the sight of her happy face and sparkling eyes disarmed her, and she passed over the affair much more lightly than Violet had dared to hope she would.

The young girl frankly acknowledged the strategy she had employed, and exonerated Sarah from all blame; but she also firmly declared that if her sister would not promise to let her alone—if she persisted in the persecution of the last few days, she would reveal to Mr. and Mrs. Bailey all that had occurred, and implore their protection and assistance in securing other guardians.

Mrs. Mencke had arrived at that point where she believed that "discretion would be the better part of valor," for she realized that her young sister's spirit was too strong for her, and that she would do what she had threatened; therefore, she resolved not to antagonize her further if she could avoid it.

"It was a shame, Belle, for you to lock me up like a naughty, unreasonable child, and I will not endure such treatment," Violet indignantly affirmed, in concluding the recital of her morning's experience.

"Well, well, child, I did not know what else to do with you; but let it pass, please. Perhaps it was a mistake, and we will let by-gones be by-gones," Mrs. Mencke responded, in a conciliatory tone. "I am glad that you have decided in favor of the European trip, and I want you to go away feeling kindly toward me. Will you come home with me now?"

"Not to-night; I have promised Nellie that I would spend it with her; but you may send for me early tomorrow, for I suppose we shall have to be rather busy during the next three weeks."

"Very well; but, Vio, you will promise me that you will not try to—" Mrs. Mencke began, anxiously, for she could not rid herself of the fear that Violet would try to meet her lover clandestinely.

"Hush, Belle; I will promise you nothing," Violet interrupted, spiritedly. "I am a woman now—I have my own rights, and there are some things upon which you shall not trench. If there is to be peace between us you must let me entirely alone on one subject."

Mrs. Mencke made no reply to this. She told herself that strategy was the only course left open to her.

She joined the Bailey family for a little while for a social chat, after which she took her leave, promising to send the carriage for Violet at ten the next morning.

The ensuing three weeks passed rapidly, and without any further trouble between the sisters to mar their intercourse.

Mrs. Mencke endeavored, by every means in her power, to keep Violet under her own eye during this time, but once or twice the young girl managed to evade her vigilance. Whether she met

Wallace or not she had no means of ascertaining, but she felt that she should be truly thankful and relieved of a heavy burden when the ocean divided them.

The day of sailing drew nigh and the voyagers, accompanied by several friends, repaired to New York, where they were to take a steamer belonging to the White Star Line.

When they all went aboard the vessel, on the morning of the tenth, Mrs. Mencke was both amazed and dismayed to see Wallace Richardson advance and greet Violet with all the assurance of an accepted suitor; while the young girl herself, though her face lighted up joyously as she caught sight of him, did not seem in the least surprised to find him there.

The fact was, Wallace had told Violet that he had a call to go to New York on business, and he would arrange to be there at the time that she sailed.

If looks could have annihilated him, he would at once have vanished forever from the sight of men; but as he met Mrs. Mencke's angry glance he courteously lifted his hat and bowed, and then went on with his conversation with Violet.

Of course it would not do to make a scene in such a conspicuous place, and the enraged woman was obliged to curb her passion; but she thanked the fates that Violet was going so far away, and she vowed that it would be a long while before she returned.

She intended to keep the young couple under her eye until the steamer started, but, in the confusion which everywhere prevailed, they managed to slip out of sight before she was aware of it, and after that she could not find them.

They were not far away, however, and their security lay in this very fact. They had simply stepped between a couple of stacks of baggage for a few last words to each other, while they became oblivious of everything save the thought of their approaching separation.

"My darling, it is hard to let you go—harder than I thought it would be, now that the time has arrived," Wallace said, as he took both her hands in his and looked tenderly into her sorrowful face.

"I almost wish I could not go, after all," Violet faltered, as the hot tears rushed into her eyes. "I will not—I will stay, even now, if you will tell me I may," she concluded, resolutely.

"No, love; that would be unwise, and I know it is better that you should go—better for you, better for me," he replied.

"But I shall come back in three months," Violet said, with an air of decision. "I could not stay away from you longer than that."

"If you feel that you must, I will not oppose it, dear," the young man returned, tenderly. "Still, if you can be contented to remain a year, I believe it would be a good plan for you to do so. Meantime I will do my utmost to attain a position which shall warrant me in claiming this dear hand when you return."

"I shall write to you by every steamer, Wallace, and you will be sure to answer as regularly," Violet pleaded.

"Indeed I shall, and I am promising myself a great deal of pleasure from our correspondence—more, in fact, than I have yet known, for our clandestine meetings have been very galling to me. I never like to do anything that is not perfectly open and straightforward," Wallace said, gravely.

"Neither do I," returned Violet; "but we were driven to it."

"True, and therefore I feel that it was justifiable. They, your guardians, would have separated us if they could; but this faithful little heart could not be won from its allegiance; and, my darling, I am sure you will still be true to me, even though the ocean divides us."

Violet's fingers closed over his with a convulsive, almost a painful clasp.

"Always; nothing—no one could ever tempt me from my faith to you, Wallace," she huskily murmured. "Oh!" she cried, with a sudden start, as a warning whistle blew, "does that mean that you must go?"

"Yes, within five minutes," he replied. "And now, my heart's queen, no one can see us; therefore give me just one parting kiss, and that must be our farewell, for I cannot take leave of you before others."

He bent and gathered her quickly in his arms, straining her to his breast with a close, yearning clasp, and pressed his lips to hers in one lingering caress.

"My love, my love, you will take the light from my world when you go," he murmured, fondly.

Then he released her, and led her forth from their hiding-place toward where her friends were gathered.

"Why, Violet, we have been alarmed about you, and our friends feared they would have to go without saying good-by to you," Mrs. Mencke exclaimed, in a tone that plainly indicated her displeasure at her sister's behavior.

But there was no time for reproaches. Everybody was bidding everybody else a last farewell, and presently the cry, "All ashore!" sounded, and there was a general stampede of all those who were not outward bound.

Wallace remained until the last moment. His was the last hand that touched Violet's, his the last voice that sounded in her ears with the words:

"Good-by, queen of my heart, and Heaven bless you!"

Then he leaped across the gang-plank, just as it was being removed.

Violet's heart was full to overflowing at this parting, and she sped down to her state-room, where, half an hour later, Nellie Bailey found her sobbing hysterically.

"Why, you silly child!" she cried, assuming a light tone, although her own eyes were full and her voice tremulous, "this does not look as if you were very much elated over the prospect of going to Europe. Are all the tears for that handsome young man who appeared so loath to leave you? By the way, Violet, was that the Mr. Richardson who saved you at the time of the inclined plane accident?"

"Yes," Violet murmured, between her sobs.

"I imagined so from something your sister said; she isn't over fond of him, is she?" Nellie inquired, with a light laugh and a mischievous glance at the averted face on the pillow in the berth, as she emphasized the pronoun. "Come," she added, presently, "let us lay out the things we are likely to need during the voyage, and put our state-room in order, for there is no knowing how soon we may be attacked by the dread enemy of all voyagers."

"Oh, I hope we shall not be sick," Violet said, diverted from her grief by Nellie's practical suggestion, and wiping away her tears. "I love the water, and I want to make the most of the time we are on the ocean. Let us make up our minds that we will not be ill."

"I suppose we can control it, in a measure, by the exercise of will power," Nellie answered, "and I will try what I can do in that respect, although I very much fear that the sea will prove to be mightier than I."

The two girls soon had their small room in order, and everything handy for the voyage, then they went up on the deck to seek their friends, Mr. and Mrs. Hawley, and the sister of the latter, Mrs. Dwight.

Mrs. Hawley eyed Violet curiously for a moment, noticing her heavy eyes and the grieved droop about her sweet mouth, then set herself to divert her mind from the recent farewell, which she plainly saw had been a severe trial.

She was one of those remarkable women who can adapt themselves to all kinds of society and circumstances. She could be delightful in a drawing-room full of cultured people; she could entertain a group of children by the hour, while the young people pronounced her the most charming companion imaginable.

It was not long, therefore, before she made Violet entirely forget herself and her recent sadness, and the young girl soon found herself laughing heartily over some droll incident of which Mrs. Hawley had recently been the amused and appreciative observer.

They were standing in a group by themselves, and by degrees became so gay and merry that two gentlemen, standing a short distance from them, became infected with their mirth.

"A gay party, isn't it, Ralph?" remarked the elder of the two.

"Jolly; I wish we knew them; and they are about as pretty a pair of girls as I have ever seen. Do you suppose they are sisters?"

"No, I do not believe it; they have not a feature or characteristic in common, as far as I can see. That golden-haired one is a perfect little Hebe; her complexion and features are perfect, her figure faultless, while she has the daintiest hands and feet that I ever saw," said the first speaker.

"Really, Cameron, I believe you are hard hit, at last," laughed his companion. "I never knew you to express yourself so enthusiastically regarding a woman before."

"I never had occasion," returned Cameron, dryly. "We must manage some way to make the acquaintance of yonder party—eh, Henderson?"

Fate seemed anxious to give him the opportunity he desired, for, just at that moment, a gust of wind lifted Violet's jaunty hat from her head and sent it flying toward the two distinguished-looking strangers, and in another moment it would have been swept into the sea and lost beyond recovery.

But the one who had been called Cameron sprang forward, and, with a quick, agile movement, one sweep of his strong right arm, caught it just as it was going over the rail.

With a gratified smile on his handsome face, and an air of courtly politeness, he approached Violet, and bowing, remarked:

"Allow me to restore the bird that took such unceremonious flight."

He glanced at the golden-winged oriole which nestled so jauntily in its brown velvet nest upon the hat as he spoke.

The fair girl thanked him, flushed slightly beneath his admiring look, and Mrs. Hawley graciously echoed her appreciation of his dexterity.

"Allow me to compliment you, sir, upon your agility," she said, in her cordial, outspoken way; "that was a leap worthy of an accomplished athlete."

"Thanks, madame," young Cameron returned, lifting his hat in acknowledgment of her praise.

Then he would have withdrawn himself from their presence, though he longed to stay, but Mr. Hawley, who had been attracted by his fine face and gentlemanly bearing, remarked:

"Since we are to be fellow-voyagers for a week or more, may I ask to whom we are indebted? My name is Hawley, of the firm of Hawley & Blake, Cincinnati, Ohio."

"Thank you," the young man replied, with a genial smile, "and I am known as Vane Cameron. I am as yet connected with no firm, but my home has for many years been in New York."

"Cameron—Cameron," repeated Mrs. Hawley, meditatively. "I wonder if he can be a relative of that Anson Cameron who married the Earl of Sutherland's daughter about the time of our marriage. It created considerable talk among the grandees of New York, I remember, for the lady was very beautiful as well as of noble blood."

Mrs. Hawley's reflection were here cut short by her husband, who introduced her to the handsome young stranger, and then he proceeded to perform the same ceremony for the other members of his party.

Mr. Vane Cameron was apparently about thirty years of age, fine-looking, neither very dark nor very light, with a clear-cut patrician face, a grandly developed form, a dignified bearing, and irreproachable manners.

He conversed in an easy, self-possessed manner with his new acquaintances for a few moments, and then craved permission to introducc his friend.

This request was cordially granted, and Mrs. Hawley ere long congratulated herself upon having secured a very pleasant addition to her party, for Mr. Ralph Henderson proved to be no less entertaining, although a much younger man, than his *compagnon du voyage*.

By a few very adroit questions, and putting this and that together, Mrs. Hawley learned that Mr. Vane Cameron was the son of Mr. Anson Cameron and the grandson of the late Earl of Sutherland, consequently the heir of the distinguished peer; and, more than that, she gleaned the interesting item that he was now on his way to England to take possession of his fine inheritance.

It is remarkable how much one woman can find out in a short time. Mrs. Hawley also learned that Mr. Ralph Henderson belonged to an aristocratic family who were numbered among the envied "four hundred" of New York.

"If I do not improve my opportunities during the next eight or nine days, it will be because my usual wit and ability fail me," the lady said to herself, after making these discoveries. "I have two pretty girls under my wing, and these young men are not backward in realizing the fact either. Violet, my pansy-eyed darling, I'll manage to make you forget that carpenter lover of yours long before your stipulated three months are at an end, or my name isn't Althea. I'd like nothing better than to write you among my list of friends as Countess of Sutherland; and Nellie, my modest little brunette, you would make a delightful little spouse for that agreeable Mr. Henderson."

CHAPTER XI.
"DEATH HAS RELEASED YOU FROM YOUR PROMISE."

The voyage across the Atlantic proved to be a most delightful one.

Vane Cameron and Ralph Henderson, by tacit consent, joined Mrs. Hawley's party, and were so entertaining and attentive that they all congratulated themselves upon having secured so pleasant an addition to their company.

By the time they reached England Vane Cameron had surrendered his hitherto impregnable heart entirely to Violet, and when he bade Mrs. Hawley and her charges good-by, after seeing them comfortably established in the hotel where they were to remain during their sojourn in London, he asked the privilege of bringing his mother—who had preceded him to England by several months—to make their acquaintance.

This was an honor which Mrs. Hawley had hardly anticipated; she well knew the exclusive proclivities of British blue blood, and was highly elated by the prospect of being introduced into London society by Isabel, only child of the late Earl of Sutherland.

It is needless to state she graciously accorded the young man the privilege he asked, and delightfully looked forward to the promised visit.

She had not long to wait, for before the week was out Lady Isabel, accompanied by her son, came to make her call, and she appeared to be no less attracted by the beauty and winning manner of Violet than young Cameron had been.

Mrs. Hawley made herself exceedingly agreeable by her courtesy and cultured self-possession, and before she left it was arranged that her ladyship would give a reception at an early date for the purpose of introducing her new acquaintances to London society.

After that there followed a whirl of pleasure and excitement such as Violet and Nellie had read about, but never expected to enjoy.

Mr. Henderson and the young girl, as he was now commonly recognized, attended them everywhere, until it began to be remarked in select circles that the son was likely to follow the example of his mother by marrying a wealthy American.

Mrs. Hawley's reports to Mrs. Mencke of all this were highly satisfactory, and the worldly minded sister congratulated herself that she had sent Violet abroad instead of insisting upon her going to Canada.

She had neither seen nor heard anything of young Richardson since Violet's departure, although Mr. Mencke had tried to post himself regarding his movements. All he could learn, however, was that he had left Cincinnati a few weeks after Violet sailed, but no one could tell him whither he had gone.

This was something of a relief, although the Menckes would have been glad to keep track of him, for a dim suspicion that he might have followed Violet haunted them.

The young girl expected to hear from her lover soon after reaching London, but three weeks went by, and not one line had she received. She was getting very anxious and impatient, but of course she did not dare to betray anything of the feeling, and so strove to bear her disappointment with as bold a front as possible.

She, however, faithfully wrote to Wallace every two or three days, and in each letter mentioned the fact that she had not heard from him, and begged him not to keep her longer in suspense.

She imagined that she exercised great care in sending her letters so that Mrs. Hawley would not suspect the correspondence, for she went down to the hotel letter-box to post every one with her own hands.

But Mrs. Hawley had received orders from Mrs. Mencke to intercept all such missives, and she, in turn, gave instructions to the hotel clerk that all epistles addressed to "Wallace Richardson, Cincinnati, Ohio," be returned to her.

Thus the lovers never heard one word from each other—though, to the woman's credit be it said, if there was any credit due her—she conscientiously burned every letter, unopened, for she was secretly very fond of Violet and could not bring herself to wrong her still further by perusing the sacred expressions of her loving little heart, or the fond words which Wallace intended only for her eye.

But Violet, though anxious, could not find much time to indulge her grief, for she was kept in such a constant round of excitement. Several times Nellie awoke in the night to find her weeping, but, upon inquiring the cause of her tears, Violet would either avoid a direct reply, or allow her friend to attribute her grief to homesickness.

One day, about six weeks after Mrs. Hawley and her party reached London, every one appeared very much surprised by the arrival of Mr. and Mrs. Mencke at the same hotel.

Mr. and Mrs. Hawley alone were in the secret of their coming, but they did not betray the fact in their greeting, and Violet, though she met her sister affectionately, was at heart very much annoyed by her arrival.

Mrs. Mencke and Mrs. Hawley improved the first opportunity to have a long, confidential talk upon all that had occurred during the period of their separation, and the former was fairly jubilant over her friend's account of the Earl of Sutherland's attentions to Violet.

"An English earl!" she exclaimed, with a glowing face. "That is positively bewildering! And you think that Violet likes him?"

"She cannot help liking him," responded Mrs. Hawley; "for he has a way that is perfectly irresistible. As I wrote to you, he is a good deal older than she is, and he possesses a quiet dignity, and a certain masterful manner that carries everything before it."

"If he will only prove himself masterful enough to conquer Violet's will and make her marry him, I shall be too proud and thankful to contain myself," said Mrs. Mencke, earnestly.

"It is very evident that he intends to do so if he can," returned her friend, "and we must leave no opportunity unimproved to help him in his wooing. We must keep Violet so busy with engagements that she will have no time to think about her carpenter lover."

Two more weeks passed, and still Violet did not hear from Wallace, and the secret suspense and anxiety were beginning to tell visibly upon her.

She lost color and spirit, and but for the fear of exciting suspicion, she would have refused to mingle in the gay scenes which were becoming wearisome to her.

There was still a ceaseless round of pleasure, receptions, parties, opera, and theatre, and everywhere the party was attended by two young gentlemen who had become so deeply enamored of the beautiful American girls.

Violet tried her best to resist the force of the stream that seemed to be hurrying her on whither she would not go, but without avail; for Vane Cameron was always at her side, and everybody appeared to take it for granted that he had a right to be there, while it became evident to Violet that he was only waiting for a favorable opportunity to declare himself her lover.

What she dreaded came at last.

They all attended the opera one evening, and a brilliant appearance they made as they sat in one of the proscenium boxes. But Violet did not enjoy the performance, and could not follow it; her thoughts would go back to that fateful day when her life was saved by the coolness and determination of Wallace Richardson. From that moment her soul had seemed to become linked to his by some mysterious and indissoluble bond.

All through the brilliant performance she sat absorbed, feeling sad, depressed, and inexpressibly anxious, and looking like some pale, beautiful spirit in her white dress trimmed with swan's-down, that was scarcely less colorless than herself.

Lord Cameron thought he had never seen her so lovely, but he realized that something was not quite right with her, and, though he had received Mrs. Mencke's permission to speak when he would, he resolved not to trouble her that night with any expression of his affection.

After their return to the hotel, Mrs. Mencke followed Violet to her room, pride and triumph written upon every line of her face.

"Have you anything to tell me, Violet?" she asked, a tremulous eagerness in her tones.

"No; what could you imagine that I should have to tell you?" the young girl replied, regarding her with surprise.

"What ails you, Violet?" Mrs. Mencke asked, with a sudden heart-throb, as she noticed her unusual pallor. "Are you sick? Has—anything happened?"

"No, I am not sick," Violet answered, with a heavy sigh; "and what could happen that you would not know about?"

"I know what I wish would happen," returned her sister, eagerly, "and what Lord Cameron wishes, too. He had eyes for no one but you to-night, and I must say I never saw you look so pretty before. Your dress is just exquisite, and it cost a heap of money, too; but that counts for nothing in comparison with the conquest you have made."

Violet could not fail to understand what all this meant. She flushed hotly, and nervously began to pull off her gloves.

Mrs. Mencke smiled at the blush; it was ominous for good, she thought.

"You comprehend, I perceive," she said, airily; "you know that you have captured a prize—that the Earl of Sutherland is ready and waiting to offer you a name and position such as does not fall to the lot of one girl in ten thousand."

"Nonsense, Belle! I wish you would not talk so to me about Lord Cameron," Violet petulantly exclaimed.

"It is not nonsense, child, for Vane Cameron has formally proposed for your hand in marriage—has asked Will's and my consent to win you if he can."

"Belle!"

Violet turned upon her sister, crimson to the roots of her hair, blank dismay written upon every feature of her fair face.

"It is true," Mrs. Mencke continued, "and it is wonderful luck for you. Just think, Violet, what it means to step into such a position! I am proud of your conquest."

Violet suddenly grew cold and pale as snow.

"Belle, you know it can never be," she began, with white lips, when Mrs. Mencke interrupted her angrily.

"It can be—it must be—it shall be; for I have given my unqualified consent to his lordship's proposal," she cried, actually trembling from excitement.

"Belle, you have not dared to do such a thing! You know that I am promised to another," the young girl cried with blazing eyes.

A queer look shot over Mrs. Mencke's face at this reply, and she opened her lips as if to make one sharp, unguarded retort. Then she suddenly checked herself, and, after a moment, remarked, in a repressed tone:

"You know well enough that that foolish escapade of yours counts for nothing, and that young Richardson has no right to hold you bound by any promise you may have impulsively given him from a feeling of gratitude."

"I hold myself bound, nevertheless," Violet returned, with tremulous lips, "and not from any feeling of gratitude either; but because I love him with all my heart."

"You shall never marry him," retorted her sister, angrily. "Are you mad to think of throwing away such a chance as this for a low-born fellow like that? It is not to be thought of for one moment; and, Violet, you shall marry Vane Cameron.

"Take care, Belle, you are going a little too far now," Violet cried, a dangerous flame leaping into her eyes. "I shall not marry Lord Cameron. I have given my word to Wallace, and I shall abide by it."

"Violet!" cried her sister, sternly, and she was now as white as the snowy lace about her neck, "there shall be no more of this child's play. You shall not ruin your life by any such foolishness. What will Vane Cameron think of me for granting him the permission he craved? It was equivalent to admitting that he would find no obstacle in his path. What could you tell him?"

"The truth—that I do not love him; that I do love some one else," bravely and steadfastly returned the young girl.

"You shall not! I should die with mortification and disappointment," cried Mrs. Mencke, wringing her hands in distress. Then bridling again, she went on, in an inflexible tone: "I will give you just one week to reconsider your folly; I will intimate to Lord Cameron that you are a little shy of the subject—that it will be just as well for him not to speak for perhaps a couple of weeks; but—hear me, Violet—if you refuse to come to my terms at the end of that time, I will take you to France and shut you up in a convent, where you shall stay until you will solemnly promise me that you will give up your miserable Yankee lover."

She turned and abruptly left the room without giving Violet a chance to reply.

Violet stood still a moment, looking wretched enough to break one's heart; then throwing herself upon her bed, she gave way to a passion of tears and sobbing.

"Oh, Wallace, where are you?" she moaned, "why don't you write to me? I feel as if I was being led into a trap, and"—with a sudden light seeming to burst upon her—"I believe they have been intercepting our letters, for I know that you would be faithful to me. Oh, I am homesick for you, and now that Belle and Will have come I know they will not let me go back at the end of three months. What shall I do? Of course I cannot marry Lord Cameron, and I shall tell him the truth if he asks me."

She lay for a long time trying to think of some way out of her troubles. At last, when she had become more calm, she arose, exchanged her beautiful evening dress for a wrapper, and then wrote a long letter to Wallace, telling him all about her perplexity and suspicions, begging him to send her some news of himself and to address his letter to Nellie.

Not having received any of his letters, she of course did not know that he had removed from Cincinnati; therefore she directed her letter as usual, and, of course, he never got it; although she slyly posted it in the letter-box on one of the public buildings of the city while she was out sight-seeing the next day.

At the end of a week Mrs. Mencke sought Violet and renewed the subject of Vane Cameron's proposal.

"I wish you would let me alone about that, Belle," the young girl responded, wearily. "It is useless for you to try to change my decision—my word is pledged to Wallace, and only death will ever release me from it, for if I live to go home I shall redeem it."

"That is your ultimatum, is it?" demanded her sister, with a face as hard as adamant.

"Yes."

"Then you oblige me to communicate a fact which, for several reasons, I should have preferred to withhold from you," said Mrs. Mencke, bending a strange look upon her.

"What do you mean?" Violet inquired, startled by her manner.

"Death has released you from your promise to that fellow. Read that," was the stunning reply, as the woman drew a paper from her pocket, and, laying it before Violet, pointed to a marked paragraph.

"Belle!" came in a low, shuddering voice from the blanched lips of the beautiful girl before her, as she seemed instinctively to know what was printed here.

"Read," commanded Mrs. Mencke, relentlessly.

With hands that shook like leaves in the wind, Violet picked up the paper. It was the Cincinnati *Times-Star*, and she read with a look of horror on her young face:

Died, on the 28th instant, Wallace Richardson, aged 23 years and 6 months.

The next moment a piercing shriek rang through the room, and Violet lay stretched senseless at her sister's feet.

"Heavens! I did not think she would take it to heart like this," cried the now thoroughly frightened woman, as she threw herself upon her knees beside the motionless girl and began to loosen her clothing and chafe her hands.

That heart-broken cry had been heard in the adjoining room, and Mrs. Hawley and Nellie came rushing upon the scene to ascertain the cause of it.

They assisted in getting Violet to bed, and a physician was immediately sent for.

"She has had some sudden and violent shock," he said at once, while he regarded Mrs. Mencke searchingly.

"Yes," she confessed, with as much composure as her guilty conscience would allow her to assume; "she read an account of the death of a—a friend, in an American paper."

"Hem!" was the medical man's brief comment, as he again turned his attention to his patient, whom, it was evident, he considered to be in a critical state.

It was long before he could restore suspended animation, and even then Violet did not come back to consciousness; fever followed, and she began to rave in the wildest delirium.

"It's going to be a neck-and-neck race between life and death," the doctor frankly told her friends, "and you must be vigilant and patient."

This unforeseen calamity, of course, put an end to all gayety.

It was thought best that Nellie should at once repair to Milan, and Mrs. Hawley left two days later to see her safely and comfortably settled at her work, after which she returned to London to assist Mrs. Mencke in the care of her sister.

It was more than a month before Violet was pronounced out of danger; and then, as soon as she was able to sit up, the physician advised a change of climate; a few weeks at Mentone, he thought, would do her good.

The poor girl looked as if a rude breath would quench what little life she had, and Mrs. Mencke, who still secretly clung to the hope of affecting an alliance between her and Lord Cameron, was anxious to do everything to build her up; consequently she immediately posted off with her invalid to that far-famed resort. She had a private interview first, however, with his lordship, from whom the real cause of Violet's illness had been kept a profound secret, and promised to send for him just as soon as her sister was able to see him.

The mild and genial atmosphere of Mentone produced a favorable change in the invalid immediately. Her appetite improved, and with it strength and something of her natural color.

But the child was pitifully sad—heart-broken. Nothing appeared to interest her, and she seemed to live from day to day only because nature was stronger than her grief.

She never spoke of Wallace, nor referred to the fact that her illness had been caused by the dreadful tidings of his death. She was patient, gentle, and submissive, doing whatever she was told to do, simply because it was easier than to resist, and, as she slowly but surely gained, Mrs. Mencke told herself that the way was clear to the consummation of her ambitious hopes.

A month passed thus, and then Vane Cameron appeared upon the scene, having been summoned by an encouraging letter from Violet's sister.

CHAPTER XII.
"YOU HAVE GIVEN YOUR PROMISE AND YOU MUST STAND BY IT."

When Mrs. Mencke informed Violet of the arrival of the Earl of Sutherland, something of her old spirit manifested itself for the first time since her illness.

"Did you send for him, Belle?" she demanded, an ominous flash leaping into her heavy eyes.

The woman colored. She did not like to confess that she had done so, but such was the fact, nevertheless.

"Why, Violet, you forget how anxious Lord Cameron would naturally be regarding the state of your health," she answered, evasively; "besides, he has waited a long time for the answer to a certain proposal, and doubtless he is impatient for that."

"He shall have it," the young girl returned, with sudden animation, a crimson flush suffusing her cheeks. "Send for him to come directly here, and I will give it at once."

Mrs. Mencke regarded her doubtfully.

"And it will be——" she began.

"No!" replied Violet, emphatically, as she paused.

"Oh, Violet, I beg of you to be reasonable," pleaded the woman, almost in tears. "Just think what your life must be! One of the highest positions in England is offered you by a young man of irreproachable character; he loves you devotedly, and there is nothing he would not do for you if you consent to become his wife. Besides a large income which he will settle upon you, you will have an elegant home in Essex County, a town house in London, and a villa on the Isle of Wight. There is no earthly reason now, whatever there may have been two months ago, why you should not listen to his suit."

Violet shivered with sudden pain as her sister thus referred to the death of her lover, and the fact that no plighted troth now stood in the way of her accepting Lord Cameron's proposal of marriage.

"No," she wailed, "I suppose there is no reason, save that I do not love him—that my heart is dead, and I have no interest in life, no desire to live."

"You may imagine now that you can never love him, but time heals all wounds," her sister returned; "and since you can now feel that you will wrong no one else by marrying him, you might at least devote yourself to him and secure his happiness by accepting him."

"Do you imagine that he would be willing to marry a loveless woman—one who had no heart to give him?" Violet questioned, with curling lips.

"He only can answer that question himself," responded Mrs. Mencke, with a sudden heart-bound, as she thought she saw signs of yielding in her sister. "Oh, Violet, do not throw away such a chance. What are you going to do in the future? How do you expect to spend the rest of your life if you refuse to marry at all?"

A thrill of intense agony ran through the young girl's frame at these probing questions.

How indeed was she to spend her life? How could she live without Wallace?

She had not thought of this before, and she was startled and appalled by the apparent blackness of the future.

"Oh, I don't know—I don't know!" she burst forth, in a voice of despair.

"As the wife of Lord Cameron you would at least have it in your power to do a great deal of good, to say nothing of the happiness you would confer upon him," suggested Mrs. Mencke, craftily.

It impressed Violet, however, and she sat in thoughtful silence for some time.

One thing had forced itself upon her during this conversation, and that was that she could not spend her life with her sister and her husband. Every day she became more and more conscious that there could never be any real congeniality and sympathy between them, and that it would be better if they should separate. But what was to become of her if she separated from them? Could she live alone—take her destiny in her own hands, and cut herself free from them? It would certainly be very lonely, very forlorn, to have no one in the world to care for her.

She knew that Vane Cameron was a man in a thousand. He was noble and amiable; whatever he did, he was actuated by pure motives, and she felt that any woman who could love him would have cause to be proud in becoming his wife.

She knew that he loved her devotedly, as her sister had said; but would he be willing to marry one who did not love him? Would it be right for her to accept all and be able to give nothing in return?

No, she did not believe he would be satisfied to live out his future in any such way.

Still she conceived a sudden resolution. She would see him; she would tell him the truth, and she believed he would sympathize with her and at once withdraw his suit, while her sister would have to accept his decision as final, and cease to importune her further upon the subject.

Having arrived at this conclusion, she leaned back in her chair, with a deep sigh, as if relieved of a heavy burden.

"Well?" said Mrs. Mencke, inquiringly.

She had been watching her closely, and surmised something of what was being revolved in her mind.

"I will see Lord Cameron," Violet quietly replied.

"And you will promise to marry him?" cried her companion, eagerly.

Violet sighed again. She was so weary of it all.

"No, I will not promise anything now; but I will see him—I will tell him the whole truth, and then——"

"Well?" was the almost breathless query, as Violet faltered and her lips grew white.

"Then he shall decide for me," she said, in a low tone.

Mrs. Mencke arose delighted, for she felt that her point was gained. She would encourage Vane Cameron to take Violet, in spite of everything, and try to make him feel that once she was his wife he would have little difficulty in eventually winning her love.

She bent over Violet, in the excess of her joy, to kiss her, but the young girl drew back from her.

"No, Belle," she said, quietly but sadly, "do not make any pretense of affection for me; you have not shown yourself a good sister; I believe you have intercepted my letters, and you have tried to ruin my life, and I do not want your kisses. I hope I shall not always feel thus," she added, regretfully, as she saw the guilty flush which mounted to the woman's forehead, "but, just now, I am afraid I do not love you very much, and I will not be hypocritical enough to pretend that I do."

Mrs. Mencke had nothing to say to this, for she well knew that she richly deserved it; but she passed quickly from the room, and at once sought an interview with Lord Cameron.

An hour later he was sitting beside Violet, with a grave and pitiful face, but with a look of eager hope in his fine eyes, which told that he had no thought of leaving her presence a rejected lover.

"Your illness has changed you greatly, Miss Huntington," he remarked, regarding her thin, white face sorrowfully, "but I hope that you will soon be yourself again, and—and now may I at once speak of what is nearest my heart? I believe in a frank course at all times, and of course you cannot be ignorant of my object in coming to you. I am sure you must realize, by this time, something of the depth of my love for you. Indeed my one hope, ever since our pleasant voyage across the water, has been to win you. Darling, words cannot express one-half that I feel; I have lived almost thirty years without ever meeting any one with whom I could be willing to spend my life until now, and all the long-pent-up passion of my nature goes forth to you. Violet, will you be my wife? will you come to me and let me shelter you in the arms of my love—let me try to make your future the brightest one that woman has ever known? My love! my love! put your little hands in mine and say that you will give yourself to me."

Violet made such a gesture of pain at these words, while her face was convulsed with such anguish, that Vane Cameron caught his breath and regarded her with astonishment.

When Mrs. Mencke had told him that Violet had consented to see him, she hinted at some childish attachment, but encouraged him to hope for a favorable issue of the interview.

He realized now, however, that this "childish attachment" had left a far deeper wound in Violet's heart than he had been allowed to suspect.

"Is my confession distasteful to you, Violet?" he gravely asked, when he could command himself to speak. "I was led to believe—I hoped that it would meet with a ready response from you."

"Oh, Lord Cameron! I do not know what to say to you," Violet began, in a trembling voice. Then resolutely repressing her emotion, she continued: "I have known, of course, that you regarded me in a very friendly way; but it almost frightens me to have you express yourself so strongly as you have just done."

"Frightens you to learn of the depth of my affection," he said, with some surprise.

"Yes—to know that it has taken such a hold upon your life and that such a responsibility has fallen upon me. I know that you are good, and true, and noble, and you have my deepest esteem; but—but oh——"

"Violet, what does this mean? I do not understand your distress at all," Lord Cameron said, looking deeply pained.

"Did not my sister tell you that I had a confession to make to you?" the young girl asked, with burning cheeks.

"No," the young man returned, very gravely; "she told me that you would receive me—that I might hope for a favorable answer to my suit. She did hint, however, that there had once been a childish attachment, as she expressed it; but I hardly gave the matter a thought since she made so light of it."

"Belle has done wrong, then, to let you hope for so much; and now, Lord Cameron, may I tell you all there is in my heart? May I make a full confession to you? and then you shall judge me as you will."

"Certainly, you may tell me anything you wish," he replied, wondering more and more at her excessive emotion. "Do not be so distressed, dear child," he added, as she covered her face with her thin hands, and he saw the tears trickling between her fingers. "I should blame myself more than I can tell you, for seeking this interview, if by so doing I cause you so much unhappiness. I will even go away and never renew this subject—though that would darken all my future life—rather than agitate you thus."

"Forgive me," Violet said, wiping her tears. "I will try not to break down like this again, and I will deal with you with perfect frankness; I know I do not need to ask you to respect my confidence."

"Thank you," he simply answered.

Violet then began by relating the accident of the incline plane and its frightful consequences; she told how, almost miraculously, she and Wallace were saved; about her illness in his home, and of their growing fondness for each other during her convalescence. When she told of Wallace's confession of his love for her and hers for him, she bowed her face again upon her hands and went on, in quick, passionate tones, as if it was too sacred to be talked about and she was anxious to have the recital over as soon as possible. She spoke of her sister's opposition to this affection and its consequences, with all the passion and trouble it had aroused, and Vane Cameron's face grew graver, yet very tender and pitiful as she proceeded. It was all told at last—Violet had concealed nothing of her affection for Wallace, nothing of her rebellion against her sister's wishes regarding her marriage with himself, and having thus unburdened her soul, she still sat with bowed head before him, waiting for his judgment of her.

There was a silence of several minutes after she had concluded, while both seemed to be battling with the emotions which filled their hearts; then Lord Cameron spoke, and the tender cadence of his voice thrilled the young girl as it had never done before.

"Poor child! poor wounded, loving heart!" he said. "I wonder how you have borne your sorrow. I know there is no human sympathy that can heal your wound—only One, who has all power, can do that. But, Violet, I can see, even though you shrink from saying it—even though you have tried to hide as much of the wrong done you by others as you could—I can see that you are unhappy from other causes than the loss of this dear one. Your heart is starving for sympathy, love, and comfort. Now, just as frankly as you have talked to me, I am now going to talk to you. You have said that the drama of your life is played out—has ended in tragedy; that you have loved and lost—your heart has exhausted itself, and you can never love again. This may be so, Violet; we will assume that it is"—his lip quivered painfully as he said it, and his face was very pale—"still, in all probability, there are many years of life before you—years which may be filled with much of good for those about you, if not of absolute happiness for yourself. Could you make up your mind to spend them with me? Do not be startled by the proposition, dear," he said, as he saw the quiver that agitated her; "you shall think of it as long as you will, and shall not be urged to anything from which you shrink. I love you—that fact remains unalterable, in spite of all that you have told me, and though your heart may not have one responsive vibration to mine, yet I feel that I would gladly devote all my future to the work of winning you to a more cheerful frame of mind—that I should be happier in doing that than in living without you. Let me take care of you. You have said you were tired of traveling—that you long for home and rest. Come to my home—you shall have all the rest and seclusion you wish—you shall live as you will; only let me give you the protection of my love and my name and throw around you all the comforting influences that I can. Forgive me if I refer to your sad past; but only for this once. The dear one whom you have honored with your love is gone; I do not ask you to forget him, or to violate, in any way, the affection that belongs to him; but, since your life must be lived out somewhere, I ask you to let it be with me. Do not allow your sensitiveness to restrain you—do not feel that you will be 'wronging me' as you have expressed it, 'by giving me only the ashes of your love;' I shall be content if you will but come. Violet, will you?"

Violet was nearer loving him at that moment than she had ever been.

How grand, how noble he seemed in his utter self-abnegation—thinking only of her and of the comfort that he might manage to throw around her broken life!

Oh, she thought, if he was only her brother, how gladly she would go with him and give him all the affection that a sister might bestow upon one so worthy.

It was a great temptation as it was, for the barriers that had come between herself and her sister, and which she knew would become stronger and almost intolerable, if she disappointed her in her ambitious schemes, made her feel as if it would be impossible to remain with her, and the world seemed very desolate.

Still, to consent to become the wife of this good man, to accept all the benefits which his position would confer upon her, to be continually surrounded by his care and thoughtful love, seemed the height of selfishness to her, when she had nothing but her broken life to give in return, and she shrank from the sacred bond and the responsibility of its obligations.

"I am afraid—it does not seem right," she faltered, yet she lifted her eyes to him with a wistfulness that was pathetic in the extreme, and which moved him deeply.

"Violet, come," he repeated, earnestly, as he held out his strong right hand to her.

"I dare not," she said, "and yet——"

"You want to—you will!" he cried, eagerly, as, leaning toward her, he clasped the small hand that lay upon the arm of her chair.

It was icy cold, and glancing anxiously into her face, he saw that she had fainted away.

The excitement of the interview, the desolation of her wounded heart, and the longing for home and rest, were too much for her frail strength, and she had swooned, even while he thought she was consenting to be his wife.

He sprang to the bell and rang for assistance, then gathering her in his arms, he gently laid her upon a sofa, just as the door opened and Mrs. Mencke entered.

"I am afraid that I have overtaxed her strength," Lord Cameron said, in a tone of self-reproach, as he lifted a rueful face to her.

"Have you won?" she asked, eagerly.

"I think so, but— —"

Mrs. Mencke waited for nothing more.

"She will soon recover from this," she interrupted, a triumphant ring in her tone, as she began to sprinkle Violet's face with water from a tumbler which she seized from a table. "Leave her with me now, and I will call you again when she is better."

The young girl was already beginning to revive, and fearing that his presence might agitate her again, Lord Cameron stole softly from the room, but looking strangely sad for a man who believed he had prospered in his wooing.

"You are better, Violet," Mrs. Mencke said, with unwonted tenderness, as her sister opened her eyes and looked around the room as if in search of some one.

She brought a glass of wine to her, and putting it to her lips, bade her drink.

She obeyed, and the stimulating beverage soon began to warm her blood and restore her strength.

"Has he gone?" she asked, glancing toward the door.

"Lord Cameron? Yes; he thought you had had excitement enough for one day, and as soon as you began to come to yourself he stole away. Do you wish me to call him back?" her sister inquired, regarding her curiously.

"No," but there was a perplexed look upon her fair face.

"He tells me that you are going to make him happy, Vio," pursued her sister, anxious to learn just how matters stood, "that you will marry him. I am delighted, dear, and I know that he will do all in his power to make your life a perfect one."

"Did he tell you that? Did I promise?" Violet cried, with a startled look and putting her hand to her head in a dazed way.

"Violet Huntington! what a strange child you are! Here you have just given a man to understand that you have accepted him and yet, when you are congratulated upon the fact, you affect not to know what you have done!" cried Mrs. Mencke, pretending to be entirely out of patience with her.

She meant to carry things with a high hand now. She saw that there had been a momentary yielding upon Violet's part, though there was some doubt as to just what she had intended to do, and she was determined to make it count if she could do so by any means, legitimate or otherwise.

"Don't be cross with me, Belle," Violet pleaded, with a quivering lip, "for I really cannot remember. Lord Cameron was so kind, so generous, and I began to say something to him—I don't know what—when I felt queer and knew nothing more until I awoke and found you here."

Mrs. Mencke saw her advantage in all this, and did not fail to make the most of it.

"Well, you must have given him to understand that you accepted him, for he told me that he had won you, and now I hope we shall not have any more nonsense about the matter. Lord Cameron is too good to be trifled with. You have given your promise, and must stand by it," she concluded, in an authoritative tone.

"Yes, if I have promised, I suppose—I must," gasped unhappy Violet, and then fainted away again.

CHAPTER XIII.
THE DAY IS SET FOR VIOLET'S MARRIAGE.

Mrs. Mencke privately informed Lord Cameron that Violet had acknowledged the engagement, and would see him again when she was a little stronger.

His lordship thanked her with a beaming face, and tried to think that he was the happiest man on the Continent, but there was, nevertheless, an aching void in his heart that could not be fully satisfied with the result of his wooing.

The morning following his betrothal he sent Violet an exquisite bouquet composed of blue and white bell-flowers, cape jasmine, and box, which breathed to the young girl, who was versed in the language of flowers, of gratitude, constancy, and joyfulness of heart.

She turned white and faint again at the sight of them, and a broken-hearted sob burst from her lips.

"Did I promise? did I promise?" she moaned. "I do not remember; but if he says I did, it must be so, for I know that he is too noble to deceive me. I wish I could die! for it seems like sacrilege to become Lord Cameron's wife when my heart is so filled with the image of another."

Mrs. Mencke came in and found her in tears, and was secretly very much annoyed, besides being a trifle conscience-smitten over the strategy which she had employed to bring about this longed-for marriage. But she exerted herself to amuse her troublesome invalid, while she told herself that she should consider it a lucky day when she got her off her hands altogether.

The second morning after matters had been thus settled, Vane Cameron was told that he might pay his betrothed another visit.

This he was, of course, only too glad to do, and his face lighted with positive joy when, upon entering her presence, he saw a cluster of bluebell flowers fastened upon her breast among the folds of her dainty white *robe-de chambre*.

He went forward and took both her hands in his, pressing his lips first to one and then the other, in a chivalrous, reverent way that touched Violet deeply, and smote her, too, with a sense of guilt and shame.

"God is good to me in granting my heart's desire," he said, in a low, earnest tone. "May His richest blessings be yours in the future, my Violet."

The fair girl could not utter one word in reply. Her heart was beating so rapidly and heavily that for a moment she thought she must suffocate, while that mute cry again went up from its wounded depths:

"Oh! Wallace, Wallace, did I promise?"

Lord Cameron saw that she was deeply agitated, and, seating himself beside her, he began to talk of subjects to distract her mind from herself and their new relations to each other.

He possessed great tact and a wonderful fund of anecdote and incident, and before he left her presence he had actually made her laugh over a droll account of an experience of the previous day.

After that he enticed her out for a drive about the beautiful bay, and having once achieved this much, it was comparatively easy to plan something for her pleasure and amusement every day.

While Violet was with him she could not fail to feel the charm of his presence, and she would, for the time, forget herself and her trouble; but the moment she was alone, the old aversion to the thought of becoming his wife, together with all her love and grief for Wallace, would revive to make her wretched.

One day, as they were nearing their hotel after a longer drive than usual, and Violet had seemed to enjoy herself more than she was wont to do, Lord Cameron ventured to broach a subject that lay very near his heart.

"Mrs. Mencke informs me that she and her husband are contemplating a tour of the Alps this summer," he remarked, by way of introduction.

Violet looked up surprised. She had not heard her sister say anything about such a tour, and there was nothing that she dreaded so much, in the present weakened state of her mind and body, as being taken about to various fashionable resorts and to be obliged to meet gay pleasure-seekers.

She sighed heavily, but made no other reply to Lord Cameron's information.

"You feel that it would be rather hard for you to make such a trip, do you not?" her companion inquired, gently. Then, without waiting for a reply, he went on: "How would you like, instead, to come with me to the Isle of Wight and spend a quiet, restful summer, interspersed perhaps, with a little yachting now and then?"

A great shock went through Violet at this, as she realized that he wanted her to become his wife immediately and go home with him.

A blur came before her eyes, a great lump seemed to rise in her throat and almost choke her.

Oh, she thought, if she could only flee away to her own room at home in Cincinnati and stay by herself, out of the sight or sound of everybody, what a relief it would be!

She shrank more and more from Belle and Will and the idea of going about from place to place with them; still, a feeling of guilt and wrong oppressed her every time she thought of marrying this good, noble man, and giving him only the ashes of a dead love in return for the wealth of his affection for her.

Yet, of the two plans, the going to the Isle of Wight, to quiet and rest, seemed the most attractive, while the yachting proposal was very alluring, for Violet was intensely fond of the sea.

Vane Cameron was conscious of the shock which had so thrilled her, but whether it had been caused by pleasure or repugnance he could not tell. He feared the latter, for his sweet bride-elect had, thus far, been very unresponsive to his love and devotion.

He sat regarding her very gravely and somewhat sadly, while she seemed to be considering his proposition.

His thought had been more for her health and comfort than of his own desire or pleasure, but he would not bias her decision one way or the other.

Finally Violet lifted her eyes to his face, while a faint flush tinged her pale cheek.

"I will do whatever you like—whatever you think best," she said, quietly.

His heart leaped as he remarked the flush, but he returned, earnestly, tenderly:

"Not what I would like, dear, but what you would prefer. I would not force you a hair's breadth against your inclination, much as I long to have you go with me. Would you enjoy the tour through the Alps with your sister?"

"No, no!" Violet cried, in a strained, unnatural voice, as she felt the net of circumstances closing hopelessly about her. "Oh, I wish I could go home!" and yet where, on the face of the earth, had she now a home?

This wistful, almost despairing cry actually brought tears to the eyes of the strong man at her side, while his heart sank heavily within him, for surely there had been no thought of him or of his great love in that homesick wail.

But bravely putting aside self, as he always did where she was concerned, he gently returned:

"You shall go home if you wish—you shall do anything you like, and I will not urge you to any step against which your heart rebels; still, if you are willing to go with me, I will gladly take you home to America. Mr. and Mrs. Mencke, I know, have no thought of returning at present, as they have told me that they intend to travel for the next year or two, and hope to see the most of Europe during that time. It seemed to me that you were not strong enough, just now, to begin such a ceaseless round of travel, and that is why I proposed the Isle of Wight. Shall we go there to rest until you are a little more robust, and then, if you wish, we will return to America?"

How good—how kind he was! And if he had only been her brother, Violet could have thrown herself upon his breast and wept out her gratitude for and appreciation of his thoughtfulness.

But to speak the words that would settle her destiny for life—to tell him that she would become his wife immediately—how could she?

Still she knew it must be one thing or the other—either a hurry and rush over Europe with uncongenial companions, or a going away to some peaceful retreat as the Countess of Sutherland.

At last, with a mighty effort to control the nervous trembling that seized her, but with a sense of despair in her heart, she murmured, in a scarcely audible voice:

"I will go to the Isle of Wight."

Vane Cameron made no reply to this, though his heart gave a great leap of gladness. He simply laid one hand gently and tenderly upon hers for a moment, then touching up his horse, drove rapidly up the avenue leading to the hotel, where upon the wide piazza, they saw Mr. and Mrs. Mencke seated among the other guests of the house.

"May I tell your sister that you have decided against the tour through the Alps?" Vane whispered, as he lifted Violet's light form from the carriage.

"Yes," she assented, and then fled to her own room, where she sank nearly fainting upon her bed.

She felt that she was irrevocably bound now; that she had given her unqualified consent to become Lord Cameron's wife. She would soon be a countess and occupy a position which half the women in Europe would envy, and yet she was utterly wretched.

A little later her sister came to her, and in all her life Violet could not remember that she had ever manifested so much affection for her.

"Vane has told me," she said, in an exultant tone, as she bent down and softly kissed Violet's forehead. "I am very glad, and I fully agree with him that it will be best for you to go quietly to the Isle of Wight until your health is fully established. He says he has a yacht there also, and intends to give you an occasional taste of the ocean which you love so much. It will be delightful. And now we must begin to think of the necessary preparations, for Vane says, if you are agreeable, he would like the marriage to take place just a month from to-day, when you will start immediately for England."

For the life of her Violet could not prevent the shiver which shook her from head to foot at this announcement, and a wild desire for death and oblivion shot through her heart.

"Well, dear, what shall I tell him?" Belle asked, after waiting some time for a response and receiving none.

"Suit yourselves—it makes no difference to me," Violet said, wearily, and though it was a rather doubtful and unsatisfactory concession,

Mrs. Mencke made the most of it; and, feeling perfectly jubilant over this happy termination to all her ambitious plotting and scheming, she stole away to impart the gratifying information to her husband, who, of late, had seemed to be very impatient of the delay to bring matters to a crisis.

They did not trouble the young girl much after that. Vane said she must not be annoyed by petty details, so he took everything that was possible upon himself.

Matters of importance, which he did not feel at liberty to decide alone, he submitted to Mrs. Mencke, who pretended to consult Violet; but it was only pretense, for she settled everything to suit herself, and the preparations for the wedding went steadily and rapidly forward.

The ambitious woman was so delighted that she felt she must have some outlet for her feelings, which would have been out of taste for her to exhibit there, so she sent notices to different American papers of the approaching marriage of her sister, "Miss Violet Draper Huntington to his lordship the Earl of Sutherland," etc. etc.

Violet kept her room most of the time, for she shrank from mingling with the guests of the hotel, since she knew there would be a great deal of gossip over her approaching nuptials, and she did not like to be conspicuous.

She drove nearly every day with her betrothed, however, and while with him exerted herself to appear interested and entertained, and grateful for his unwearied kindness.

He was very considerate of her feelings—he seldom referred to their approaching marriage, but sought by every means in his power to keep her mind engaged with amusing and pleasant topics.

The ceremony was to be performed in the English church of the place, and Mrs. Mencke had sent to Paris for a suitable trousseau for the occasion. She had spared no expense, for she was determined that the affair should be as brilliant as circumstances would permit.

The day preceding that set for the wedding Violet was so ill—so nervous and prostrated by her increasing dread and sense of wrong as the fatal hour drew near—that she did not rise until noon, while it was nearly evening before she felt able to grant Vane an interview which he particularly requested.

He startled back appalled, when, as he entered her parlor, she turned her wan, colorless face toward him.

"You are ill! I had no idea that you were so sick!" he cried, in a voice of deep concern and surprise, for Mrs. Mencke had made light of Violet's indisposition.

"No, not ill, only tired and a little nervous," she replied, trying to smile, reassuringly.

He sat down beside her and began to tell her about the arrangements he had made for going "home," and she was touched to see how, in every detail, he had had only her comfort and pleasure in mind.

"Shall you like it?" he asked, when he had sketched the proposed journey to her.

"Yes, thank you; you are very kind," she tried to say, heartily, but, in spite of her effort, the tone sounded cold and formal.

The young man's face fell. He had so hoped to see hers light up with anticipation.

"Is there anything that you would like changed? Would you prefer to go another way, or to take in other places on the route?" he asked, wishing, oh, so earnestly, that she would express some preference, or even make some objection to his plans; anything would be more endurable than such apathetic acquiescence.

"No, let it stand, please, just as you have it," she answered, in a somewhat weary tone.

"Have you everything you wish? Are there no little things that you need—that have been overlooked—for—to-morrow?" he asked, wistfully, his voice dropping to a tender cadence at that last word, as he realized how nearly the one great desire of his heart was within his grasp.

Was it his imagination, or did a shiver of repulsion run over Violet's frame at this reference to their wedding-day?

She was as white as the fleecy shawl that was thrown about her shoulders, and there was a pathetic droop about her lovely mouth that pained him exceedingly.

"No, thank you," she quietly replied; "Belle has attended to everything."

He arose, feeling disappointed. If she had made but a single request of him, no matter how simple, it would have made him so happy to execute it; but his hands were tied—he could not force favors upon her.

"I will not remain longer, dear," he said, gently; "I want you to get all the rest possible to-night, so as to be strong for our journey to-morrow."

Violet arose also, and stood pale and motionless before him. She was very lovely, and he never forgot the picture she made, with the crimson light of the setting sun flooding her white-robed form, tinging her pale face with an exquisite color, and giving a deeper, richer tint to her golden hair.

Oh, if he had but been sure of her love, how supremely happy they might be, he thought, with all the bright prospects before him.

An irrepressible wave of tenderness and longing swept over him, and, involuntarily reaching out his arms, he drew her gently within his embrace.

"My darling," he whispered, "you are all the world to me. I pray that I may be able to prove to you by and by, how wholly you occupy this heart of mine."

He lifted her face with one hand and searched it earnestly for a moment, then, bending forward, he pressed his lips to hers in a lingering caress.

It was the first time that he had kissed her, or made any outward demonstration of his great love since their betrothal.

Violet broke away from him, with a low, thrilling cry of anguish, and sank, pale and quivering in every nerve, into the chair from which she had just arisen.

That caress had recalled the last passionate kiss of farewell that Wallace had given her just before the steamer left its pier in New York, while it had also revealed to her the fact that he would always be more to her, even though he were dead, than Lord Cameron, with all his love, his goodness, and generosity, could ever hope to be, living.

He was deeply hurt, however, by this repulse and her cry of despair. He stood for a moment looking down upon her, mingled pain and remorse for what he had done plainly written on his face. Then he said, in a repressed tone:

"Forgive me, Violet; I will try not to wound you thus again."

She threw out her hand to him with an appealing gesture, conscience-smitten, for his tone plainly told her how deeply she had hurt him.

"Forgive me," she said, contritely, a little sob pointing her words.

He took the hand and pressed it gently.

"I have nothing to forgive, dear. Now good-night, and try to sleep well," he returned kindly, and then went softly out from her presence, but looking grave and troubled.

CHAPTER XIV.
"THERE WILL BE NO WEDDING TO-DAY"

"Oh, if my mother were only alive!" burst passionately from Violet's lips, as the door closed after her betrothed. "My heart is broken, and there is no one in the wide, wide world to whom I can tell my trouble. I have no friends, no home, and am forced to marry a man whom I do not love, in order to find one. Belle, who ought to care for me, sympathize with, and comfort me, thinks only of the wealth and position I am to secure, and"—a bitter smile curling her lips—"is even greatly elated at the prospect of getting rid of me in such fine style. I cannot—I cannot bear it; and to-morrow—to-morrow I am to be bound for life!"

She sprang wildly to her feet, a bright spot of fever burning upon each cheek, and began pacing the floor with nervous tread. For an hour she kept this up, going mechanically from one end of the luxurious apartment to the other, apparently unconscious of what she was doing.

In the midst of this almost frantic state of mind Mrs. Mencke came sweeping in upon her.

"What ails you, Violet?" she demanded, regarding her with anxious eyes. "You have been moving about incessantly during the last hour. You must not work yourself into such a nervous state, or you will be wholly unfitted for the ceremony to-morrow. I want you to look your best, and you will surely be pale and hollow-eyed, if not positively ill, if you keep on at this rate. Besides, Lady Isabella arrived a short time ago, and has asked to be allowed to see you for a little while."

"Oh! I cannot see her to-night, Belle. Let me alone for the few hours that remain to me," Violet moaned, as she threw herself upon the lounge and buried her hot face in the cool, silken pillow.

"The few hours that remain to you, indeed! One would think you were about to be executed, instead of married to an earl. Do not be so insufferably childish," returned her sister, impatiently. "There will be no time to-morrow for you to see Lady Cameron, and it is uncourteous, uncivil to refuse her request."

Violet made no response to this; she was too weak and wretched to assert herself, and she knew that Belle would carry her point regarding this interview as she had done in all other things of late.

Mrs. Mencke brought her some quieting drops, which she obediently swallowed, and after a few moments began to grow more composed.

"I will tell Lady Cameron that you are nervous and tired, and ask her not to stay long," Belle said, when she saw that Violet was more calm; "but you must see her for a few minutes, and I hope you will have the good taste not to offend her in any way," she concluded, significantly.

"Very well; let her come," Violet answered, resignedly, and thinking it better to have the ordeal over as soon as possible.

She had always liked and admired Lady Cameron; had always enjoyed her society, and, under other circumstances, would have been glad to see her now; but everything and every one connected with her approaching marriage seemed positively hateful to her, in her present state.

Mrs. Mencke did not wait for her to change her mind, but went immediately to tell her ladyship that Violet would see her, and a few minutes later, there came a gentle knock upon the door of the young girl's room.

Before she could arise to admit her visitor, it was softly opened, and a lovely, sweet-faced lady of about fifty years entered.

She was clad in a simple yet elegant costume of silver-gray silk, trimmed with rich black lace. A cluster of pearls gleamed fair and white at her throat, and a dainty little cap of costly lace rested lightly upon her soft, brown hair, which as yet had not a visible thread of silver in it.

"Do not rise, dear," she said, as Violet attempted to do so. "Your sister has told me that you are still far from being well, and that I must not stay long. Let me sit right here beside you," she continued, drawing a low rocker close to the lounge, and then, bending down, she kissed Violet fondly upon the forehead.

Violet returned her greeting with what composure she could, but the observing lady could easily see that it required a great effort, although she imagined that embarrassment was the cause.

"I knew that I could not see you to-morrow," she resumed, "and I felt as if I must have just a few minutes' chat with you on this last evening of your maiden life. You have no mother, dear, and though I am sure your sister has tried to do everything that was wise and kind, yet she cannot quite take the place of a mother at such a time as this, and my heart yearned to come to you."

Violet was deeply moved by these kind words, and she clasped more closely the hand that had sought hers in such fond sympathy. Still her heart ached more keenly, if that were possible, than before, while a feeling of guilt stole over her—a consciousness of wrong toward this loving mother in the injury she felt she was about to do her son.

"I was wishing for my mother just as you came," she murmured, a little sob bursting from her lips.

Lady Isabel leaned forward and wound her arms about the slight form of the girl.

"Then, dear child, let me take her place, as far as I can," she said, in a low, winning tone; "and to-morrow you will have the right to call me by that sacred name, while I shall have a dear daughter. Ah, Violet, I cannot tell you how much I have always wanted a daughter—one who would be a companion and a confidante. But I have had only my son until now. My dear, I know we shall love each other, and I am looking forward, with more delight than I can express, to the future when you will belong to us and brighten our home with your fresh young life. I have been drawn toward you from the first day of our meeting in London, and if Vane had asked me to select a bride for him, I could not have chosen one more to my mind. I know that you will make him a very loving and faithful wife." How Violet cringed beneath those words, which so plainly told her that Vane had not confided to his mother the doubtful relations that existed between them! "He is a noble fellow," the fond woman went on; "he was always a good and dutiful boy, and has been such a comfort to me. Better than all, Violet, he is a true Christian, and it is delightful to hear him talk of his plans regarding the welfare of his tenants, and of the improvements he hopes to make in the condition of the poor upon his estates. Do you know," she continued, with a sweet seriousness that was very charming, "that I think it is a great thing—a wonderful thing for an earl to be such a Christian, and one who wishes so earnestly to carry his Christianity into his every-day life? There is so much responsibility in such a position, and such an opportunity for doing good. You are a Christian also, are you not, Violet? and you will sympathize with and help Vane carry out all his plans? What is it, dear?"

This last anxious question was drawn forth by the violent start which Violet had given, as a new and solemn thought suddenly burst upon her at these probing questions.

"Am I wearying you—are you feeling ill?" she added, regarding her with deep concern.

With a great effort Violet controlled the trembling that had seized her, and strove to reply calmly:

"No, I am not ill, dear Lady Cameron, but your asking me if I am a Christian made me suddenly remember something that I had not thought of before."

"What was that, dear?" Lady Isabel questioned. "Unburden yourself just as you would to your own mother on this last night of your single life."

An expression of pain clouded Violet's brow, but after a moment she said, gravely:

"Yes, I have called myself a Christian for more than a year, and I believe my strongest desire is to do what is right always; but life has so many temptations that I know I have often failed. I will try—to do right in the future," she went on, but seemingly strangely agitated, her companion thought. "I will do what I can to—to make Lord Cameron—at least, I will try not to hinder him in any good work. I would like to make him happy and you—dear Lady Cameron, I truly wish that I might make you happy also," Violet concluded, raising her head from her pillow and looking eagerly, wistfully into the beautiful face beside her.

The lady bent and kissed her again, though she wondered a little at the undertone of pain and passion that rang through her words.

"With such a spirit I am sure you cannot fail to be a help to Vane, and I know we shall all be very happy," she said fondly.

Still Violet continued to regard her with that earnest, wistful look, while the nervous trembling, which she strove so hard to conceal, began to be apparent in spite of her efforts.

"I hope," she said, timidly, appealingly, "that you will always believe in me. I am liable to be mistaken in my view of what is right—promise me, oh, promise me, that, whatever I may do, you will trust me—you will believe that I want to be true, and that you will never cease to think kindly of me."

She clung to her companion with passionate longing, her hot little hands grasping hers with a painful, trembling clasp, while she seemed so completely unstrung by some inward emotion that Lady Cameron was alarmed.

"My dear child, this will never do," she said, regarding her anxiously, "you must not allow yourself to become so excited, and I blame myself for directing our conversation into such a serious channel. I must run away at once and leave you to get calm. Of course, my love, I shall always trust you, while you already have such a firm hold upon my heart that I do not believe I could cease to love you if I would. There, you shall not talk any more," as Violet opened her lips as if to speak; "good-night, pleasant dreams, and a refreshing slumber. This," with a light laugh, "is the last kiss I shall ever give Violet Huntington; when next my lips touch yours you will be somebody's dear wife."

With a lingering caress the beautiful woman released her from her arms, and then stole softly from the room, thinking what a sweet, lovable wife Vane would have on the morrow.

But if she could have seen Violet as she lay there on her couch after she had gone, she would have marveled more than she had done over her previous excitement.

She clasped her hands across her eyes as if to shut out some dreadful vision, and seemed to cower and shrink as if some one was smiting her with a stinging lash.

"Oh, what have I done!" she moaned. "A Christian, and on the point of perjuring myself before God's altar! A Christian, and weakly yielding to what I know would be a sin of deepest dye! A Christian, and consenting to take the poison of my wretchedness—of a heart that is filled with a hopeless love for another—into a good man's life and home! No—a thousand times no! I have been blind, wicked, reckless. Vane Cameron is too good a man to have his life hampered and ruined thus, and I honor him far too much to do him such wrong, now that I see it in its true light. Oh, if he were but my brother, with his noble principles, his strong, true heart and boundless sympathy, I could stand by him, help him to carry out the good that he has planned, and devote my whole life to him; but as his wife—never!" and she broke into a perfect tempest of tears and sobs as she arrived at this crisis.

Daylight faded; the last crimson flush died out of the western sky; darkness settled upon the mountain-tops that overlooked the beautiful bay, and gradually wrapping itself about them like a mantle, finally dropped like a pall upon the gay watering-place and the adjacent village, which all day long had been in a fever of excitement and expectation over the prospect of the grand wedding that was to occur on the morrow.

Nothing else had been talked of for a week, and everybody was anxious to see the beautiful girl whom the distinguished English earl had won, but who had so resolutely secluded herself that but very few had had even a glimpse of her face; but on the morrow everybody would have an opportunity to judge for themselves, whether she was one who would honor the high position which had been offered her.

About nine o'clock Mrs. Mencke went up to her sister's room to see if she needed anything before retiring.

She tried the door and found it locked.

"Are you in bed, Violet?" she called, in a low tone, with her lips at the key-hole.

"No, Belle, but I am busy with a little writing which I wish to do," Violet answered, in calm, even tones. "But never mind me—go back to your dancing; I can take care of myself and would rather not be disturbed by any one again to-night."

"I will come up again in half an hour," Mrs. Mencke returned, not satisfied to leave her thus for the night.

"No, do not, Belle, please—I prefer that you should not," pleaded her sister.

"Will you be sure to take your drops? You will need all the strength that you can get for to-morrow," persisted Mrs. Mencke.

"Yes, I will take them; I know that I shall need strength," was the grave reply.

"All right; good-night, then, and a good rest to you," said Mrs. Mencke, and the rustle of her silken garments on the stairs, a moment later, told Violet that she had gone back to the gay company below which she enjoyed so much.

Two hours later, when she came up to bed, she stopped again before Violet's door, as she was passing to her own room, and bent her head to listen.

All was quiet within, except for the ticking of the clock which stood on a bracket near the door, and which, somehow, sounded strangely clear, and almost seemed to give an ominous click with each motion of its pendulum.

She did not try to enter; she thought if Violet was sleeping quietly it would be unwise to disturb her, and so she moved on to her own chamber, yet with a somewhat anxious and unsatisfied feeling at her heart.

She slept very soundly, and did not awake until nearly eight o'clock the next morning. Her husband had gone to Nice a couple of days previous, and was to return on the first train that day, so there had been no movement in her room to disturb her.

When she realized how late it was, and how much there was to be done, for the wedding had been set for eleven o'clock, she sprang from her bed, and hastily throwing on her clothing, went immediately to Violet's apartments.

The door yielded to her touch, and she entered the parlor, to find no one there.

She passed on to Violet's chamber, and rapped upon the door.

There was no answer, and entering, she was surprised to see that it was empty, and somewhat startled, also, to see that the bed was nicely made, and the room in perfect order.

"What can this mean?" she muttered, and then rang the bell a vigorous peal.

A servant answered it immediately.

"Have you been called to attend Miss Huntington this morning?" she demanded.

"No, madame."

"Have you seen her anywhere about the house?" Mrs. Mencke questioned, greatly perplexed by her sister's strange movements.

"No, madam."

"What! did you not put her room in order this morning?" she asked, sharply.

Again she was doomed to hear the simple, respectful, "No, madame."

More and more perplexed, and not a little alarmed, Mrs. Mencke hastened out into the hall, and was proceeding down stairs to seek Lord Cameron, when she met him just coming up to inquire for his betrothed.

He greeted her with his usual courteous manner; then, observing her troubled look, became suddenly grave.

"What is it?" he quickly asked. "I hope Violet is not ill."

"No—I do not know—I—I—have you seen her?" faltered and stumbled Mrs. Mencke, in a tone of distress.

"Seen her?" the young man replied, greatly surprised; for on this morning, of all others, Violet would, of course, be supposed to be invisible. "No; certainly not," he added, recovering himself. "Is she not in her room?"

"No, and it looks as if it had not been occupied during the night," Mrs. Mencke whispered, with pale lips.

"Do not tell me that," Lord Cameron said, sternly, his face growing ashen pale at the information.

He turned, and leaping two stairs at a time, was at the top in a moment, and striding forward toward Violet's room.

Reaching it, he stopped, his innate delicacy forbidding him to enter without permission, and waited until Mrs. Mencke joined him.

They went in together, and he observed with a terrible heart-sinking the perfect order in which everything had been left in both rooms.

Mrs. Mencke explained that she had questioned the chambermaid, but that she knew nothing about Violet's movements.

"She may have gone out for a walk—to get the air," the wretched groom-elect remarked, but he was white to his lips as he said it.

"Gone out for a walk on her wedding-morning, when there was scarcely time to prepare for the ceremony! I wish I could even believe it possible that she would do such an unheard-of thing," said Mrs. Mencke, in a tone of despair, and feeling nearly paralyzed by this sudden and inexplicable absence.

Nevertheless they exerted themselves to ascertain if the missing bride-elect was anywhere about the premises, Lord Cameron, with the proprietor of the hotel, to whom alone he confided his trouble, going out in search of her.

Meantime Mrs. Mencke went back to Violet's rooms to ascertain if anything was missing, but everything appeared to be in its accustomed place. Every drawer was daintily arranged, as she was in the habit of keeping them; all her jewels, laces, and ribbons were in their respective boxes; even the rings, which she usually wore, lay upon her pincushion, where she always put them before taking a bath.

Her dresses hung in her wardrobe—all but the traveling dress which she had worn when she came to Mentone. It was a dark-gray cloth, trimmed with narrow bands of blue silk. The hat to match, with its bows of blue velvet, and a single gray wing, together with a thick blue vail, were also missing, and a pair of thick walking-boots, together with a light traveling shawl.

Beyond these few things nothing, as far as she could ascertain upon so hasty an examination, was gone; not even a change of clothing, toilet articles, or a traveling-bag, things which Violet would be sure to need if she had contemplated flight.

Mrs. Mencke was somewhat reassured after these investigations, and tried to think that her sister had gone out for a walk—possibly to the town to post the letter she had been writing the previous night, rather than to wait for it to go later with the hotel mail.

Still, she was terribly anxious, and her face was pallid with fear and anxiety.

She had staked so much—far more than any one save herself knew—to achieve this brilliant marriage for Violet, and it seemed more than she could bear to have it fail at the last moment, and after all the heavy expense of the beautiful trousseau from Worth's.

She wandered restlessly from room to room in an agony of suspense, Lady Cameron following her and vainly trying to speak words of comfort and cheer, while they waited for the return of those who had gone to search for the missing one.

Lord Cameron came back after a time, accompanied by Mr. Mencke, who had arrived on the first train from Nice, but he brought no tidings of Violet.

"There will be no wedding to-day, even if she is found," he said, with a stern, set face, "so let all preparations be stopped at once."

Then without another word, he went out, mounted his horse, and rode away toward the mountains.

The wretched day passed, and evening shut down again upon the place, where but one theme was thought of or talked about. Many believed that the young girl had gone out for a walk in the early morning and had, perhaps, fallen into some ravine among the mountains, or into the sea and been drowned.

There were only a few who thought otherwise, and these were Mr. and Mrs. Mencke, Lord Cameron, and his mother.

Mr. and Mrs. Mencke did not lisp their suspicions that Violet might have fled from an uncongenial marriage to a suicide's fate; but Lord Cameron, who remembered his last interview with his betrothed, had a terrible fear that such might be the case; while Lady Cameron, having told him of Violet's strange excitement and remarks of the evening previous, suggested that she might have fled to escape wronging him and being untrue to herself.

"It may be so," the wretched young man said, "but oh, I fear she is dead. I shall search for her until I am satisfied of either one thing or the other."

When Lord Cameron had said there would be no wedding, even if Violet were found, Mrs. Mencke went away and shut herself in the room where Violet was to have dressed for her bridal, and where, spread out before her, were the lovely dress of white silk tulle, with its delicate garnishings of lilies of the valley and white violets the beautiful Brussels net vail, with its chaplet of the same flowers, the dainty white satin boots, gloves, and handkerchief; and there she gave vent to the rage, disappointment, and grief which she could no longer contain.

It was the most wretched day of her whole life, and she afterward confessed that there, for the first time, in the presence of these voiceless accusers of her for her treachery and heartlessness toward the young girl whom she should have tenderly cherished and shielded from all unhappiness, her guilty conscience began to upbraid her, and remorse to sting her with their relentless lashings.

CHAPTER XV.
"SHE IS MY WIFE."

It was later in the season than people were in the habit of remaining at Mentone; but the unusual attraction of a wedding in high life had induced many to delay their departure and so a large number had tarried, much to the gratification and profit of hotel proprietors and other natives, only to be disappointed by missing the wedding, after all.

Everything possible was done to obtain some clew to the missing girl, but all to no purpose. Three weeks went by, and every one, save Lord Cameron, had given up all hope of ever solving the sad mystery. He alone still patiently kept up his search day by day.

By the beginning of the fourth week, Mr. and Mrs. Mencke both agreed that the girl must be dead, and announced their intention of leaving in a few days for Switzerland. Mrs. Mencke was so confirmed in her opinion that Violet was not living that she assumed mourning for her, and while she remained in Mentone her deeply bordered handkerchiefs were never out of her hands, and were frequently brought into ostentatious use.

The day before the one set for their departure was intensely warm and oppressive, and everybody was almost prostrated by the heat.

Lady Cameron and Mrs. Mencke could only exist by lying, lightly clad, in hammocks swung upon the north piazza of the hotel, while Mr. Mencke idled away the hours as best he could, in the smoking and reading-room, or in imbibing mint juleps.

Lord Cameron, as was his invariable custom, had departed, in spite of the heat, upon one of his long rides immediately after breakfast. His quest for the girl whom he had so fondly loved was becoming almost a mania.

He had grown thin and pale; his appetite failed, until he seemed not to eat sufficient to keep life in him. He was depressed, and absent-minded, and so nervous and restless that his mother suffered the keenest anxiety lest all this strain upon his mind and body should end in insanity!

"Oh, what an interminable day this has seemed!" sighed Lady Cameron to her companion, as, soft on the saltry stillness of the air, there came to them the sound of a distant church clock striking the hour of six. "I hope I may never pass another like it—I could neither read nor work, while my thoughts and the dread of something—I know not what—have nearly driven me wild."

Mrs. Mencke shivered, in spite of the heat, at these words. She also had felt as if she could never live through another twelve hours like the past, and she believed if she could but once get away from the place where she had suffered so much of disappointment and wretchedness, this terrible oppression and weight would in a measure disappear.

Tomorrow they would go, and she longed for tomorrow to come. During the latter part of the afternoon she had simply lain still and watched the lengthening shadows, which told that the sun was declining and evening drawing on apace, and longed for night and slumber to lock her senses in oblivion.

"I believe the name of Mentone will always give me a chill after this," she said, in a husky tone.

"Hark! is not that the sound of a horse's hoofs?" cried Lady Cameron, starting up to look down the road. "Yes, there comes Vane and—Mrs. Mencke, he is riding at a break-neck pace! Can he—do you believe he has any—news?"

The woman was so overcome by the thought that the last word was uttered in a whisper, while her eager eyes were intently fastened upon the approaching horseman.

Mrs. Mencke started to a sitting posture, and waited with breathless interest for Lord Cameron to arrive.

Nearer and nearer he came, and now they could see that his noble steed was flecked with foam.

Vane checked his headlong speed as he caught sight of the two figures upon the piazza; but, as he entered the grounds of the hotel, both ladies could see that his face was frightful in its ghastliness. Instinctively they knew that he was the bearer of evil tidings.

Arriving at the steps, he threw his bridle to a man who approached to take his horse, then turned to enter the hotel.

"Vane—you have—news!" his mother said, in an awe-stricken voice, as she went forward to meet him.

He glanced up at her, and the sympathy and love written on her gentle face seemed to unman him for a moment.

He staggered, reeled, and then caught at a post, while he put his hand to his head and groaned aloud with anguish.

"Tell me," gasped Mrs. Mencke, coming toward him, her own face now as white as his, "have you heard anything of—Violet?"

He nodded, but hid his face from the gaze of the two women, while a shudder shook him from head to foot; then he said, in a hollow tone:

"Yes—she is found."

"Found!" repeated his startled hearers, in shrill, tense voices. "Where? Alive?"

He shook his head at that last word.

"Dead!" whispered Mrs. Mencke, hoarsely.

"Dead," said Lord Cameron, in an awful tone and with another groan.

Then with a mighty effort he partially recovered his composure, made them sit down, and told them as briefly as he could all about his dreadful day.

He had started out that morning determined to make one last vigorous effort—to spare neither himself, his horse, nor his purse to gain some clew; then, if he learned nothing of the fate of his lost love, he would give up his search and go home to England with his mother.

He followed the coast along the gulf, as he had done a dozen times before, but intending to extend his search farther than he had yet done. He rode many miles, until the heat became so intense that he was forced to turn back without as yet having made any discovery.

Suddenly, however, as he was nearing Mentone, he saw a group of fishermen gathered around something which they had evidently just drawn from the water at the foot of a cliff, along the edge of which the highway ran.

Approaching nearer, he saw what appeared to be a long black object, and knew that it was contemplated with horror by the spectators, for the men's faces were gray and awe-stricken.

A nameless fear seized upon his own heart, and leaping from his horse, he fastened him to a tree, and springing down the cliff with all the speed he could force into his faltering feet, he saw, while a groan of despair burst from him, that the object lying upon the beach was the body of a woman.

Such a horror he had never looked upon before—he hoped never to look upon again.

The woman was clad, not in black, as he had at first thought, but in a dark gray suit trimmed with bands of blue silk. Upon the head was a grey hat, also trimmed with blue, and having a gray wing among the folds of velvet, and wound about this was a thick blue vail.

"Violet?" moaned Mrs. Mencke, with a shiver, as Lord Cameron reached this portion of his tale.

"Yes, Violet, without any doubt," he answered, in a hollow voice, "for the clothing all corresponded exactly with your description of what she wore away; but otherwise she was past all recognition, excepting the hair, which was golden like hers, though sadly matted and disheveled by the action of the sea. What her object was in leaving the hotel we can probably never know; perhaps it was simply a walk—I hope that was her object," the young man said, something like a sob bursting from him; "but she must have wandered too near the edge of the cliff, missed her foothold, and fallen into the sea. The coast is very bold near there—overhanging the water in many places, while the road runs very near the edge of the cliff. It was a terrible fate for the poor child, and the experiences of this day will haunt me as long as I live."

It was a horrible story, gently as he tried to break it to them, and the hearts of his listeners stood still with awe and misery. And yet, dreadful as it was, they all felt that the certainty of knowing that Violet was no more, did not equal the agonizing suspense which had tortured them during the last four weeks.

There was not much sleep for any of them that night, and Lord Cameron looked as if he had just risen from a long illness when he appeared the next morning.

He was calmer, however, than on the previous evening, and went about his sad duties with a sorrowful dignity which deeply impressed and touched every one.

Of course all thoughts of any of the party leaving Mentone for the next few days were given up, for their loved dead must be cared for before they could turn their faces northward.

The authorities would not allow the body to be removed from the place; but ordered that the young girl should be buried there without delay.

After this was attended to, the few mourning friends, together with many sympathizing residents of Mentone, gathered in the church, where the grand wedding was to have taken place, and a simple memorial service was observed, after which they all repaired to the spot where the unfortunate girl had been laid to rest.

Lord Cameron had chosen the spot, which was a little remote from other graves in the place of burial and beneath a beautiful, wide-spreading beech. The low mound had been covered with myrtle and a profusion of choice flowers, the greensward was like velvet about it, and not far away could be seen the deep blue sea which Violet had loved so much.

Mrs. Mencke appeared to be greatly overcome as she visited this lonely grave, and many glances of sympathy were bent upon her by those gathered about; but they could not know of the guilty secret which lay so heavily upon her conscience and caused remorse to outweigh whatever of natural grief she might otherwise have experienced. She alone knew that she was wholly responsible for all the sorrow and trouble which had thus overtaken the fair girl in the very morning of her life.

The next day they all spent in resting, for they had arranged to leave Mentone the following morning.

Lady Cameron and Mrs. Mencke remained in their rooms until evening, only coming down to join the gentlemen after tea for a little while.

They were gathered in a small private parlor, where each seemed to strive to assume a cheerfulness which no one felt.

Suddenly there came a sharp, imperative knock upon the door.

Lord Cameron arose to open it, and found himself face to face with a young man several years his junior, and who would have been regarded as strikingly handsome but for the worn and haggard look upon his face, and the wild, almost insane expression in his restless eyes.

Vane bowed to him courteously, then inquired:

"Can I do anything for you, sir? Whom do you wish to see?"

"Lord Cameron, Earl of Sutherland," was the brief but stern reply.

"I am he," the young man began, when his visitor unceremoniously pushed his way into the room, closing the door behind him.

At this act Wilhelm Mencke and his wife started to their feet, one with a cry of surprise and dismay, the other with an oath of anger, while both had grown deathly pale.

"Pardon me, sir, but are you not somewhat brusque and uncourteous in your demeanor?" Vane demanded, with some hauteur. "Who are you, and what do you want?"

"I want to meet the woman whom report says you are to marry or have married. I want to meet her here and now, in your presence," was the quick, passionate, quivering response.

Lord Cameron shuddered and grew white to his lips at this imperative demand, and wondered if the man was mad.

"That is impossible," he said, in a husky voice. Then he added, in a conciliatory tone, for something seemed to tell him that the man was in great mental suffering, though he had not a suspicion of its cause: "But pray explain why you make such a request. Who are you sir?"

"My name is Wallace Hamilton Richardson," tersely returned the stranger.

Vane Cameron recoiled as if the man had struck him a blow instead of simply stating his name.

He was so much overcome by the announcement that those observing him feared he was upon the point of fainting, strong man though he was.

"Wallace Richardson—from America?" he whispered, hoarsely.

"Yes."

"I—I thought you were dead! She believed you were dead!" the young lord returned, with ashen lips.

"Dead!" repeated Wallace, wonderingly, his hitherto inflexible face softening a trifle. "Oh, say it again—does Violet really believe that I am dead?" and the eager, quivering tones rang sharply through the room.

"Yes, she believes so; it was so announced in one of the American papers," Lord Cameron replied, with something more of composure, but never losing that first look of horror.

Like a flash Wallace wheeled about and faced Wilhelm Mencke and his trembling wife.

"Then that was some more of your miserable work!" he cried, in a terrible voice, "a diabolical plot to separate us. From the first you have left nothing undone to part us, and so, when all else failed, you reported me dead, knowing well that she would never marry another while she believed me to be living. Oh! I see it all now, and my love, my love, I have wronged you!" he concluded, in a tone of anguish.

When he had turned with such fiery denunciation upon them, Mrs. Mencke shrank from him with such an expression of awe, fear, and guilt upon her face, that she was instantly self-condemned; every one in the room was as sure that she had caused that lying paragraph, announcing Wallace's death, to be inserted in the paper to mislead Violet, as if she had openly confessed it.

"Did you do it—did you drive that poor child thus to promise to become my wife?" demanded Lord Cameron, in a voice that was like the ominous calm before a tempest.

The woman was speechless; but her guilty eyes drooped beneath his stern look, for she knew that her miserable secret was revealed.

"You do not know what you have done," Wallace cried, growing wild again, "but you will pay dearly for your treachery—ha! ha! you little dream how dearly it will cost you, when the consequences of your wretched plot shall be noised abroad from the aristocratic summit upon which you have hitherto so proudly stood, and from which you will soon be ruthlessly hurled."

Wilhelm Mencke, having by this time begun to recover somewhat from the shock of Wallace's unexpected appearance, commenced to bluster:

"Look here, you young upstart," he cried, growing very red in the face, and assuming a threatening attitude, "all these charges and accusations may or may not be true—we won't discuss that point just now; but whether it is or not, it can be no possible concern of yours. I should like to know what you mean by bursting in upon respectable people in this rude way. What was Violet to you?—what right or business have you to interfere with whatever she might have chosen to do?"

"The most sacred right in the world, sir, for—she is my wife!"

CHAPTER XVI.
"I MUST FIND HER—I MUST FOLLOW HER."

This thrilling and unexpected announcement was electrical in its results.

Mrs. Mencke gave vent to a shriek of horror, and sank, weak and trembling, upon a chair, while her husband gazed at the young man with a look of blank astonishment and dismay; indeed, for the moment, he seemed almost paralyzed by the astounding declaration, for if Violet was indeed Wallace's wife, he and his wife had been criminally guilty in trying to drive her into a marriage with Lord Cameron, and in view of what the consequence might have been had they succeeded and Violet had lived, he had every reason to feel appalled.

Lady Cameron, also realizing all this, bowed her blanched face upon her hands and sat quivering as if with ague. What a terrible fate had been spared her son; but at what a fearful cost!

Lord Cameron alone betrayed no surprise, made no comment, though he still remained as colorless as when Wallace had first revealed his identity; while he stood regarding the young man with a sad, pitying look, for he saw that Wallace did not suspect what they yet had to tell him—had not even noticed that they spoke of her in the past tense or that Mrs. Mencke was clad in deep mourning.

There was an oppressive silence in the room for the space of three or four minutes then Wilhelm Mencke started forward, his phlegmatic nature for once all aflame.

"It is an infernal lie!" he cried, shaking his massive fist before Wallace's face; "all an infernal lie, I tell you, made up for the occasion, with the design, perhaps, of claiming her money. But you'll find, my would-be smart young man, that you have tackled the wrong parties this time."

Wallace made no verbal reply to this coarse outbreak, but, quietly slipping one hand within a breast-pocket, he drew forth a folded paper, which he opened and held before the man.

"Read," he said, briefly.

With rapidly fading color, with eyes that grew round and wide, with mingled conviction and dismay, Wilhelm Mencke read the marriage certificate, which proved that Wallace Hamilton Richardson and Violet Draper Huntington had been legally united, by a well-known clergyman of Cincinnati, about three weeks previous to the sailing of the young girl for Europe.

The man knew it was the truth, and this conviction was plainly stamped upon his face as he read; but he was so enraged by the fact, and also by the secret fear that Wallace might make him some trouble pecuniarily, that he lost control of his temper and reason.

A coarse, angry oath escaped him, and then he cried out, as he grew crimson with passion:

"It is a —— forgery, cleverly executed for the purpose of gaining his own ends."

Lord Cameron colored and drew himself up with dignity, while he remarked, with marked displeasure:

"Mr. Mencke, allow me to request you to refrain from profanity in the presence of my mother."

"Beg pardon, your lordship," said Mencke, looking somewhat abashed, "but I am so upset by this blamed trick that I forgot myself entirely."

"It is no trick, sir—it is the truth," quietly returned Vane Cameron.

"What do you mean, Lord Cameron? How can you know anything about it?" cried Mrs. Mencke, forgetting, for the moment, her weakness and agitation in her surprise at his positive declaration.

"Violet told me—she confided the fact of her marriage to me," he calmly returned.

"She told you," Wallace cried, his face lighting, his voice dropping to a tender cadence, as he began to realize how true Violet had been to him, in spite of her apparent faithlessness.

"Yes, when I asked her to become my wife," replied his lordship; then he added: "But sit down, Mr. Richardson, and let us freely discuss this matter, so that you can clearly understand it."

Vane rolled forward a comfortable chair for his visitor, a sad deference in his manner, which betrayed how strongly his sympathies were enlisted for the young man, who still had no suspicion of the sad news in store for him. He then seated himself near him and proceeded to relate all that had occurred in connection with his proposed marriage with Violet.

He would not tell him at once that the ceremony had never taken place, for Wallace was still greatly excited, and he felt that his news must be all broken to him gradually, or he would be completely unnerved.

"Evidently you have not learned that Miss Huntington was very ill for several weeks in London," he began.

"No," Wallace said, with a start.

"Yes, she was very sick with brain fever. The attack was caused by reading the notice of your death, and for a month her life was nearly despaired of. When she began to recover, her physician recommended that she be brought to Mentone for a change, and Mrs. Mencke acted immediately upon his advice. Just previous to her illness I had confided my feelings to Mrs. Mencke, and solicited her permission to address her sister. It was freely given, but, of course, I could not avail myself of it while Miss Huntington was so ill, and it was arranged—without her knowledge, I have since learned—that I was to follow her hither when she should have gained somewhat in strength. She had been here about a month when I received word that I might come. A few days later I was granted an interview, during which I confessed my affection and asked her to become my wife.

"She told me frankly at once that she did not love me well enough to marry me, and then, with sudden impulse, asked if she might make a confession—might open her whole heart to me. Of course this request was readily granted, and then she told me of her love for you, Mr. Richardson; how it had originated, and how, when"—bending a grave look upon Mrs. Mencke as he said this—"sorely pressed and alarmed by the fear of being sent away from home and deprived of her liberty, she had begged you to advise her what to do, and you told her that the only safe-guard that you could throw around her would be to make her your wife——"

"Yes," Wallace here interrupted, "Violet had been threatened with being sent to a convent unless she would promise to cast me off. Such a fate seemed to possess excessive terrors for her, and, being fully convinced that nothing could change our affection for each other, I suggested that we should be privately married, and then, if she was deprived of her liberty, it would be in my power to aid her by claiming her as my wife."

"Yes, that was what she told me in substance," said Lord Cameron. "She stated that you were married, but that you did not propose to claim her, because of the opposition of her friends, until a year or two should elapse and you were in a better position to make a home for her; that you advised her to travel and see all of the world that was possible, while you pursued your profession. Then came your separation, and she made no secret of the unhappiness that this caused her, or of her absorbing affection for you, and she spoke of the intense anxiety that she experienced because she received no letters from you after leaving home."

Surely Lord Cameron, with his usual noble self-abnegation, was doing all in his power to soothe Wallace's wounded heart and prepare him for the trial before him.

"But I wrote twice every week for more than two months," Wallace here interposed, "without receiving a single letter from her. This fact also we doubtless owe to the sisterly interposition that has been so vigilant and active regarding her welfare," he concluded, bitterly.

"Her grief and despair over your supposed death," continued the young earl, "was too deep for expression, and she said that life seemed hardly worth the living. She told me that she dared not become my wife, feeling thus; that her heart was dead, her dream of life was over, and she would not wrong me by giving me the ashes of her love in return for the devotion I offered her."

Lord Cameron paused a moment here, as if the memory of that never-to-be-forgotten interview was too much for him; but presently he controlled himself, and went on:

"I take upon myself all the blame for what followed," he said, "for I still urged her to give herself to me. I knew she was not happy here—that she was still weak from her illness and weary of travel, and longed for rest and quiet. I told her I would be content if she would but allow me to throw around her the protection of my name and love, and let me take her, just as she was, into my heart and home. Her answer was, 'I dare not, and yet——' That simple qualification made my heart bound, for I accepted it as a sign of yielding.

"'And yet you want to—you will?' I said, assuming that that was what she meant, and as I clasped her hand to seal the compact, I saw that she had fainted. Later her sister came to me and said that it was all right—that Violet had said she would marry me. Of course I was elated, for I believed that I should win her in time—that eventually she must yield to my love and devotion, when her wounded heart should have a chance to heal, and I was satisfied to take her thus, even though she had frankly said she could never love me as a wife should love her husband. Still, as time passed, I began to fear that she regretted her promise, and during an interview with her, on the evening previous to the day set for our marriage, I was deeply pained and troubled by her manner and a certain wretchedness which she could not conceal. But I reasoned that when the wedding was once over, and we were quietly settled in our home, she would gradually grow content."

Wallace had listened thus far with absorbing interest. At times when Lord Cameron spoke of Violet's faithfulness to and love for him, of her despairing grief over his supposed death, and her reluctance to become the wife of another, his face would light up for an instant or grow tender with love, as his emotions moved him; but gradually, as the narrator drew near the end of his tale, he grew nervous and restless, the tense lines of pain settled again about his mouth, his eyes grew dark and moody in expression, while the spasmodic twitching of his nerves could be plainly seen by every one in the room.

"'When once the wedding was over,'" he interposed hoarsely, at this point of the story; "that was—a month ago—to-day——"

"Yes, that was the date set for the ceremony," Vane Cameron responded, with a sinking heart, as he bent a pitying look upon the young and terribly stricken husband.

Bitter as his own grief and disappointment had been when he lost Violet, they now seemed to dwindle into nothing in comparison with Wallace's greater suffering and the terrible tidings which he yet had to reveal to him. His heart sank with a sickening dread; no duty had ever seemed so hard before.

"I—I read a notice of it in a Cincinnati paper, and I started for England at once——" Wallace began excitedly.

"You started at once!" said Lord Cameron, surprised. "It was announced a month previous."

"I know—I know; but I did not get the paper for some time after," was the agitated reply. "At the time Violet left for Europe I was called to New York to consult with an architect about going into partnership with him and accepting an important contract. The partnership was consummated, the contract accepted, and I have been in New York ever since. This was why I did not get the news earlier—it was a mere chance that I got it at all. The paper stated that you were to start immediately for your residence on the Isle of Wight, consequently I went directly there, thus losing much more time. But—oh, I cannot stop for all these details now," the young man cried, with a ghastly face, the perspiration standing in great beads upon his brow, while he was terribly excited. "Of course Violet is not your wife, even though ten thousand ceremonies were performed over you. She is mine—mine! Oh, Heaven! am I going mad? Where is she? Tell me—tell me! Why are you still here? Why did you not go to the Isle of Wight? Why do you not speak? Why do you keep me in such suspense?"

It was dreadful to look upon him, and no pen could portray the anguish that was written upon his countenance, that vibrated in his hoarse, quivering tones.

"We—did not go because—that marriage ceremony never took place," said Lord Cameron, gravely, but inwardly quaking over what he must tell him next.

Wallace sprang to his feet, a thrilling cry of joy bursting from him.

"Never took place!" he repeated, panting for breath. "Thank Heaven! Violet, my love! you are still my own! Oh, say it again—say those blessed words again!"

"Be calm, I beseech you, Mr. Richardson," said Lord Cameron, pitifully, while convulsive sobs broke from Lady Isabel; "do not allow yourself to become so unnerved and you shall learn all. I told you, if you remember, that Violet—nay, do not frown when I speak of her thus," the noble young man gently interposed, as Wallace's brow grew dark, to hear that loved named drop so familiarly from his lips, "for had I known the truth, I would have scorned to wrong either of you by even a confession of my love. But I told you that she appeared strangely during my last interview with her. I offered her a caress—I tell you this," he interposed, a crimson flush mounting to his brow, "that you may have all the comfort possible in knowing how wholly her heart belonged to you—and she shrank from me in pain, if not with absolute loathing. Later on, during the same evening, my mother saw her for a few minutes, and she made some remarks which seemed very strange at the time, but which were readily comprehended later; for the next morning when her sister went to her room, to help her prepare for her bridal, she was not there. She had gone—left the house and the place, and no one knew whither."

A cry of mingled thankfulness and anxiety broke from Wallace at this, and his sorely tried nerves, so long strung to their utmost tension, gave way, and sob after sob burst from his overcharged heart as he sank weakly back in his chair.

It was a pitiful sight to see that brave, strong young man weep thus over the discovery of the faithfulness of his loved one.

It was almost more than Lord Cameron could bear and retain his composure, while Lady Cameron wept unrestrainedly.

Wilhelm Mencke and his wife sat stolidly by viewing this affecting sight, one racked with feelings of mingled anger, guilt, and remorse, the other uneasily considering the chances of trouble for himself regarding the disposition of Violet's fortune.

But Wallace soon mastered his emotion; he was not one to remain long inactive when there was anything to be done.

"My faithful, true-hearted little wife!" he murmured, as he dashed aside his tears, new hope and courage already glowing on his face, "her love and instinct were stronger than the force of circumstances. But," starting again to his feet, "I must find her; I must follow her to the ends of the earth, if need be, and when I do find her, as I surely shall,"—with a stern glance at Mr. and Mrs. Mencke—"nothing save death shall ever separate us again."

A chill ran over every listener at these confident words, and an ominous silence fell over the shrinking group.

"Have you any idea whither she went? Has any one tried to follow her?" Wallace asked, turning to Lord Cameron, and wondering why he should look so ghastly; why Lady Cameron's sobs should have burst forth again with renewed violence.

"Every possible effort was made to find her; day after day we have searched for her," began his lordship, falteringly.

"And you have learned nothing—gained no clew?" impatiently demanded the anxious young husband.

"Nothing—until the day before yesterday."

"Ah! then you have news at last!" cried Wallace, eagerly. "Tell me!—tell me!—what have you learned?"

"Heaven help me! how can I tell you?" exclaimed Lord Cameron, in an agonized tone. Then with a great effort for self-control, he solemnly added: "Mr. Richardson, be brave—Violet is dead!—drowned! we found her two days ago. She doubtless missed her footing during her flight in the night, and fell into the sea."

But these last words fell upon unheeding ears, for when Lord Cameron said that she was "dead"—"drowned"—Wallace had cast one horrified, despairing look around upon those white, hopeless faces, and then, without a word or cry, as if smitten by some mighty unseen power, he fell forward on his face and lay like a log upon the floor, at Vane Cameron's feet.

CHAPTER XVII.
LORD CAMERON AND WALLACE BECOME FIRM FRIENDS.

"Help me!" Vane Cameron commanded of Mr. Mencke, as he stooped to assist the fallen man, his noble face full of pity and compassion for him.

They lifted Wallace and laid him upon a lounge, where Vane, after loosening his necktie and collar, strove to revive him by sprinkling his face plentifully with cold water and chafing his hands vigorously.

But Wallace showed no signs of recovering; he lay motionless, breathless—like a man dead, and at last, becoming alarmed, Lord Cameron sent a servant for the nearest physician.

Upon his arrival, and after an examination of Wallace's condition, he pronounced it to be an attack of coma produced by hemorrhage in the brain, caused by excessive excitement and long continued anxiety of mind.

"It is a serious attack," he said, gravely, "but the poor fellow is young and has a splendid physique; if he can hold out long enough—until the clot is absorbed—he may recover. Is he a relative of milord?"

"No, I never saw him until this evening," Vane answered, "but I want everything possible done to save his life, and I will be responsible."

The energetic little French doctor needed no better incentive than this, for the wealth and generosity of the young English earl had been common talk in the town ever since his arrival, and he threw himself into the work of effecting Wallace's recovery with all his heart. Every luxury that Vane could think of or the doctor suggest, was supplied for his benefit and comfort.

Mr. and Mrs. Mencke took a hasty leave the day following the disclosures related in the foregoing chapter.

Their treachery and unnatural harshness toward Violet had been unmasked, and Lady Cameron and her son did not take any pains to conceal their condemnation of such atrocious conduct; consequently Violet's sister and her husband were anxious to escape from Mentone as quickly as possible.

"You must go home also, mother," Vane said to Lady Isabel, after their departure, "it will not do for you to remain longer in this enervating climate."

"And what of you, my son?" the fond mother questioned, anxiously.

"I shall stay with him until he recovers, or at least until he is able to be moved farther north," the young man quietly responded.

"Vane— —"

"Do not oppose me, mother, please," he interrupted, "he is a stranger in a strange country, with not a friend to minister to his need or comfort; and, if I am not mistaken, he has only a scant supply of money."

"But the nurse and physician can look after him, and the bills can all be sent to you, if you wish," urged Lady Cameron.

"The nurse and physician will both do their duty more faithfully if I am here to watch them," Vane answered, inflexibly. "For her sake," he added, in a low tone, and with white lips, "I shall do my utmost to bring him back to health, while if, in spite of all, he dies, I shall lay him by her side, and then take up the broken thread of my own life as best I can."

Lady Cameron stole to his side and wound her arms about his neck.

"Vane," she murmured, while tears streamed over her cheeks, "my noble boy! it is like you to do this and like the Master who said, 'I was a stranger and ye took me in.' But it breaks my heart to hear you speak in that hopeless tone. I know—I feel sure that the 'broken thread of your life,' as you express it, will be joined again. I cannot contemplate with resignation that you, with your noble character and grand possibilities for doing good, should carry this unhealed wound to your grave. But I shall not go home to leave you here," she added, resolutely; "if you stay to care for this poor, suffering stranger, I shall stay to look after you."

"Mother, I cannot permit it," Vane began, but she interrupted him.

"I am inexorable," she said, firmly. "You know that the warm weather is not depressing to me, as to most people, and anxiety would prey upon me more than the climate, so it will be useless to urge me further."

Thus it was settled, and those two royal-hearted people remained for another month in that deserted hotel, and devoted themselves to the care of Wallace Richardson during his critical illness.

He was very, very ill, but as the physician had said, possessed a splendid constitution, and, after a fierce battle with disease, he began slowly to recover—at least his physical health.

But his mind seemed sadly clouded, a condition caused by the pressure of a clot of blood upon his brain, the doctor said, and time alone would show whether he would ever entirely regain the use of his mental faculties; absorption was the only process by which it could be achieved, and this might be slow or rapid, as his general health improved.

At the end of four weeks it was thought that he might safely be moved; indeed, the physician advised it, thinking he would gain strength faster in a more invigorating atmosphere, and Vane determined to convey him directly to the Isle of Wight, whither he had intended taking Violet.

It seemed almost like the mockery of fate that, instead of taking the woman whom he had loved and hoped to make his wife to this beautiful summer home, he should remove hither the man whom she had loved and secretly married, to nurse him back to health.

The change proved to be very beneficial, and Wallace began to gain strength, both physically and mentally, almost immediately.

Possibly the change in medical treatment had also something to do with this improvement, for Lord Cameron placed him under the care of one of the most skillful physicians of London, who happened to be summering on the island.

He did not appear to regard the case so seriously as the French doctor had done.

"He will be all right again in a couple of months," Doctor Harkness said. "Give him plain, nourishing diet, plenty of moderate out-door exercise, and keep his mind free from all exciting subjects."

Time proved the truth of this prophecy; there was a steady improvement in Wallace from the moment of his arrival upon the island, and twelve weeks from the day of his attack he was pronounced a well man again.

During his convalescence, as he came, little by little, to realize his position, together with the kindness and care which had been thrown around him during his illness, he tried to manifest his appreciation of it.

The first time he referred to the subject was one delightful afternoon, when the two young men were sitting together upon the broad piazza of Lord Cameron's elegant villa, which overlooked the sea.

Vane had been reading to his companion an amusing story, which both had seemed to enjoy thoroughly. When he finished it and closed his book Wallace looked up and remarked, gratefully:

"What a good friend you have been to me, Cameron! I hope you do not think me unappreciative, but I have only just begun to have sense enough to find it out."

"I trust we are good friends," Vane answered, cordially but evading a direct reply to his gratitude, "and that we shall continue to be such throughout our lives."

He had grown to admire the young architect exceedingly during the long weeks that he had so patiently borne his weakness and enforced idleness; while, as his mind gradually became stronger and clearer, he saw that he was no ordinary person, that he possessed great ability—a strong character, and unswerving principles of rectitude.

"Thank you," Wallace answered, gratefully; "I hope so, too. But how am I ever to repay you for your unexampled kindness? It is a problem beyond my ability to solve."

"By pledging the friendship I desire, and saying no more about the obligation—if any there is," Vane replied, with a genial smile, and holding out his hand to his companion.

Wallace instantly laid his within it, and the two men thus sealed the compact with a violent but heart-felt clasp.

Later Wallace spoke of Violet for the first time since his illness, and begged for more information regarding her sojourn at Mentone and the circumstances of her flight, though he touched as lightly as possible upon the revolting story of the discovery of the body upon the beach and its burial; but he would not even hint his suspicion of suicide.

The subject was a depressing one to both, and to change it Vane said, after a long pause:

"If you feel like it, would you mind coming with me into the library to look over some plans that came from London to-day? I am about to erect a school building for the children of my tenants, and also a home for aged people and orphans. Perhaps, being an architect, you can make some suggestions that will be useful to me."

This was merely a ruse to divert Wallace's mind from the sad and exciting train of thought into which he had fallen; but the young man arose with alacrity at the mention of plans. He dearly loved his profession, and was already beginning to be anxious to get into active service again.

He followed his friend to the library, where they found the plans spread out upon a table, and both soon became deeply interested in discussing them.

Wallace was quick to discover that they were defective, and far from being practical, in many respects. They were imposing, and looked well on paper, but he knew that when completed the buildings would be very disappointing in various ways.

He modestly pointed out the defects, but in a way that betrayed he knew his business thoroughly, and Lord Cameron, who would never have discovered them until the buildings were completed, became disgusted with the plans, and said at once that he should discard them entirely.

"Nay, do not be too hasty in your condemnation. I am afraid I have been too critical," Wallace said, regretfully. "With some changes, you might still use them; but, if you will allow me, I will make you some drawings, giving you my ideas regarding these buildings; then, perhaps, you can combine the two sets, and get something more to your mind."

"Do," said Lord Cameron, eagerly; "and if they prove to be what I want, you shall have the price Mac Cumber is going to charge me for these—it is no mean one, either."

"The price!" exclaimed Wallace, flushing. "No, indeed! Do not mention such a thing after all your bounty to me during these many weeks."

"Ah, but that was on the score of friendship, you know," lightly returned Vane. "That is all settled for. Remember your pledge. This will be business."

Wallace made no reply, but the settling of the firm lines about his mouth plainly indicated that he meant to have his own way in this matter.

He went immediately to work, all his old enthusiasm awakening the moment he took his pencil in his fingers.

He was not yet strong enough mentally to apply himself very closely, neither would Lord Cameron allow him to be imprudent; but by working a few hours every day he made good progress, and at the end of a couple of weeks laid before Lord Cameron two sets of plans which, for convenience, beauty of design, and elegance of workmanship, far exceeded anything that he had even seen.

"You are a genius, Richardson!" he exclaimed, after he had thoroughly examined them, and Wallace had explained everything. "You have utilized every square foot of space, and that, too, without infringing in any way upon the beauty and proportions. I shall use these plans, and Mac Cumber would do well to come and take lesson of you."

Wallace was of course very much pleased with this high praise, while he was no less gratified when, the following week, Lord Cameron proposed that they should take a trip to his estate, so that he might judge if the proposed site for the new buildings were just what it should be, or whether it could be improved upon by choosing some other.

The next seven days were spent in Essex County, at the country seat of the young Earl of Sutherland, and where Wallace was entertained as an honored guest, while every day the bond of friendship between the two men became more firmly cemented.

The site proved all that could be desired, and Wallace assured his friend that the buildings would make a very fine appearance upon it when completed.

After that Vane said that he must see some of the "lions of London," and he took him up to his town house, where they spent two weeks very enjoyably.

It was now about the first of October, and Wallace, claiming that he was now as well as ever, said that he must return to his business in New York.

Dr. Harkness was consulted, and expressed the opinion that he was able to go, and, accordingly, the day of his departure was set for the fifth.

"I am very loath to let you go," Vane said, regretfully, as, on the evening before his departure, they sat together in his "bachelor nest," as his smoking-room was called.

"I shall regret the separation as much as you possibly can," Wallace replied, gravely, "but I must go back to my work. I have but one object in life now—my profession. I shall devote all my energies to it, and try to forget my great loss in making a name for myself."

"There can be no doubt that you will do that, with your talent," Lord Cameron replied; then drawing an envelope from his pocket, he quietly passed it to him. "Do not open it until you reach New York," he said, with some embarrassment.

"Forgive me if I do," Wallace said, cutting the end and drawing forth the paper within it, for he was confident that he knew the nature of its contents.

He found a check on the Bank of England for a hundred pounds.

"Cameron! I cannot take it," he said, flushing hotly.

"I beg you will," said Vane, earnestly.

"I should never respect myself again if I did," Wallace returned, with emotion. "You are more than welcome to the plans, if this check was intended as a remuneration for them, while I shall never cease to feel that I owe you a debt which I can never repay for all your kindness to my loved one, not to mention the vetoed subject of my obligations to you."

"But—have you funds sufficient for your needs?" Vane asked, flushing.

"Yes, for all present needs," his companion answered. "I was paid five thousand dollars for the injuries which I received in that accident I told you of, and I took a letter of credit for a thousand when I came abroad, so I have abundant means for my expenses to America."

CHAPTER XVIII.
THE FACE AT THE WINDOW.

Lord Cameron admired Wallace's independence, yet while he saw he would hurt him deeply by insisting upon his acceptance of the check, he could not feel satisfied to accept as a gift the valuable plans which he had executed for him.

He therefore said no more about the money, but, before he slept, he wrote several letters to prominent parties in New York, whom he knew, in which he spoke with highest praise of Wallace's talents as an architect, and solicited their influence and patronage for him in the future.

"Perhaps these may prove to be of more advantage to you than the contents of that other envelope which you rejected," he remarked, with a smile, as he slipped a half dozen letters of introduction into his hands just before they retired.

"You are very thoughtful, Cameron," Wallace said, appreciatively; "and I will thankfully make use of these."

The fifth of October, the date of Wallace's departure, dawned a bright, lovely morning.

Lord Cameron had engaged to accompany him to Liverpool, determined to delay their parting to the last moment, and dreading, more than he could express, the return to his estate in Essex County, when he would begin to realize something of the loneliness of his own situation. Wallace's illness, and the care which he had been forced to give him, he now realized had been a great blessing to him, for it had prevented, in a measure, his brooding over his own troubles.

Vane had made thoughtful provision for his friend's voyage, supplying him with everything he could think of to make his passage comfortable and pleasant, and the two men, after taking an affectionate leave of Lady Isabel, who also had become very fond of Wallace, drove away to catch the express for Liverpool.

As they were passing through one of the busy thoroughfares of the city, their progress was hindered for a few moments by a blockade of vehicles.

While waiting for an opportunity to advance, another carriage, going in the opposite direction, slowly passed them—for the stream of teams was not blocked on the other side of the street—and when it was directly opposite them the face of a woman looked forth from the window for an instant, then the coach passed on, and she was lost to view.

An agonized cry had burst from Wallace at that moment, and that, with his fixed stare at the passing carriage, caused Lord Cameron also to glance that way; but he only caught a fleeting glimpse of the outline of a delicate face framed in golden hair, then it vanished beyond his sight.

"Violet!" gasped Wallace, with ashen lips, and trembling violently from head to foot. "Did you see her? Oh, let me out, quick! quick! I must find her!"

He was terribly agitated and unnerved, almost frantic, in fact, and Lord Cameron greatly feared another attack such as had previously prostrated him.

He reached out his hand, and pushed him firmly yet kindly back upon his seat.

"Be quiet, Richardson!" he said, with gentle authoritativeness. "It could not have been Violet. It was but a delusion, a fancied resemblance, or a trick of the imagination. Violet is dead. Did I not see her with my own eyes? Did I not care for her, and lay her to rest beneath the shade of that grand old beech?—while you yourself have seen her grave."

"Oh, but it—the face—was so like—so like!" murmured Wallace, still fearfully overcome.

"My friend," Vane continued, while he tried to control his own startled nerves, "you must not allow yourself to be so unnerved by a fancied, or even a real resemblance to the loved one whom you have lost. It is not unlikely you may meet it again some time, but you must bear it bravely. This great sorrow has been sent upon you, and you must meet it with courage and resignation, as one who believes in God should meet the trials which He sends upon you. There is work in the world for you to do, or your life would not have been spared; take it up, carry it on to its fulfillment, and do not ruin your health, your brain, your great talent, by allowing the ghost of your lost happiness to haunt and weaken you thus."

The young man spoke gravely and very earnestly, but his own face was almost as pallid as Wallace's and it was easy to see that he had been deeply moved by what had occurred. It might even be that he was striving to fortify his own sore heart and wounded spirit with the admonitions that he was giving his friend.

Wallace wiped the perspiration from his face, and strove manfully to recover his self-possession; but it was no easy thing to do, and it was long before he regained his natural color, or ceased to tremble visibly.

"I know what you say must be true," he returned, when he could speak, "and my common sense tells me that I was deceived—that the face could not have been Violet's; and yet—if—I could follow and find the woman who looks so much like her—who seemed to be her exact counterpart, I believed it would comfort me—would help to ease this ceaseless aching, this never-ending longing of my heart."

"It would not," said Lord Cameron, positively; "it would but unsettle you the more; and now that I come to think of it the more, that face—though I caught but the merest glimpse of its outline—was thinner and older than Violet's."

He immediately changed the subject, and strove to divert the mind of his friend from the painful incident, but while he endeavored to talk and appear like himself, he was secretly greatly shaken by what had occurred.

Most of the journey to Liverpool was spent in discussing Lord Cameron's plans regarding the school for the children of his tenants and the home for aged people and orphans, and the young earl exacted a promise from Wallace that, when the buildings were completed and ready for occupancy, he would come again to England to be present at their dedication, and pronounce his verdict upon them.

"You will not need to be absent from your business more than three weeks or a month," he said, "and I am sure you will have earned the right to that much of a vacation by that time. However, I shall see you again before then, since I do not intend to entirely desert the land of my birth, even though my home must be in England, and every year I shall make a short trip to America. I am not going to lose sight of my friend either; remember, Richardson, we are pledged to each other for life."

The hand which he extended with this remark was warmly grasped, and both young men felt that their souls were "knit unto each other," in a bond as strong and tender as that which had united David and Jonathan of old.

The steamer was to sail at sundown, and the little time that intervened, after their arrival in Liverpool, the two friends spent in looking over the mammoth vessel.

When at last the signal for departure sounded, they parted with a lingering hand-clasp and a simple "God bless you;" but Lord Cameron, as he journeyed back alone to his princely home, felt as if half the light had suddenly gone out of his life.

Wallace had a quick and comfortable passage, and, having cabled the time of his departure, and the name of the steamer, found his partner awaiting him at the pier upon his arrival in New York.

He greeted him with great warmth, which had in it an undertone of genuine sympathy for his troubles, and then informed him that he had just secured a contract for a sixty-thousand-dollar building; remarking, too, that he hoped Wallace felt in the spirit for work, as they would have their hands full during the coming year.

"Work will be the mainspring of my life after this," Wallace briefly returned, but he appeared gratified with the encouraging report of business which his partner had given him.

He threw himself heart and soul into his profession from that day. He worked at his office from morning until evening, when not out upon duties of inspection, and for hours in his own room at night; worked to keep his mind from dwelling upon his great sorrow, and until he was so weary in body that sleep came to him, unbidden, as soon as his head touched his pillow.

He took the earliest opportunity possible to present his letters of introduction to the parties whom Lord Cameron had addressed in his behalf.

These recommendations proved to be worth a great deal to him, for to be the valued friend of an English earl and a man of genius as well, were facts calculated to give him prestige with even the most conservative, and business flowed in upon the firm of Harlow & Richardson in such a continuous stream that they bade fair to have more work than they could handle.

At the close of the first year, after Wallace's return, they found they had cleared twenty thousand dollars, while they had contracts ahead for another twelve months, besides applications that were constantly coming in.

Wallace had never been in better health than during this time. He loved his work and forgot himself in it, and was fast winning a name and fame that promised to place him, not far in the future, at the head of his profession; while already rumors of his success had somehow been set afloat in his old home in Cincinnati, and people there were beginning to talk of that "promising young Richardson" whom they had once known only as an humble carpenter.

He had acquired also during this year both strength of character and dignity of bearing, and was a grand looking young man.

He went, now and then, into society, for Mr. Harlow, who was some years his senior, had a delightful home and a lovely wife, and they insisted upon his visiting them occasionally. In this way he met many agreeable people, who, in their turn, solicited his presence in their homes.

But society had comparatively few attractions for him, even though several ambitious mothers smiled encouragingly upon the rising young architect, and many fair, bright-eyed damsels shot alluring glances at him.

But he had no heart to offer any one, and met all these advances with quiet but dignified courtesy.

He heard regularly from Lord Cameron, who was throwing all his energies toward pushing his benevolent schemes to completion, and the buildings which Wallace had planned would, he wrote, be finished and ready for occupancy by another spring.

He had intended to visit America before this, his last letter said, but the press of business and the delicate state of his mother's health had thus far prevented; he hoped, however, before many weeks should pass to tread again the familiar streets of New York.

He also stated that he had met Mr. and Mrs. Mencke once during the past year. It was during the London season, and he and his mother had run across them at a brilliant reception—a circumstance that surprised him somewhat, as he did not suppose they would go into society so soon after the death of their sister.

The meeting had occurred in this way.

After making an extended tour of the Alps, Mr. and Mrs. Mencke had returned to London, to meet Mrs. Hawley, who was to spend a few weeks there and then go on to Milan, to remain for the winter with Nellie Bailey, who had concluded to devote another year to her beloved music before returning to America.

Mrs. Hawley was a woman who dearly loved society, and always had a long list of engagements—one who had it in her power to be so charming could not fail to be a welcome guest wherever she went—consequently, it was perfectly natural that she should wish her friend to participate in her enjoyment.

Mrs. Mencke at first faintly demurred upon the ground of being in mourning, but Mrs. Hawley, who did not believe in mourning anyway, easily overruled her scruples.

"What is the harm?" she questioned. "You cannot do Violet any good by secluding yourself, and no one here knows you well enough to gossip about you. It would be different, perhaps, if you were at home, where people have known you all your life."

So Mrs. Mencke, who liked gay life as well as any one, smothered her conscience, and, never doing things by halves, went everywhere.

It was at a reception given by the American Consul that she met Lord Cameron and his mother, Lady Isabel having been an intimate friend of the gentleman's family when her home was in New York.

Mrs. Mencke, ignoring entirely the barriers that had arisen between them at Mentone, appeared delighted to meet her "dear friends," but the greetings upon their part were decidedly cool, while Lady Cameron looked the reproaches she could not utter at Mrs. Mencke's gay manner and attire, and uttered a sigh of regret that the gentle girl, whom she had begun to love as a daughter, should so soon have been forgotten by her only relative.

"Are you in London for any length of time, Lady Cameron?" Mrs. Mencke inquired, secretly hoping that she might get an invitation to visit her at her town-house.

"Only for a week or two longer, as my son's affairs call him to his estate in Essex," was the somewhat formal reply.

"Indeed! and have you been in town long?"

"About a month."

"Really? I wonder that we have not met before, then," Mrs. Mencke remarked, with some surprise.

"It is not strange," said Lady Cameron, with a sigh, "for my son and I are still too sad to care to go much into company, and we should not have been here this evening but for a special request of your consul, who is an old and valued friend."

Mrs. Mencke colored vividly at this reply, and began to make excuses for her own presence there; but Lady Cameron, with a disapproving glance over her elegant and showy costume, only bowed with reserved courtesy in reply, and then, as Lord Cameron accosted an acquaintance who was approached, she excused herself and turned to greet her friend, leaving Mrs. Mencke boiling with rage over their distant reception, and bitterly disappointed at not having secured an invitation even to call upon them.

She felt humiliated as well as angry, and too wrought up to longer enjoy the gayeties of the evening, she retired at an early hour from the reception.

The unhappy woman had other causes, aside from the failure of her matrimonial schemes and the contempt of the Camerons, for anxiety and unhappiness.

Her husband, during the last few months, while visiting various resorts, had developed an alarming taste for gambling, and had, to her knowledge, lost large sums of money; while he seemed perfectly reckless in his expenditure, and she felt sure, though she did not yet dream the worst, that their own as well as Violet's fortune was fast melting away.

Deep and frequent potations at the cup, too, were showing their effect upon him; he was growing more gross and coarse, and his temper suffered in proportion with the continuous nervous excitement under which he was laboring.

All this must have an end sooner or later, she knew, but she was not prepared to have it come so soon as it did.

Four weeks after her meeting with the Camerons the man returned to her, late one night, from a terrible orgie. His face was bloated and crimson from drink; his eyes wild and blood-shot, his hair disheveled, and his clothing soiled and disordered.

Coming rudely into his wife's presence, he cried out with a shocking oath:

"It's all gone!—hic—every—dollar we had in the world, and, Belle, we're—hic—beggars!"

"What do you mean, Will?" his wife demanded, with a sinking heart and white face.

"Are you deaf?" he bawled, with another oath. "We're—hic—beggars, I tell—hic—you. I've just—hic—rattled away the hic—last dollar."

There was a scene then, as might be expected, for Mrs. Mencke was not a woman to tamely submit to such wrong and abuse, and the thought that the whole of her own, as well as Violet's fortune, had been squandered at the gaming-table and the race-track was more than she could bear. She could talk as few women can talk, and when she had ceased her denunciations, Wilhelm Mencke was completely sobered, and sat pale and sullen and cowed before her.

She did not realize how exceedingly bitter and stinging her denunciations were until the next morning, when, upon rising, she found the jewel-box, in which she kept the jewelry which she commonly wore (her diamonds and more valuable gems being locked in a trunk, fortunately) together with all that Violet had possessed, was rifled of its contents and her husband gone, together with his traveling-bag and a change of clothes.

The desertion of her husband was the most humiliating of all her troubles; but her proud spirit would not yield to even this blow. She calmly stated that her husband had been suddenly called home and that she was to follow him by the next steamer.

Fortunately she had considerable money with her, and she settled every bill with a grave front, and finally took her departure from the hotel with as much pomp and state as she had maintained throughout her sojourn there.

A week from the day of her husband's flight she was crossing the Atlantic alone, and immediately upon reaching New York proceeded to Cincinnati in the hope of saving something by the sale of her house and furniture. The house had already been disposed of, though she learned that not much had been realized on it, for it had been heavily mortgaged and the sale was a forced one.

This fact told her that her husband was in America, although no one had seen him, for the sale had been made through an agent, and she tried to feel thankful that he had had the grace to leave her the furniture. This she turned into money, but it did not bring her a third of its real value, for she was forced to sacrifice it at auction.

Where now was the proud woman's boasted wealth and position? Where now her vaunted superiority over the "low-born carpenter" because of his poverty?

Gone! for she had not—aside from some valuable jewels and clothing—a thousand dollars in the world, while she had the exceeding mortification of realizing the stern fact that she would be obliged to seek some employment in order to live honestly.

It was the bitterest drop in her already bitter cup, and too proud to remain in the city where she had hitherto been a leader in society, she suddenly disappeared from the place and no one knew whither she had gone.

CHAPTER XIX.
A RETROSPECTIVE GLANCE.

It was on the fourteenth of May, nearly a year and a half previous to the sudden downfall and disappearance of Wilhelm Mencke and his wife, that a curious incident occurred which has an important bearing upon our story.

At the foot of one of the mountains which skirt the Gulf of Genoa just a few miles east of the line which separate France and Italy, there stood at that time the dwelling of a well-to-do Italian peasant.

That the man was above the majority of his class, his neat homestead, his thrifty fields and vineyards, and the general air of comfort which pervaded his dwelling plainly betokened.

But he was a stern, harsh man, bestowing little affection upon his family, yet exacting unquestioning obedience and diligent toil from every member, to help him maintain the thrift for which he was noted and to fill his pockets with money.

On a dark and starless night, long after Tasso Simone and most of his family were wrapped in slumber, the door of his dwelling was softly opened, whereupon a slight, girlish figure stole forth and sped noiselessly across the vineyard of olive trees, toward the highway which skirted the gulf.

Upon reaching the road, the flying fugitive moderated her pace, but walked on with a firm, elastic step toward Mentone, which was the nearest town over the French line.

For an hour she walked steadily on, appearing to be perfectly familiar with the way, even in that intense darkness, until finally she paused before a low, rude building, or shed, which had been constructed out of rough boards to protect fishermen from the hot rays of the sun, while cleaning their fish for market.

She sat down to rest just outside upon a rude bench, which she seemed to know was there, and opening a parcel which she carried in her hands, she began to eat of its contents.

Suddenly she paused and listened, for a slight movement behind her, within the shed, had attracted her attention.

A sigh that was almost a moan had greeted her ears.

She did not move for several moments, but waited for the sound to be repeated.

Soon she heard it again; a long-drawn, sobbing sigh like some one deeply grieved or in distress.

The girl arose, and, without a trace of fear in her manner, made her way within the shed, showing by her quick, decisive movements that she was as familiar with the ground as with her own home.

Here she struck a match and lighted a piece of candle, which she took from her pocket, when she saw, with evident amazement, a beautiful girl lying asleep upon a shawl which had been spread over a pile of seaweed in one corner of the place.

The light also revealed the fugitive, whom we have followed thus far, to be a slight, graceful form, straight as an arrow, and having a wiry energy and resolution in her every movement which betrayed unusual self-reliance in one so young.

She was very light in complexion, having yellow hair, black eyes, and bright, rosy cheeks, a somewhat unusual combination in one who was a native of that Southern clime.

She was dressed in the costume of the country, and with a neatness and trimness that made her seem almost dainty in the homely dress, while on her head she wore a large, coarse straw hat, over which a bright handkerchief had been thrown, and was tied under her pretty, rounded chin.

She softly approached and leaned over the sleeper, astonishment depicted upon every feature of her young face; and well she might look surprised, for the lovely girl who lay upon that wretched bed of sea-weed was richly and tastefully clad, and bespoke the petted child of luxury and fortune.

She knelt beside her, and, laying her hand lightly upon her shoulder, said, in low, musical Italian:

"Wake, signorina."

The touch aroused the fair sleeper, and she started up affrighted; but, upon seeing the kindly face of a young girl about her own age bending above her, her expression of terror changed to one equally surprised with that of her companion.

"Why is the signorina sleeping here in this miserable place?" the peasant girl asked.

But her companion could not understand or speak Italian, and shook her head, intimating that she did not know what she had said.

To her surprise the girl then addressed her in broken French, repeating her question, and then the fair stranger, appearing to think it best to confide in her, answered, though with some embarrassment:

"I am in great trouble, and I am running away from it. I have walked a long distance, but became so weak and faint I could go no farther, and stumbled in here to rest, and must have fallen asleep from weariness."

A look of pity and sympathy swept over the peasant girl's face.

"Mademoiselle is hungry, perhaps?" she remarked.

"Yes; I had no supper. I could not eat and am faint. I have been ill and am far from strong."

The girl stuck her candle upon a rock and then, going outside the shed, brought in her own lunch which she had left lying upon the bench. It consisted of some coarse bread and cheese, some cakes fried in olive oil, with a few dried figs, and all wrapped in a clean linen cloth.

"Eat, mademoiselle," she said, as she placed it upon her companion's lap.

The beautiful stranger seized a fig and quickly disposed of it with evident relish; then she suddenly paused and asked:

"But do you not need this yourself? I must not rob you."

The girl shrugged her shoulders, and shook her head.

"Eat, signorina, eat," she said, mixing her French and Italian; and the other, without waiting to be urged further, and apparently ravenously hungry, quickly disposed of everything save the cheese.

"You are very good," she said, gratefully, when the last fig was eaten. "I thank you very much." Then with sudden curiosity, she inquired: "But how do you also happen to be abroad alone at this hour of the night?"

Again the peasant girl shrugged her shoulders, and a dark look of passion swept over her face.

"I, too, am running away," she said. "I do not like my home; I have a step-father; he is cruel, harsh, and wants to marry me to a man I do not love."

"How strange," murmured her companion, a look of wonder coming into her beautiful eyes, while an expression of sympathy crept over her lovely face.

"My father owes him for a fine pair of mules, just bought," the girl resumed, a look of scorn gleaming in here eyes, "and Beppo will call the debt square if I marry him. I will not be exchanged for brutes—I will not be sold like a slave, and to one I hate and loathe, and I fly from him," she concluded, indignantly, the rich blood mounting to her forehead.

"Where are you going?" questioned the other, eagerly.

"To Monaco, to find service in some family, as maid or nurse, until I can earn money to go to some school to learn to study," was the earnest reply.

"You are not an Italian?" the fair stranger said, inquiringly.

The girl shook her head, a sneer curling her red lips.

Evidently to be an Italian was not very desirable in her estimation.

"My mother is Swiss, my own father was French," she briefly answered.

"Ah! that is how you happen to be so light and to speak the French language. Will you tell me your name?"

"You will not betray me? You will not set them on my track, if I tell you?" said the peasant girl, apparently longing to confide in the beautiful maiden, but secretly questioning the wisdom of so doing.

"Surely not. Am I not flying from trouble also? Besides, I am going to another country," was the reassuring reply.

"I am Lisette Vermilet," the girl then said. "I am eighteen years old. I have worked from sunrise till sunset every day for seven long years, in the field, in the vineyard, or the dairy, ever since my poor, foolish mother married her tyrant husband. I do it no more. I take care of myself and be no man's slave, and I marry whom I will, when the right one and the right time come. But first," she continued, eagerly, her face lightning with intense longing, "I study; I learn about the world and other things, like some lovely French girls I saw at

Mentone last year, who told me all about the flowers, the birds, the earth, and the sea. Oh! I weep when I think of how much there is to know, and I have lost it all—all!" and her voice grew tremulous with repressed feeling as she concluded.

"Poor child! you surely ought to have an education if you want it so much," said her sympathetic listener, in a kindly tone, while she regarded the girl's eager face almost affectionately. "But are you not afraid that your cruel step-father will go after you and bring you back?"

"Tasso Simone would beat me black and blue if he should catch me," she said, with a shiver, as if she recalled some experience of the kind. "Ah! if I had but a disguise he would not know me—I get away better."

A bright idea seemed suddenly to strike her companion, for her face lighted eagerly.

"Let us exchange clothing," she exclaimed, "then no one will recognize either of us."

"Ah! but the signorina has such beautiful clothes, while mine are so poor," sighed Lisette, in a deprecatory tone, but with a wistful glance over the daintily made traveling suit, at the tasteful hat, and expensive boots which her companion wore.

"Never mind; yours are neat and whole, and no one would ever think of looking for me in them, while you will be much more likely to succeed in eluding your cruel father in mine," the young stranger persisted.

"The signorina is very kind," Lisette said, gratefully, as, with an impulsive movement, she bent forward and kissed the fair white hand that lay within her reach, while it seemed to her simple heart that she should feel like a princess in that lovely dark-grey cloth dress, with its daintily stitched bands of blue silk.

Alas! she did not dream that it was to become her shroud.

Yes, as has doubtless been surmised, it was Violet whom Lisette Vermilet had found lying asleep upon the pile of sea-weed in the fisherman's shed.

After refusing to admit her sister to her room on the night previous to the day appointed for her wedding, she had continued her occupation of writing for some time. When she was through she read over what she had written, and then deliberately tore it into atoms.

"No, I will not tell them anything," she muttered, with a frown; "I will just go and leave no trace behind me. It may seem unkind to Lord Cameron, but some time I will explain it all."

She then arose and dressed herself in her traveling suit, tied a dark-blue vail about her face, and brought a thick shawl from her closet. She then began to lay out a change of clothing and her toilet articles, but suddenly stopped in the midst of her work.

"No, I will not burden myself with anything," she murmured, thoughtfully. "I am not strong, and I need all the strength I have to get myself away; besides, I can easily buy what I need in any town."

She hastily drew on her gloves, without observing that the rings, which she usually wore and which she prized very highly, were still lying upon her cushion where she had left them before taking her bath. She did not even think to take her watch, which she sadly missed and regretted afterward; her only thought was to get away as quickly as possible from all danger of violating her conscience and of wronging a noble and generous man.

She then put out her light and sat alone in the darkness, waiting for the house to become quiet so that she could steal forth unobserved.

Two hours passed, all in the house seemed to be at rest, and she noiselessly crept out of a window upon the piazza, made her way swiftly around the house to where a flight of stairs led to the ground, and then sped away in the darkness, with no definite idea whither she was going.

She took the highway leading away from Mentone, because she dreaded lest some one should meet and accost her in the town. She had a dim idea that if she could get to San Remo, which was about twelve miles east of Mentone, she could take a train going north without being discovered, and accordingly she bent her footsteps in this direction.

Her way led along the cliffs overhanging the sea, before mentioned, and how she, to whom the way was entirely strange, should have escaped the fate which every one afterward supposed to have been hers was wondered. But escape it she did, and after safely passing this perilous point she descended the hill, and then the road closely followed the beach for some distance.

Here she came upon the rude hut, or shelter, which has been described, and being foot-sore and weary with her long walk, she spread her shawl upon a mass of sea-weed which she found in one corner, and throwing herself upon it soon fell into a profound slumber, from which she was awakened by the light touch of Lisette Vermilet.

With this brief explanation of Violet's flight, we will return to the two girls who were discussing a change of apparel.

Violet was much strengthened by the food which she had eaten and greatly refreshed by her nap, while she was encouraged by the presence of the young girl, who was also, strangely enough, flying from a fate similar to her own.

She overcame the scruples of Lisette, and insisting upon the plan she had proposed, the two girls, under cover of that rude shed, made the exchange, Violet declaring that every article be transferred in order to make the disguise more complete. She only reserved her shawl, as, in traveling, she knew she would need it.

"Now," she said, when their task was completed, "can you tell me the best way to get north. I am going to England, and from there to America, and I want to get away from this region as soon as possible."

"Mademoiselle would do well to come with me to Mentone and take a train from there," Lisette replied.

"Oh, I could not do that," Violet cried. "I have just come from Mentone, and would not go back there for anything."

It will be observed that she had refrained from saying much about herself thus far, for she did not wish even this simple girl to know the circumstances which had caused her flight.

Lisette thought a minute, then she told her to go on to a village about a mile distant, where, in a couple of hours, a train would make a brief stop at a crossing.

This, she said, would bear her back in the same direction she had come, but she could go on to Nice, where she could take an express direct for Paris.

Violet, much as she dreaded passing through Mentone again, saw that this would be the wisest course to pursue, and decided that she would follow the girl's advice.

"You will not betray that you have met me, if any one should question you, and you will keep out of sight of people in Mentone as much as possible," Violet pleaded.

"Surely I will not betray you, signorina, and I will not show myself by daylight in Mentone," Lisette said, earnestly, "and you will get away without any trouble, for a peasant girl can go about alone in this country where an English lady could not. Take courage, signorina; nothing will harm you, and may the Holy Virgin go with you."

"I feel anxious about your passing through Mentone," Violet said. "If you should be seen there tomorrow you would surely be stopped, for my clothing would instantly be recognized by those who will search for me; they would compel you to tell where and how you met me, and then they would telegraph ahead and have me stopped."

"Do not fear, signorina," Lisette responded. "I shall pass through Mentone before light, for I am a rapid walker. I go straight to Monaco, and seek service in some French family going to Paris."

Violet looked relieved at this.

"Have you money?" she asked.

"I have forty francs, signorina. I have saved for eighteen months every sou I could get."

Eighteen months saving eight dollars!

Violet regarded the girl with sorrowful astonishment.

"That is very little; let me give you some more," she cried, and eagerly opening her well-filled purse, counted out some gold-pieces amounting to fifty francs more.

"No, signorina, not a sou," Lisette returned, firmly, as she waved back Violet's extended hand. "My heart is heavy now with all you have done for me—giving me these beautiful clothes in exchange for a poor peasant's dress. I cannot take your money."

"Please," persisted Violet. "I have plenty, and can easily spare you this."

But the girl made a proud gesture of dissent.

"The signorina must go; and I must get on also," she said, gravely. "Keep to the straight road until you come to the track in the village.

You can get no ticket, but the guard will charge you a couple of francs for your fare. Adieu, signorina."

She was about turning away, when Violet stopped her.

"Lisette," she said, holding out her hand, "good-by. You have been very kind to me, and I shall always remember you kindly. I hope we shall meet again some time."

Tears were in Lisette's eyes as she responded in a similar strain, and then led Violet from the shed.

"That way, go; adieu!" she said, pointing eastward; then raising the hand she held, she pressed her lips impulsively to it and dropped it.

With a softly breathed farewell in response, Violet turned and walked quickly away, while Lisette went back into the shed, put out her candle and threw the end away, after which she turned in the opposite direction and began to climb the steep hills or cliffs, along which the highway led toward Mentone.

Violet went on her way in the darkness, her heart beating rapidly with fear lest she should encounter some rude fisherman or peasant who would stop and question her.

She was foot-sore and weary long before she came in sight of the village, for a mile was a long distance to her unaccustomed muscles, while Lisette's heavy shoes hurt her tender feet sorely.

But, guided by the lights along the railroad track, she found her way to the crossing the girl had told, her about, and, sinking down upon a pile of sleepers by the road-bed, she uttered a sigh of relief that she had reached the end of her long walk.

She did not have a great while to wait, for presently the cars came thundering along, and soon she was on the train for Nice, whence she took an express for Paris. Now she felt safe from pursuit, as she was being whirled northward at the rate of forty miles an hour.

CHAPTER XX.
VIOLET RETURNS TO AMERICA.

Meanwhile the kind-hearted peasant girl, Lisette, feeling as if she had suddenly been changed into another being by some good fairy—and she certainly looked like a different person, clad as she was like a lady—was walking at a swinging pace toward Mentone, and—her doom.

She intended to walk until the day began to dawn, and then beg a ride to Monaco in one of the market-carts which made daily trips from the country to that city.

It was still very dark, and the road, which lay up a steep hill, was very narrow, and ran dangerously near the cliffs which overhung the sea.

The girl had worked very hard the previous day, while she had slept none that night, for she had been too much excited, over the thought of leaving her home, to rest, and she now began to experience a feeling of weariness and languor stealing over her. It was the reaction coming on, while added to that was a feeling of dread and loneliness over the uncertainty of the future.

More than this, she found the boots, which Violet had insisted must go with the rest of her costume, were too tight to be comfortable, and this greatly impeded her progress.

She climbed to the top of the cliffs and there sat down by the roadside upon a huge bowlder, where she had rested many a time before, to recover herself a little before going on.

The stone was an irregular one, with a projection which formed a support for her back, and leaning against this, she was overcome by weariness before she knew it and fell into a sound sleep.

It did not seem as if ten minutes had elapsed since she sat down, though in reality it was more than half an hour when the sound of a galloping horse aroused her.

She started to her feet, a cry of terror and dismay breaking from her. It was still so dark that she could see nothing any distance away, but the sound of that swiftly advancing horse made her heart beat with fearful throbs.

Was it some pursuer coming in search of her?

Had her flight been discovered at home, and was her tyrannical step-father coming to force her back into wearisome servitude? or, worse yet, to sell her to another man equally brutal and unkind?

She started to flee, but, not being able to clearly distinguish the road, while she was sadly bewildered by having been so suddenly aroused from her sleep, she turned in the wrong direction and made straight for the edge of the cliff.

It was very strange—as familiar as she was with every inch of the ground between her home and Mentone—that she could have become so confused and lost as to her location, and it was only when she caught the ominous sound of the washing of the waves against the rocks below that she became conscious of her danger.

But she was rushing at such headlong speed she could not save herself; a low shuddering cry of terror burst from her lips as she suddenly lost her balance; there was a short interval of silence, followed by a heavy splash in the waters below, then the waves closed over the unfortunate girl, and the ocean held the secret of her fate, as well as of Violet's mysterious disappearance.

The cliff was very high at that point, and projected considerably over the sea, which was very deep just there.

The girl sank at once to the bottom, and her clothing probably becoming entangled among the rocks, her body was held there for some weeks, and only disturbed and washed far below to the point where the fishermen had found it after a storm of considerable violence.

It was, of course, unrecognizable, but every article which she wore tended to prove that she was Vane Cameron's lost bride-elect. As such he claimed her, without a doubt as to her identity, and, as we already know, laid her to rest beneath the shadow of the venerable beech in one corner of the church-yard at Mentone.

Lisette's parents never once suspected what her fate had been.

Upon discovering that she had fled, her iron-hearted master had started in search of her, vowing that she should pay dearly for daring to run away from him, and the future that he had planned for her.

He learned that a peasant girl, answering to her description, had boarded the westward-bound train at the village, in the early morning, and had left it again at Nice.

He hastened hither at once, and was told that such a girl had been seen in the waiting-room of the station; but further than that he could get no trace of her, and was finally obliged to return to his home, where, upon the other members of his family, he vented his disappointment and anger over the loss of such valuable help.

The mother, who was far superior to her husband in every way, grieved long and bitterly over the loss of her first-born, but it was many months before she learned the truth regarding her untimely end.

Violet's journey to Paris was accomplished with very little weariness and nothing of incident. Her first business upon reaching the French metropolis was to go to a lady's furnishing house, where she purchased a simple but comfortable outfit, after which she proceeded to a respectable *pension,* which she had heard highly recommended by some Americans whom she had met in London.

It was fortunate that she had a liberal supply of money in her possession. She had never been stinted, for it was supposed that she was the heir to a large fortune, and a certain income was paid to her quarterly. Since she had been joined by her sister and her husband she had not had occasion to use much money, as Mr. Mencke had settled all her bills, and she had several hundred dollars in her possession at the time of her flight.

This fact, together with the discovery that she could find a very safe and pleasant home for a time in the *pension,* where she was stopping, somewhat changed her original plan of returning directly to America, and she resolved to remain in Paris a while for the purpose of perfecting herself more fully in French, and also to take a few finishing lessons in music, for she had determined to make use of these branches in supporting herself in the future.

She threw her whole heart into her work, and few people would have recognized in this grave, studious girl, the bright, laughing, care-free Violet who had been such a favorite among her friends in Cincinnati the year previous.

She put herself under the best of teachers, and made the most of her time and opportunities; thus nearly four months slipped by, and then she resolved to go home to America.

It was the last of September when she left Paris for London, where she remained several days to make preparations for her voyage, before proceeding to Glasgow to take the steamer, she having decided to sail from there, because she could obtain a comfortable passage at cheaper rates on the Anchor Line, and it was now becoming necessary for her to husband her funds a little.

It was the fifth of October when she left London for Glasgow, and it was her face that Wallace had seen looking from that carriage window as he was detained for a few minutes by a blockade in the street.

Violet, however, was wholly unconscious of her proximity to her lover—or her husband, as we now know him to be. She was deeply absorbed in her own thoughts, and was gazing at nothing in particular; therefore, the carriage that she was in had passed Lord Cameron's without her having a suspicion that she had attracted the attention of any one.

She was driven on to the Midland Grand station, where she took a train for Glasgow, and that evening boarded the Circassia for New York, where she arrived eleven days later—three days after the return of Wallace, who had sailed on a faster vessel.

One can imagine something of the loneliness and desolation which this young and delicately reared girl experienced upon finding herself adrift and an utter stranger in that great city and with but little money in her purse.

She longed to learn the circumstances of Wallace's supposed death, her grief over which had been newly aroused on returning to her native land.

She had known before leaving for Europe that he had received an offer of partnership with some New York architect; but he had not mentioned the name of the gentleman before she left, and not having received any of his letters, she did not know whether he had closed with the offer, and therefore, did not know where to go to make any inquiries relative to his movements after her departure.

She dare not go to Cincinnati to ascertain—she dare not write to ask anything about him, for she was determined that her sister should not know where she was. She had become entirely alienated by her unkindness, and felt that she would much prefer to toil for her daily bread than to go back to her and be subject to her arbitrary control again.

"There are hundreds of girls as young as I, even younger, who have to support themselves, and I believe I am just as capable of earning my own living," she mused, considering her future. "At any rate, I am determined to make the trial, and if I find I cannot earn a living there will be time enough then to appeal to the court to appoint a different guardian for me, and demand my money from Wilhelm."

The poor child had yet to learn that there was no money to demand.

She found a quiet, respectable boarding-place a few days after her arrival in New York, and then took time by the forelock, by inserting the following advertisement in two of the daily papers:

A LADY, JUST RETURNED FROM EUROPE, and fitted to teach music and French, would like a few pupils. Address H, at this office.

Two days thereafter Violet received a single letter in answer to her advertisement, and it read thus:

"If H. will call at No. —— Fifth avenue, she may learn something to her advantage."

Violet was greatly disappointed to receive only one response; but she argued that one pupil might open the way for others; so she dressed herself with great care, took her music-roll under her arm, and made her way to the address mentioned.

"No. —— Fifth avenue" proved to be a palatial residence, with the name Lawrence gleaming in silver letters upon the door, and Violet's heart sank a little as she mounted the marble steps, for she feared that she might not be competent to teach in an aristocratic family such as doubtless inhabited this elegant mansion.

Her ring was answered by a colored servant, in livery to whom she stated her errand, giving him her card, whereupon she was ushered into a reception-room upon the right of a magnificent hall.

Everything about her bespoke unlimited wealth, while the most perfect taste was displayed in the harmonizing tints of everything, the costly pictures, statuettes, bric-a-brac, and curios.

Ten minutes elapsed. It seemed an age to anxious Violet; then the rich draperies of the archway leading into the hall were swept aside, and a tall, finely proportioned man of perhaps fifty years entered her presence.

He was distinguished-looking, with clear-cut features, an intelligent, expressive eye, and a grandly shaped head; but there was a worn look on his brow, a sad and anxious expression on his face that bespoke care and sorrow.

"Miss Huntington, I presume," he remarked, bowing gravely yet courteously to her, as he glanced at the card which she had sent him by the servant.

"Yes, sir," Violet replied, and taking the letter, which she had received that morning, from her hand-bag, she passed it to him, while she added: "I have come to inquire if I am to find a pupil here. I judged that such must be the fact, since the letter was in response to my advertisement."

Mr. Lawrence did not reply immediately; he seemed to be studying the beautiful girl before him—the sad though lovely face, which was crowned with such a mass of gleaming gold; the graceful figure, in its simple but tasteful costume, while the small hand, so neatly incased in its perfectly fitting glove, and the little foot, in its natty walking-boot, did not escape his observation.

It was easy to perceive that he was favorably impressed by his fair visitor, for when he did speak, he was more kind and courteous than before.

"I was impressed, Miss Huntington, when I read your advertisement, that you were a young lady in search of employment," he said; "and as I am also looking for some young lady to fill a vacancy, it occurred to me that, although you had advertised for 'pupils,' you might be persuaded—if we should be mutually pleased with each other—to devote yourself to one, provided the remuneration were sufficient."

"Ah! you are looking for a governess," Violet remarked, with a quiet smile, and in no wise displeased by the proposition.

"Not a governess, according to the common acceptation of the term," the gentleman returned, in a sad tone. "But let me tell you exactly how I am situated, and what I desire; then you can decide as to the desirability of the position. I have a daughter," Mr. Lawrence resumed, after a moment of thought, "who is in her twelfth year. She is blind——"

"Blind!" repeated Violet, in such a tender, sympathetic tone, and with such a compassionate glance that her companion's face lighted with a grateful smile.

"Yes," he answered, "she was born totally blind. It is a peculiar case, and I have been told there is only one other on record like it. It is called cataract of the lens; but when my child was nine months old a noted oculist, whom we consulted, thought that an operation might be performed which would at least give her a portion of her sight. Of course, I was willing to consent to anything that would mitigate, even to the smallest extent, her heavy affliction. The cataracts were punctured through the pupils, and she saw, very faintly at first, but, as time elapsed and the cataracts began to be absorbed, her sight strengthened somewhat. Her sight is very limited, however; she can see to get about the house, and distinguishes objects of any size with the aid of glasses, but not well enough to read, and whatever she learns is taught by reading aloud to her. She has a remarkable memory, as most blind people have, I believe, and she is extremely fond of music, both vocal and instrumental. Do you sing, Miss Huntington?" Mr. Lawrence asked, suddenly breaking in upon his account of his little daughter's condition.

"Yes, sir, I have spent more time upon vocal culture than upon instrumental music," Violet responded, and this assurance drew forth a smile of approbation from her host.

"I have had many governesses for her," the gentleman resumed, "and she has spent two years in an institution for the blind, though for the last six months I have been obliged myself to teach her all that she has learned. And now I come to the most trying portion of my story," he added, a slight flush tinging his face. "I feel it is only right that I should be perfectly frank with you in the matter, and so feel obliged to tell you that Bertha possesses a very strong, an almost indomitable will, and there are times when she becomes sullen and unmanageable. She will not study, she will not practice, or do anything which she imagines is required of her; and thus, for a time, the whole household is in a most uncomfortable state; for while she refuses obedience to others, she is equally insistent upon requiring instant compliance with all her demands. When the fit passes she is again gentle, merry and lovable. Now, my object in sending for you Miss Huntington, was, providing I was favorably impressed with you, to ask if you would consent to devote all your time to one pupil instead of several. The position will require a steady, persistent, even temperament—one of mingled gentleness and firmness—and I believe I see lines of decision in your face; you have a strong will, have you not?"

"I have been told that I have," Violet replied, smiling, "but"—growing very grave again—"whether I possess firmness sufficient to cope with the will you have described, I cannot say. I have never had any experience in the government of children; but I should say that tact would prove more effective in the management of your daughter than an obstinate insistence regarding obedience."

Mr. Lawrence's face lighted at this remark.

"That is the wisest observation that I have ever heard any governess make regarding the control of Bertha," he said. "Miss Huntington, will you make a trial of it for a while?"

Still Violet looked grave. She felt that the responsibility would be a great one, and she trembled for the result.

Yet her sympathies were enlisted both for this careworn, perplexed father, and for his afflicted child, while, too, the idea of a permanent, pleasant home was an attractive feature to her.

"Money would be no object," Mr. Lawrence continued, as she did not reply, "if the right person could be obtained, and if you could but achieve a strong influence over the child and sway her by tact, or by any other method, I would gladly give you any price you choose to name. Somehow I feel impelled to urge you to come to us—the very fact that you hesitate to accept the position assures me that you are wise in the consideration of all projects."

CHAPTER XXI.
VIOLET MAKES AN ENGAGEMENT.

Violet was deeply touched by the sad account to which she had listened. It seemed very hard that this poor child, who lived amid all this luxury, and who was surrounded with everything to make life delightful, should be so deprived of the enjoyment of it, and the young girl's heart yearned toward the unfortunate little heiress; her eyes grew moist and tender with pity; her face shone with a sincere sympathy, and the anxious father, as he watched her, felt an increasing desire to secure her services for his afflicted daughter.

"I fear that I am too young and inexperienced to assume such a responsibility," Violet began, at length. "Truth compels me to tell you frankly that I have never taught, and that only recent reverses have driven me to the necessity of earning my own living. Do you think that Miss Bertha's mother would approve— —"

She checked herself suddenly, for the expression of pain which swept over her companion's face warned her that she had touched upon a tender subject.

"I should have told you, to begin with, Miss Huntington, that Bertha has no mother—she died at the time of Bertha's birth, and my poor little girl has had to grow up without a mother's love or care," Mr. Lawrence replied, with evident emotion. "As far as your youthfulness is concerned," he resumed, after a moment of thought, "I am inclined to think that it is in your favor, and that you will succeed better with Bertha on that account. I am afraid that I have made a mistake heretofore in employing companions who were too mature to sympathize with her in her childish tastes and desires, as a younger person would perhaps have done. If you should decide in favor of the position, you would of course reside here with us, and your time would be chiefly occupied with Bertha, for she needs constant care. I would like her to have regular lessons—by that I mean you would have to read aloud what she was to learn, and talk it over with her until it became fixed in her memory. Then—your advertisement stated that you desired pupils in French; do you speak the language readily?"

"Yes, sir; I have studied years under a native teacher, while, during most of the past year I was abroad, the last four months I spent in Paris and devoted exclusively to perfecting myself in music and French."

"I am gratified to learn that," Mr. Lawrence said, "because I wish Bertha to be able to speak French as readily as she can English, as I intend to take her abroad at no distant day—to Paris—to see if something more cannot be done to improve her sight. As for music, you will have no difficulty in teaching her that, for the child is passionately fond of it, and is never so happy as when she is at the piano or organ. You perceive that you would have to be both teacher and companion—I hope I do not frighten you with all these requirements, Miss Huntington," the gentleman interposed, smiling, "but I wish you to fully understand, at the outset, what your duties will be. Do you object to giving up your plan of having a number of pupils and taking one instead?"

"Oh, no," Violet answered, thoughtfully; "I think, on the whole, that I should prefer to do so, if I were sure of my competency for the position. It appears a great responsibility to have the care and training of a motherless girl like Miss Bertha."

"Are you fond of children?" Mr. Lawrence inquired.

Violet's face lighted, as she replied:

"Yes, indeed, although I have been very little with them during my life; while my heart goes forth with a strange yearning toward your little daughter, and I believe I would really like to devote myself to her—at least, make the trial—and see if I cannot make the time pass agreeably and profitably to her."

Mr. Lawrence was very much gratified at this response. He saw that Violet was wholly sincere in what she said, while her apparent sympathy for his afflicted child touched him deeply.

"I am very much pleased to hear you say that," he remarked, with a genial smile, and Violet was greatly surprised that he did not ask for references regarding either her character or qualifications. "Now, would you like to see Bertha?" he asked. "I suppose we shall be obliged to secure her sanction to this arrangement, for, to be perfectly frank with you, her intuitions are very keen; she is a child of strong likes and dislikes, and unless she is favorably impressed with a person, it is almost impossible for that one to influence her."

Violet's heart sank at this, for if her future was to be governed by the capricious fancies of a willful child, she feared that a very trying experience lay before her.

Nevertheless she signified her desire to see this young autocrat, who appeared to exercise such supreme control in that household. Rising, she followed Mr. Lawrence from the room, up a wide, richly carpeted stair-way, to a large, sunny apartment which overlooked the busy street.

It was a very pleasant room, and furnished with every luxury and device to amuse, that the most exacting nature could desire.

In a large, richly upholstered chair, by one of the windows, sat a very pretty girl of about twelve years. She had a clear, beautiful complexion, with brown hair, rather massive features for one so young, but upon which there were plainly written great strength of will and decision of character; yet there was a sweet expression about her mouth which bespoke a loving nature, and at once attracted Violet.

Her eyes were blue, but it was evident that they were very defective in sight, though they were partially concealed by the glasses which she wore.

She was amusing herself with some gayly dressed dolls that lay upon another chair in front of her, while a maid sat near by, engaged in dressing another.

The child looked up eagerly as the door opened, for she had recognized her father's step; her lips wreathed with fond smiles, which plainly indicated that she was devotedly attached to him.

"Why, papa!" she exclaimed, in a tone of surprise; "I didn't know that you were at home. Did you bring me some candy? Who is that with you?" she added, quickly, as she caught the sound of Violet's light steps.

"I have brought you something far better than candy," her father responded, with a tender note in his voice; "I have invited a young lady to come up to see you. Miss Huntington, this is my little daughter, Bertha."

"Come here, Miss Huntington!" the child said, imperatively, and Violet went at once to her side, greeting her in her gentle voice.

"You are very good to come to see me," the child said, more courteously than she had previously spoken, for Violet's sweet tones had attracted her. "I like your voice. Put your face down and let me see it."

Violet knelt beside her chair, thus bringing her face on a level with Bertha's.

The young girl strained her gaze to get a view of it, but this not proving satisfactory, she passed her fingers lightly over Violet's delicate features, their touch lingering longest upon her sweet lips.

"You are lovely," she said, naively, after the examination. "Are you one of papa's especial friends?"

Violet smiled, and a dash of exquisite color shot into her cheeks at the form of the question.

"No, dear; I am simply here to ascertain if I will be a suitable governess and companion for you," she answered, thinking it best to come to the point at once.

"Oh!" and Miss Bertha's tone changed instantly. Evidently the subject of a governess was not an acceptable one to her. "I hate governesses; they are stiff and proper. Do you get cross and ill-natured when little girls don't mind you, Miss Huntington?"

Violet laughed out in her musical, merry way at this personal question.

"Because if you do," the child went on, gravely, "I don't want you. All my governesses have been cross and wouldn't let me do as I want to. What a nice smile you have!" she rambled on, her fingers lingering caressingly about Violet's mouth, "and you laugh out so prettily I like to hear it. You are pretty and—and nice, aren't you?"

"Perhaps it would be just as well, dear, not to discuss those points at present," Violet returned, with some embarrassment, for Mr. Lawrence's smiling eyes told her that he fully concurred in his daughter's admiring remarks; "but I hope I could never be cross or ill-natured toward any little girl," and the sudden tenderness that leaped into her tone seemed to add, as plainly as words could have done, "who could not see."

"I reckon you are nice," said Bertha, reflectively. "Do you like dolls?" she asked, as she laid her hand upon the group in her lap.

"Yes, indeed," and Violet laughed and flushed consciously. "Do you know," she added, confidentially, "after I became so old that I was ashamed to be seen playing with them, I used to beg to be allowed to dress them for fairs and for the children of my friends? Of course under those circumstances I could not be accused of playing with them, and yet, between you and me, I had a very nice time with them."

Violet thereupon began making some inquiries regarding the doll family before her, and quite an entertaining conversation was kept up for several minutes, greatly to the amusement of Mr. Lawrence and the maid, who had never before seen a would-be-governess put herself so *en rapport* with her prospective pupil. They had always seemed to think they must be "stiff" and "proper," as Bertha had said.

"Do you play the organ and piano, and can you sing?" Bertha inquired, eagerly, after the subject of dolls had been exhausted.

"Yes; would you like me to play you something?" Violet asked, as she began to draw off her gloves.

"Yes, yes!" cried the child, an earnest look of expectation and pleasure flashing into her face.

Violet went directly to a fine Steinway piano that was in the room, and without the slightest consciousness or embarrassment, thinking only of contributing to the young girl's employment, played a couple of selections with great expression and correctness.

"Now sing," commanded Miss Bertha, upon the conclusion of the second piece; and Violet sang a lovely little ballad in her clear, pure, cultivated tones.

There was not a sound in the room until the last note died away; then Bertha exclaimed, in a voice that thrilled with feeling:

"Oh, that was beautiful!"

Violet glanced at her, and saw that great tears were rolling down her cheeks, and she told herself that there must be much of good in a nature that could be so affected by music.

She could easily perceive that she had a strong will and was of a somewhat arbitrary temperament; but she believed that she had been antagonized and confirmed in these faults by unwise government.

She went again to her side, saying in a tender tone:

"You are fond of music, aren't you, dear?" and as she spoke she gently wiped her tears away with her own dainty handkerchief.

The child, moved by some sudden impulse, caught her hand and kissed it passionately.

"I like you, Miss Huntington, and you shall stay with me!" she cried.

"Bertha," interposed her father, reprovingly, "you should not speak in such a way, and that is a matter which Miss Huntington will have to decide for herself."

"Will you stay?" urged Bertha, appealingly, and still clinging to the hand she had kissed.

"Yes, dear, if you think that you could be happy with me," Violet answered, and Bertha asserted confidently that she could—that she should be unhappy without her, while she promised that she would "be good" and attentive to her lessons; that she would even "try real hard" to learn the multiplication table, which had hitherto been a sharp thorn in the flesh, and a bone of contention between herself and her former governesses.

Mr. Lawrence was very much pleased to observe how readily Violet appeared to acquire an influence over the willful, headstrong girl, who had in every previous instance rebelled against the engagement of a governess, and he felt that he would be very fortunate in securing her services.

"I am exceedingly gratified that you are willing to undertake the charge," he said, gratefully.

"I almost wonder at your willingness to trust her to me," Violet answered, smiling, yet her lips quivered slightly, for it seemed like a very sacred charge to her.

"On account of youth and inexperience, I suppose," he returned; then added, reassuringly: "But, as I said before, I believe that will be in your favor, although I warn you that you will have to exercise firmness and judgment at all times. But when can you come to us, Miss Huntington?"

"Whenever you wish," she replied.

"At once?—to-morrow?"

"Yes, sir; I have but to give up my lodgings and have my trunk removed."

"That will be perfectly delightful, papa," Bertha exclaimed, eagerly, "and you will sing and play to me; you will amuse me every day, will you not, Miss Huntington?"

"Yes, to a reasonable extent; but, in return, you will try faithfully to learn all that I wish to teach you?" stipulated Violet.

"Yes, I will try," the child said, earnestly, as she again pressed her lips to Violet's hand.

"Now, my pet, you will have to excuse us," said Mr. Lawrence, rising. "I have a few more arrangements to make with Miss Huntington, and we must not detain her longer."

"I wish you did not need to go at all," Bertha said, wistfully.

"Perhaps you will be wishing to send me away before a great while," Violet remarked, with a quiet laugh.

"No, indeed; I am sure I shall never want to give you up," persisted the child, confidently.

Violet bent to kiss the sweet face upraised to hers, and then followed Mr. Lawrence from the room, having first promised to "come early to-morrow."

CHAPTER XXII.
VIOLET AND HER UNRULY PUPIL.

Mr. Lawrence led Violet back to the reception-room below, remarking, as he courteously rolled a chair forward for her:

"I cannot tell you how pleased I am, Miss Huntington, with the cordial reception that Bertha has given you. It is seldom that she is so strongly attracted by a stranger, and if you can but retain your influence over her I am sure you cannot fail to do her good. I know that you will not be easily discouraged."

"To be 'forewarned is to be forearmed,' you know, sir," Violet smilingly responded; then she added more seriously, and with a firmness which told her companion that she was far from lacking in decision of character: "As I have already told you, I know but very little about teaching and less about governing, from personal experience, but, while I mean to do my duty faithfully and be all that is kind or considerate toward Miss Bertha, I believe it will be better for both of us, if I insist upon obedience and a cheerful compliance with my wishes—upon a regular routine, during certain hours of the day, after which I shall be pleased to attend to her pleasure and amusement."

Mr. Lawrence's smile told Violet that he approved of the course which she had suggested, even before he replied:

"I agree with you most heartily, Miss Huntington," he said, "and if you can, by any means, put your theory into practice, you will succeed in doing more than any one else has ever done. Bertha is perfectly well and strong, with the exception of her imperfect sight, and she ought to have regular duties; but she is so willful and obstinate at times that others have found it impossible to make her learn her lessons. She is naturally affectionate and tender-hearted, and good when she is not crossed; then there comes a severe trial of patience. But she is always repentant and remorseful after her willfulness until—she is crossed again. Now, what will you consider adequate remuneration for the giving up of your own plans and assuming the responsibility which I desire to commit to you?"

Violet regarded her companion with unfeigned surprise.

This was a new way of making terms with a governess, she thought—to request her to set her own price for her services.

"That is a matter which I supposed you would regulate yourself," she remarked, flushing slightly, "at least until we can ascertain whether I am to be successful in my position. I hope that Miss Bertha and I will get on very agreeably," she concluded, earnestly.

"I feel very sure that you will," Mr. Lawrence replied, confidently. "My family," he continued, "consists only of my daughter, my housekeeper, and myself, besides the servants. I fear it may be somewhat dull for you here, at times, as we live so quietly; but we will endeavor to make it as pleasant as possible for you. We will enter into no formal contract at present—I would not ask you to pledge yourself to remain any length of time, until you have an opportunity to realize what your duties and responsibilities will be; but if—while you do remain—a hundred dollars a quarter will be sufficient for your needs, I shall consider myself fortunate in securing your services for that amount."

"The sum will be ample, thank you," Violet returned, secretly thinking it a very generous offer, while she began to realize that she was also very fortunate in securing so pleasant a home and such a remunerative position, instead of having to trust to promiscuous pupils for her living.

Still, she knew that it would be no light task to have to be eyes for the blind, and subject to the willfulness and obstinacy of a capricious and over-indulged child. That there would be many severe trials in her position she did not doubt, but there would also be comfort in having the protection of a home, and, perhaps, the occasional companionship of a cultured gentleman like Mr. Lawrence.

She arose to take her leave now, and Mr. Lawrence himself accompanied her to the door instead of calling a servant to show her out.

He bade her a courteous good-day, saying he should hope to see her as early as convenient on the morrow, and offering to send his carriage for her if she would give him her address.

Violet thanked him, but declined his kind offer, for she was not quite sure at what hour she would be ready to leave her lodgings, as she had two or three errands to do in the morning.

But about eleven o'clock the next day she arrived at her future home, where she found Mr. Lawrence just going to his office down town.

He greeted her warmly, waiting until her trunk was brought in, and directed that it should be carried up to the blue room.

Then, as he was about leaving he remarked, with earnest hospitality:

"Pray make yourself perfectly at home, Miss Huntington, call upon the servants for anything you want, and command me at any time."

Violet thanked him, and then followed her trunk to the blue room, which she found to be a lovely apartment with an alcove, adjoining Bertha's sitting-room, and furnished with all the comfort and elegance to which she had been accustomed to all her life in her own home.

And now a strange, new life opened before her.

Hitherto she had lived a life of ease and pleasure; with plenty of money at her command, she had been able to gratify every whim or caprice; in her luxurious home, servants had waited upon her, and she had been petted and indulged, and, as a general thing, allowed to have her own way.

Now she was to serve and be subject to an arrogant and overbearing child.

She knew that her duties would call for unlimited patience and self-control, and now that she found the die was cast, she was almost appalled to think that she had dared to assume so much.

To all intents and purposes, she was alone in the world—separated and alienated from her sister and her husband; cut off, as she believed, by death, from her beloved young husband, she had no one to whom she could turn in any trouble or emergency.

But the varied experiences of the last four months had begun to develop powers within her, which she had never before dreamed that she possessed. She had grown strong, resolute, and self-reliant in character; she had learned to plan for herself financially, and to feel that life had been given to her for some other purpose than simple enjoyment and pleasure.

The gayety and impulsiveness which had characterized her previous to her troubles, had given place to a sweet and quiet dignity, a charming gentleness and grace which were very attractive, and so, with a brave, firm heart, and an unwavering trust in the strong Hand, on which she had begun to lean during her illness in Mrs. Richardson's home and under her influence, she bravely took up the burden of her lonely life, and resolved to do her very best in the trying position she had assumed.

But she had many sad hours, nevertheless; the bright past would sometimes arise, like some alluring phantom to remind her of her former happy, care-free life, and mock her in her present loneliness and sorrow, and for the time being the deep waters would seem to roll over her soul and threaten to swamp her beneath their cruel waves.

But she never yielded to such depression long—her bruised heart would always rise above her sorrow after a time, and turn with trusting confidence to the Comforter in whom her faith was every day growing stronger.

Bertha Lawrence, as has been seen from her father's account, had been an over-indulged child all her life.

From the hour when he had first discovered the dreadful fact that his motherless little girl was blind—a discovery which had nearly unsettled his reason—he had felt that the devotion of himself and all that he possessed could not make up to her for the loss of her sight, and he had spared nothing that would contribute to her comfort or enjoyment. He had literally showered luxuries and expensive gifts upon her from the very first, and once, when a friend had chided him for his lavishness and extravagance, he had replied that he "should regard a fortune as well spent if it would give her pleasure."

This, of course, was mistaken kindness, though prompted by tenderest love, for pleasure and unlimited gratification palled upon her after a while, and this course of indulgence only developed a selfish spirit and an unusually strong will, which she had inherited from both parents.

If she was crossed ever so lightly, a spirit of antagonism and obstinacy was instantly aroused, which it sometimes took days to overcome, and was often made worse by servile coaxing and bribing on the part of those who had the care of her, this being considered the easiest way to get along with her.

Violet had a trial of this nature not very many days after she assumed her duties as companion, and governess, and how she met it will be developed.

Miss Bertha always took her breakfast in her private sitting-room, because, as she retired early, she awoke earlier in the morning than the other members of the family, and it was thought best that she should not wait to eat with them.

When Violet learned this, she at once said that she would take her breakfast with her charge, if it would be agreeable to her.

Bertha thought this was very kind, and a delightful arrangement, and for a few days everything moved along harmoniously.

But one morning there came a storm to dispel this unusual calm.

Bertha had given orders for something that she particularly wanted for breakfast, but through some misunderstanding or oversight, it was not provided, although the table was very nicely laid with broiled chicken, hot rolls, Lyonnaise potatoes, and an omelet, the latter usually being a favorite with the young lady.

"Where are my oysters?" Miss Bertha demanded, with a frown, after the servant had named over the various viands upon the table, and she discovered that her order had been ignored.

"The man did not bring them, Miss Bertha," the girl answered.

"But I want some broiled oysters," persisted the unreasonable child.

"I am very sorry, I am sure——" began the servant, when Bertha interrupted her, angrily:

"That doesn't make any difference; I'm going to have the oysters, and I shall not eat any breakfast until I get them."

A threat of this kind usually resulted in somebody flying around to procure the desired delicacy, for the child was stubborn enough to keep her word, and it was believed it would never do to allow one born to such luxury to fast.

"I am sure this is a very nice breakfast, Bertha," Violet here interposed. "This broiled chicken is delicious; those hot rolls are just a lovely brown, and the sight of that golden omelet makes my mouth water."

But Bertha would not be coaxed—that had been tried too often already without avail. She threw herself back in her chair, a sullen, determined look on her face.

"Come, dear; I am really quite hungry," persevered Violet, as she took her by the hand to lead her to the table.

Bertha snatched it rudely away.

"I do not want any breakfast," she pouted.

"But it is very nice, and you can have the oysters to-morrow morning," urged Violet.

"I want them now. Mary, send John for them at once, and then have them cooked immediately," the child commanded, arbitrarily.

"But, miss, it would take a long time, and you would be half famished before you got your breakfast," remonstrated Mary.

"I don't care; I will have them!" Bertha insisted, passionately.

"No, dear, not this morning," Violet said, kindly, but firmly, and thinking it best to take matters into her own hands and settle them once for all. "Mary, roll Miss Bertha's chair to the table, and we will eat what we have."

The girl turned to obey, but Bertha struck at her, saying that she was to be let alone; she would not have any breakfast.

Violet thought a moment; then, with a significant glance at the servant, she said, quietly:

"Very well, Mary; if Miss Bertha does not care to eat, of course she need not. I will, however, have my breakfast now, as this nice chicken will be getting cold. You may pour out a cup of coffee for me, if you please."

She seated herself at the table and began to help herself to the various viands, and entirely ignoring the presence of the sulky girl on the other side of the room.

The servant looked very much amused at this new departure, while Bertha appeared speechless from astonishment.

She had never been dealt with in this manner before, and did not exactly know how to meet such treatment.

Violet was assured, and indeed Mr. Lawrence had told her, that Bertha was a perfectly well child; therefore, she thought it would do her no harm to fast, and she was not at all troubled by her refusal to eat, at least not more so than what the unpleasant occurrence caused her to feel.

She proceeded quietly with her own employment, talking a little now and then with Mary, but not once addressing Bertha.

When she finished her meal, she asked, as a matter of form merely:

"Bertha, is there anything you would like from the table before Mary removes the service?"

"No; I want my oysters," was the pouting reply.

"Very well; then, Mary, you may take the things away, and you can tell the cook that we will have the broiled oysters to-morrow morning," Violet said, composedly.

Bertha lifted her head, a look of blank dismay written on every feature. Her face flushed an angry red, but apparently she did not know just what to do under the circumstances, and so continued to remain sulkily silent.

She was too proud and obstinate to succumb and eat anything, although the cravings of her healthful appetite were making themselves keenly felt, and so the tempting breakfast was removed.

When the servant finally disappeared, after brushing up and putting the room in order, Bertha's passion broke all bounds.

She threw herself prone upon the floor, and began to cry and sob violently.

Violet paid no attention, however, to this outbreak, but taking up a book, appeared to be reading, although she was so excited and troubled by this first conflict with her pupil that she was unconscious that her book was upside down.

The child cried for nearly half an hour, and not one word was spoken during that time. At last Bertha arose from her prostrate position, and moved toward the electric button which governed a bell in the kitchen.

"What are you going to do, Bertha?" Violet quietly asked.

"I am going to have my oysters," was the sullen yet determined reply.

"No, dear, you cannot have any oysters this morning; you must wait for them until to-morrow," Violet said, with a ring of decision in her tone which plainly indicated that there would be no repeal of the sentence. "If you are really hungry, Mary may bring you a cup of chocolate and some toast."

"I hate chocolate and toast, and I want my breakfast. Nobody ever dared to treat me so before. I will have oysters," she concluded, shrieking out those last words passionately.

Violet made no reply, and the child stood irresolute for a few moments, then threw herself into a chair and began to swing her feet back and forth violently, kicking the frame with every movement.

This uncomfortable state of affairs lasted until the clock struck nine, when Violet laid aside her book, saying, pleasantly, and as if nothing unusual had happened:

"Come, Bertha, it is time for our lessons."

She arose and wheeled the small table, upon which their text books were always kept, toward the bay-window where Bertha liked to sit, and seating herself, took up a history and began to read aloud, as was her custom.

"No," cried Bertha, in an irritating tone, "I am not going to have any lessons this morning. I want my breakfast."

Violet was astonished at such persistent obstinacy in one so young; but she was determined that she would not yield to it. She felt that if she conquered in this first conflict she would be reasonably sure to come off victor in other encounters, while if she allowed herself to be beaten she might as well give up her position at once, for she would be able to do the child no earthly good without a curbing influence over her.

So she went quietly on with her reading, whereupon Miss Bertha clapped her hands over her ears as if to shut out the sound of her teacher's voice.

Violet was not going to waste her breath reading to the four walls, so she shut and laid down her book with a heavy sigh, and wondering how long this would last, and what she ought to do next.

CHAPTER XXIII.
VIOLET GAINS A SIGNAL VICTORY.

The child was only pretending not to hear.

She caught the sound of her much-tried companion's sigh, and instantly her lips began to twitch and curve slightly in a smile that had suspicion of triumph in it.

Violet saw it, and instantly the lines about her own mouth grew firmer and more resolute.

"She thinks to tire me out and gain her point," she said to herself, "but I am going to settle who is to rule, once for all, for if I cannot have her respectful obedience it will be useless for me to remain here."

She arose and passed into her own room, but presently returned bringing with her a dainty little basket in which there lay some fancy-work and bright flosses.

Resuming her seat by the window, she busied herself with her embroidery, apparently oblivious of the fact that there was any one else in the room.

The hour that followed was tedious in the extreme to both teacher and pupil, for not one single word was spoken during that time.

When the clock struck ten—the hour generally devoted to music—Violet arose, and, going to the piano, began to play.

Instantly Bertha's chubby hands went up to her ears again, but her young teacher, without appearing to notice the movement, kept on, and did a faithful half-hour's practice for herself.

Then she began to sing a sweet little ballad which she had learned soon after her mother's death. It was plaintive, and told the story of a lonely little heart longing for mother-love, and she had not reached the end of the second verse when she saw the tears streaming over Bertha's little face, and knew that her wedge had entered the obstinate little soul.

Still she pretended to ignore her, keeping on with her song until she had finished it, then she went back to her work in the window.

Presently a timid, somewhat uncertain voice said:

"Miss Huntington."

"Well, dear."

"May—may I have oysters for my lunch?"

"Ah! those oysters! Were ever such tender things so hard to be disposed of?" But she took courage from the form of the request and the appealing tone.

"No, dear," she quietly answered.

"Why?" imperatively.

"Because I have said, once, that you cannot have them, and have given Mary orders to provide them for your breakfast to-morrow morning," was the calm response; then she added: "Now, let us talk no more about the unpleasant subject, but attend to our duties. It is time for your geography lesson."

"I do not want my geography. I must do my history first," was the rebellious response.

"The history hour is past, and will not come again until to-morrow," Violet replied.

She knew that the child was very much interested in her history—she always listened attentively while she read it to her, and seldom had to be prompted in repeating it; but the lessons had all been assigned for certain hours in the day, and she did not intend to break her rules or be governed by the caprices of this spoiled girl of twelve.

"I don't care; I shall not do my geography until I have done my history," retorted Bertha, angrily.

"Bertha," said Violet, gravely, "we are going to do the lessons in their regular order every day, for if we jumble things we shall never have any system. Now, I hope you are going to do right, because only those who do their duty are happy. I know you are unhappy now because you have done wrong this morning, and it makes me sad also. We did not begin the day just as we should, but let us go on and finish it as well as we can, and try to do better to-morrow."

"No-o; if I cannot do my history, I shall not do anything else," the girl answered, defiantly.

"Very well," Violet said, coldly, "then there will be no lessons to-day, nor reading of any kind."

"Oh! aren't you going to read to me from that nice book that papa brought to me yesterday?" Bertha demanded, anxiously.

"No, I cannot read to any little girl who will not obey me."

"I never obey anybody but papa," was the pouting rejoinder.

"Your father wishes you to obey me, Bertha, and—if you do not I shall be obliged to go away. I shall never ask you to do anything save what I believe to be right, and if you cannot give me your obedience I shall have to find some other little girl to teach."

A look of dismay passed over Bertha's face for a moment; but having always won the victory in all previous battles with other governesses, she imagined that she would win this, eventually.

"I don't care—I am not going to do any lessons today," she said, shortly, and Violet felt severely tried—indeed, almost discouraged.

But she had made up her mind not to yield her point, and so kept quietly on with her work.

Bertha brought out her dolls and began to play with them, and for a couple of hours she managed to get on very well. At the end of that time she grew tired of being so by herself, and begged Violet to read to her.

"Come here, Bertha, if you please," Violet said, without replying directly to her question.

Bertha, wondering at the grave tone, went and stood before her teacher.

"Can you see my face, dear?" she asked.

"Yes," the child said, peering up at her curiously.

"Can you see my eyes?"

"Yes, I see them," Bertha replied, bringing her face very close to Violet's.

"Tell me how they look."

"They look kind of—sorry, and your face is like papa's when he is grieved and displeased with me."

"I am sorry and grieved; more grieved than I can tell you, to have had this trouble with my little friend," Violet said, sadly. "You know, dear, that you are not doing right, and that I should be doing you wrong and injury to let you have your own way. You would not respect me or believe me truthful if I should give up to you. I have told you just how the lessons must go on, and I shall make no change, and if you cannot do as I wish, you must amuse yourself as best you can."

"And you will not read me any stories at all today?" and there was a suspicious tremor in the young tones, for the child dearly loved this recreation, and Violet was a very entertaining reader.

"No; the stories only come after lessons, you know."

Bertha went thoughtfully back to her dolls, and played by herself until luncheon was brought up, when she sat down at the table and ate heartily, for by this time she was very hungry.

No mention was made of oysters, and Violet earnestly hoped that that battle would not have to be fought over again.

After luncheon, blocks and other playthings were called into service, and the child busied herself with them during the greater part of the afternoon.

Now and then she would ask some question of Violet, who answered kindly and pleasantly, but always without looking up from her work or appearing to be in the least interested in Bertha's employment.

When twilight began to gather, Bertha left her toys and came to sit down by her teacher—who had now laid aside her work—her young face wearing a very sober look. After a while she slipped one hand into that of Violet, who clasped it kindly and drew her still nearer.

"Will you please sing me something, Miss Huntington?" the child asked, after a while.

"I should be very glad to, Bertha, but I cannot today," was the grave reply.

Nothing further was said upon that subject, and presently they fell to talking in a quiet, social way, and this was kept up until dinner was announced, when Violet and her pupil went down, as was their custom, to eat with Mr. Lawrence.

"How have the lessons been getting on to-day, little daughter?" Mr. Lawrence inquired during the meal, and observing that Bertha was more quiet than usual.

The child grew suddenly crimson, hesitated a moment, and then said:

"I didn't feel much like lessons to-day. Will you take me out for a drive to-morrow, papa?"

It was evident to all that Miss Bertha wished to change the subject introduced by her father, and Mr. Lawrence smiled as he glanced significantly at Violet, thus showing that he understood there had been trouble in the school-room.

"Perhaps so, dear," he answered. "We will see how the lessons get on to-morrow," and then he began talking of other things.

After dinner, however, he asked Violet if there had been any disturbance, and she gave him a truthful account of all that had occurred, remarking, as she concluded:

"I believed that if I could be firm at the outset and make the dear child understand that I must have her obedience, it would be better for all of us. If I had allowed her to conquer me in this, I am convinced that it would have been but the beginning of trouble, and I could be of but little service to her."

"You are right, Miss Huntington," Mr. Lawrence said, bestowing a glance of approbation upon her, and secretly well pleased with this evidence of her decision of character, "and it would have been far better if Bertha had had a firm rule like this from early childhood. All her other governesses have yielded to her, and I fear I have not carried as steady a hand with her as I should have done. Keep on as you have begun, Miss Huntington, and you will secure my unbounded gratitude, if you can conquer this singular obstinacy which has seemed to possess the child all her life."

Violet was much relieved to find that he regarded her course of action so sensibly, and she felt strengthened to go on as she had begun.

The next morning the much-contested oysters appeared upon the breakfast-table, and they were broiled to a delicious flavor.

No remark was made about them until Violet put a bountiful supply upon a plate and told Mary to pass them to Miss Bertha.

"I do not want any oysters, and I shall not eat any," that young lady asserted, much to Violet's dismay, for she had flattered herself that there would be no trouble on that question that morning.

"Then give them to me, if you please, Mary," she quietly said, then helped Bertha to a nice bit of steak, which she requested the girl to cut up for her.

"I wonder if we are going to have yesterday's experience repeated," the young teacher said to herself, but she could see by the expression on Bertha's face that she was greatly disappointed at being taken at her word. She had evidently expected to be coaxed to eat her oysters, and when she was not, she was ashamed to ask for them. "I am sorry for her," thought Violet, with a sigh, "but I do believe the lesson will do her good, and will never need to be repeated."

She began to chat pleasantly upon other subjects, and the meal was finished in the most friendly manner.

At nine o'clock Violet took up the history, and began to read the neglected lesson of yesterday, while Bertha paid earnest attention to every word, after which she gave a very clear account of what she had heard.

She then went to her practice without a word of objection, and performed her work faithfully, after which her other lessons were taken up as usual.

All during the day she was obedient and respectful, and when the lessons were completed, Violet, with a tenderer feeling for her than she had yet experienced, read her the most charming story that she could find.

By the middle of the afternoon Mr. Lawrence paid them a visit, and finding his daughter in a sunnier mood than usual, looked the pleasure he felt.

He told them that he had come to take them to drive in Central Park, and a few minutes after they were rolling rapidly out toward that beautiful spot, behind a pair of handsome bays.

That evening, just before it was time for Bertha to retire, she stole softly to Violet's side, wound her arms about her neck, and, peering eagerly into her face, shyly remarked:

"Miss Huntington, your eyes do not look 'sorry' tonight."

"No, indeed, dear; they ought to look very bright and happy, after such a delightful day as we have had," Violet answered.

"It has been a good day, hasn't it?" Bertha questioned, laying her head fondly on her teacher's shoulder.

"Yes, and all days will be 'good days,' if we do right," was the gentle response, as Violet passed her arm around the child and drew her closer to her.

"I wonder, Miss Huntington, if you will get to love me by and by," Bertha said, wistfully, after a little pause.

"I love you now, dear," was the sweet-voiced assurance.

"Truly."

"Yes, truly and dearly," and a soft kiss emphasized the statement.

"But— —"

"But what, Bertha?"

"You didn't love me yesterday."

"Oh, yes, I did, my dear child."

"How could you? It did not seem like love when you were so—so stern and set."

"I certainly should not have shown love for you it I had allowed you to have your own way."

"Shall you always be so?"

"'So'—how?"

"Why, set—determined."

"I hope I shall always be firm enough to do what is right, dear."

"Is it right to make little girls do what they do not want to?"

"Yes, if what they wish to do is wrong."

"Don't you ever say 'yes,' when you have once said 'no,' Miss Huntington?"

"I do not mean to, Bertha, for I am afraid that a certain little girl, whom I know, would not trust or respect me if I should," Violet answered, gravely.

"I love you," said the child, impulsively, and Violet felt that she had won no mean victory, and the one influence of which would be felt as long as she retained her present position.

Those three simple, earnest words told her that, by continuing firm during their recent contest, she had gained an influence and hold upon the young girl's heart that she would never lose, and she resolved to persevere in the course she had laid out for herself.

It was easy to resolve when her pupil was in such a delightful mood, but it was not so easy to execute, and Violet had to exercise all the patience and self-control of which she was possessed, for during the next few weeks there were several repetitions of willfulness and obstinacy on the part of her pupil, although she never held out so long again and was more easily conquered each time.

She finally seemed to realize that her governess meant just what she said—that sooner or later she must yield her the obedience which she demanded; and after a while it became evident to Violet that she was really trying to conquer her antagonistic disposition, and was truly anxious to please her.

There were many struggles and many failures, for over-indulgence had pampered her disposition and fostered a selfishness which was not easily mastered; but the strong will was now being bent in the right direction, and the fruits of firmness and decision were making themselves manifest; while, as Violet was always patient and gentle, tender in reproof, and sympathetic whenever Bertha manifested sorrow, the child gradually grew to love her almost to idolatry.

Six months after the young teacher took up her abode in that elegant home, one would hardly have recognized the docile, obedient child, and every one in the house marveled at the change in her.

Study grew delightful to her; she made rapid progress in her music, and became so gentle and courteous to the servants, so affectionate and companionable with her father, that she was like a sunbeam in the house.

CHAPTER XXIV.
VIOLET MEETS WITH AN ACCIDENT.

Violet's life became more and more pleasant as time went on. Her pupil continued to make marked and steady progress in her studies, while in music she was becoming wonderfully proficient. She also grew more cheerful and equable in temperament, and Mr. Lawrence was constantly congratulating himself upon having secured such a treasure for a governess.

He was not long in discovering, also, that she was a very cultivated young woman and exceedingly companionable as well, for, while Violet was conscientious in the discharge of her duties toward her charge, she did not neglect any opportunity to improve herself.

She took up a course of reading which could not fail to expand her mind and enlarge her views of life; kept herself informed regarding passing events, while she devoted the greater portion of her evenings, after Bertha had retired, to music, both vocal and instrumental.

No one who had known her in the old days in Cincinnati would have believed it possible that she could have changed in so short a time from a careless girl into this self-contained yet gracious woman, who charmed every one with her sweet dignity, her beautiful face, and cultured conversation, and Mr. Lawrence was not slow to appreciate his good fortune in having so lovely a woman in his home.

"She would grace the highest position in the land," he told himself, one night, when, at his request, she had presided over his table at a select dinner party, bearing herself with so much ease and grace, and displaying so much tact, that he was charmed and his guests eloquent in their praises of her.

From that time he began to show her, in a quiet way, numberless little attentions. If he heard her express a desire, it was unostentatiously gratified within twenty-four hours. If she mentioned a book or picture, it appeared as if by magic—the one among the collection upon Bertha's shelves, the other somewhere upon the walls of her sitting-room, while every day the choicest of flowers found their way, by some unseen agency, to the little table which was devoted to Violet's especial use.

Once or twice every week Mr. Lawrence would come home to luncheon, bringing opera or theater tickets for a matinee, and though Bertha and the housekeeper were always included in these pleasures, for form's sake, it was evident that the gentleman was most anxious to contribute to the enjoyment of the fair governess, for he always managed to ascertain her preference, and in this way Violet had opportunity to hear the best histrionic and musical talent.

Every pleasant afternoon he would plan a drive or a visit to some picture-gallery or museum of art for her and Bertha, who, notwithstanding her imperfect sight, enjoyed listening to a description of the beautiful and interesting things about her, while it was something new and delightful to have her papa such a devoted and faithful attendant.

One day, for a change, they drove out to one of the reservoirs which supply New York city with water.

Violet had been unusually happy all the week; her pleasant life, the kind care and attention so constantly thrown around her, all contributed to make the world seem a very delightful place once more, even though its chief joy and light for her had been removed.

She and Bertha had been in an unusually gay mood for them, and Mr. Lawrence thought he had never seen Miss Huntington look so pretty and appear so charming.

Her musical laugh, her ready repartee, her bright and animated countenance, amused and cheered him, making him feel younger by a score of years than he really was.

They rode about the reservoir, over the broad smooth drives for a while, and then Bertha begged that they might get out and walk about, for she wanted to get nearer the water.

Mr. Lawrence, always willing to indulge her, acceded to her request, and all three alighting, he told the coachman to drive slowly about until he should signal for him.

Then they spent half an hour or more strolling along the water's edge, to Bertha's great enjoyment, after which Violet expressed a wish to see the inside of the gatehouse, for she had never had an opportunity to visit one.

They proceeded thither, it being quite near, and, Mr. Lawrence having obtained permission of the keeper, they went in to view the huge vaults, together with the massive engine, by which the engineer controlled the waters which swept with such ceaseless roar through the caverns below and on toward their various channels in the city.

They all became very much interested in watching the ponderous machinery, and there was a strange fascination in the endless hurry and rush of the water beneath them.

But all at once, nobody could ever tell afterward how it happened, Bertha made a misstep, and would have fallen beneath the railing and in among the machinery had not Violet darted forward, seized her by her clothing, and drawn her quickly out of harm's way. In doing so, however, she herself fell, or was thrown, with great force against the railing, and when Mr. Lawrence led them both farther away, she was very pale and quivering from head to foot, from mingled pain and fright.

"Are you hurt, Bertha?" she asked, bending over the weeping girl, who had been terribly startled by the accident.

"I guess not, but—oh! my heart beats so I cannot breathe," she panted, in reply.

"I am very glad—I—was—afraid——"

Violet could get no further, but reeled dizzily, and would have fallen if Mr. Lawrence had not sprung to her side, and, throwing his arm about her slight form, asked, with great anxiety:

"What is it, Miss Huntington—are you hurt?"

"My arm," Violet murmured, with white lips, and, glancing down, he saw that her left arm was hanging helplessly by her side.

"Ah! you must have hurt it when you fell against the railing," he said, his face and tone both expressing great concern. Then he added: "Can you lift it? Can you move it?"

Violet made an effort to do so, but the pain it produced was intolerable, and the next moment she was lying unconscious in Mr. Lawrence's arms.

He laid her gently upon the floor, and took advantage of her insensibility to make an examination of the injured member, when, to his consternation, he discovered that it was broken just above the elbow.

Bidding Bertha stay close beside her teacher, he then darted out of the building, and, his carriage fortunately being within hailing distance, he signaled for the coachman to come there.

Without waiting for Violet to recover consciousness, he, with the assistance of one of the men who belonged in the gate-house, lifted her into the carriage, placing her as comfortably as possible upon one of the seats, and then bade the coachman drive with all possible speed back to the city.

Mr. Lawrence had saturated his handkerchief with water before starting, and now devoted himself to the task of reviving the insensible girl, by bathing her face, and chafing her uninjured hand to restore circulation.

Violet soon began to come to herself, but only to experience intense suffering, while her bruised and broken arm had begun to swell frightfully.

"This is very unfortunate—I am very sorry," Mr. Lawrence said, deep solicitude expressed in both tone and countenance, while Bertha sat beside him weeping silently from sympathy.

Violet tried to bear her pain with fortitude. She made no outward demonstration or complaint; but her colorless face, contracted brow, and the wild look in her eyes betrayed but too plainly that her suffering was excruciating.

The fleet horses made good time, and in less than an hour they were home.

Violet was tenderly lifted from the carriage and borne to her own room, whither the housekeeper and servants were summoned to attend her, while Mr. Lawrence himself went for a surgeon.

Mrs. Davis was a kind and motherly woman, and seemed to know just what needed to be done in this emergency. She cut away the sleeve of Violet's dress and underclothing, thus releasing the wounded arm from its painful bondage, and then wrapped it in wet cloths to reduce the swelling and allay the inflammation.

Twenty minutes after a skillful surgeon was on the spot, ether was administered to his patient, then the broken bone was quickly and nicely set, the arm bandaged, and Doctor Ashley declared that it would be as good as new in the course of three or four weeks.

When Violet came to herself again, the agonizing pain which she had suffered before the administration of ether was gone, and though she was weak and feverish, she was comparatively comfortable.

But the shock to her system had been severe, and she was obliged to keep her bed for several days, although she told Mrs. Davis and

Bertha that it was simply a pleasure to be sick when every one was so kind and attentive to her.

Of course Mr. Lawrence did not see her during this time, and he began to be conscious of an oppressive feeling of loneliness; the house seemed empty, desolate, without her.

This sensation followed him everywhere he went; at table he could not eat as usual, while his glance constantly roved to Violet's empty chair. In his library, where usually he could find plenty of entertainment, and even in Bertha's sitting-room, where he spent much time trying to amuse her, and to make up to her as much as possible for the loss of her companion, he was conscious of something wanting.

"If I miss her like this for a few days, what shall I do if she ever goes away to stay?" he asked himself one evening, when he was feeling more lonely than usual.

A wave of hot color mounted to his brow; then receding as quickly, left his face blanched with a sudden discovery and an unaccountable feeling of dread.

"What is all this?" he muttered, half angrily; "am I, after all these years, going to lose my head over a girl not half my age?"

He sprang to his feet and began to pace the floor with a nervous, uncertain tread, while during the next few days he appeared as if oppressed by some heavy burden.

Before a week had passed from the day of Violet's accident, she was up and anxious to resume her usual duties.

Mr. Lawrence went up stairs, one morning, to Bertha's room to amuse the child, as he had been doing of late, and found the young teacher sitting beside her pupil at the piano, trying to direct her practice, and his fine face at once assumed a look of undisguised disapproval, even though Violet glanced up and bade him a smiling good-morning.

"My dear Miss Huntington, this will not do at all," he said, gravely; "you are not to try your strength or take up your regular duties until your arm is entirely well, and you have fully recovered from the effects of your injury."

"But, I assure you, I am feeling nicely. If this left hand of mine was only at liberty, I should be wholly myself again," Violet replied, bending a regretful look upon the helpless member in its sling.

"That may be; but I am nevertheless going to prohibit all lessons, at least until you can dispense with this," the gentleman replied, as he softly touched the spotless handkerchief suspended about her neck.

"What shall we do with ourselves, Bertha, if papa is going to be so tyrannical?" asked Violet, in a tone of mock despair, but bestowing at the same time a grateful glance upon her patron for his consideration.

"The days are very long, papa, when I don't attend to my lessons with Miss Huntington," Bertha said, with a sigh; "but I love her so well that I do not want her to do anything to make herself ill."

"That is my good girl," Mr. Lawrence replied, heartily; "but I imagine we can arrange everything satisfactorily. Suppose we begin by seeing what we can do with the two hours between now and lunch-time," and he drew a new book from one of his pockets as he spoke; "I think I have something nice here for you both."

He wheeled an easy-chair into the bay-window, where the sun shone in most invitingly, and made Violet occupy it; then, with Bertha on a hassock at his feet, he began to read a recent and extremely interesting story.

The two hours slipped by on magic wings and then, as Mary appeared with a tray of tempting viands, Mr. Lawrence invited himself to lunch with them, and they had a right merry time together as they ate.

A little later he ordered the carriage, and they all went for a drive, returning just in time to prepare for dinner.

Violet had not dined with the family since her injury, for, having only one hand at her command, she was sensitive about appearing awkward. But to-day Mr. Lawrence particularly requested that she would favor them with her presence again, if she felt able to come down.

She flushed.

"I am so helpless——" she began, when he interrupted her, saying, with a strange note in his voice, which she had never heard before:

"And for that very reason, I wish to make myself useful to you; besides, Bertha and I are very lonely without you."

The color grew deeper upon Violet's cheek, for both his look and tone were very earnest; but she promised to come down to dine with them, and then ran up to her room to make some slight change in her attire.

During dinner Mr. Lawrence was kindly attentive. He cut her meat for her, and unostentatiously prepared whatever would be awkward for her to manage, talking all the while upon some entertaining subject, and made himself so agreeable and helpful throughout the meal that Violet was glad that she had consented to resume her place at the table.

After that she came down every day, and grew quite used to having him care for her, and found it very pleasant, too.

"He is like a dear, kind father, only a great deal more thoughtful and attentive than most fathers would be," she told herself, when thinking it over afterward, and how he had interposed in every way to prevent her from feeling awkward in accepting his attentions.

Mr. Lawrence kept his word—he would allow no more lessons while she was crippled, but planned some amusement or pleasant trip for every day, until she was entirely well.

Once she remonstrated against the idle life she was leading.

"Mr. Lawrence," she said, "I do not feel right about this. I ought to be at work—I am not earning my salt."

"And why should you?" he asked, gravely.

"But I came here to perform certain duties, and I am doing nothing but playing—just drifting along, and having a pleasant time," she explained.

"I hope so; but I am very sorry if you feel any weight of obligation, when that should rest upon me," he returned, in the same tone as before. "Miss Huntington, do you imagine that it is nothing to me that you saved my child from some serious accident—perhaps from death? Do you think me so ungrateful as not to wish to do everything possible for you, when you have suffered so much in your efforts to save her? I hope we shall hear no more about your earning your salt—that, and everything else, has been already earned a good many times over," he concluded, with a luminous smile.

Violet had not thought of it in this way before, but she was effectually silenced, and objected no more at anything he chose to do for her.

One rainy morning, they had an unusually merry time over a humorous story which Mr. Lawrence read to them.

"What a jolly time we are having, papa!" Bertha remarked, with a long-drawn breath of content, when the story was concluded.

"You are right, pet, and I only hope you will always be as happy," her father returned, fondly, as he stroked her glossy hair.

"Of course, I am sorry that Miss Huntington's arm had to be broken," the child continued, naively, "but we have had such a delightful time during these last three weeks that I wish it could always last, don't you?"

"It would be very pleasant, Bertha," said her father, musingly.

"I think we three make just the nicest chums," the little miss went on; "wouldn't it be fine if we could stay so and always be together?"

Mr. Lawrence's fine eyes were resting upon the fair face of his child's governess at that moment, and there was a strangely wistful look in them, a tender, tremulous expression about his handsome mouth, also.

"It would, indeed, dear," he said, more as if speaking to himself than in answer to her, but in such an intensely earnest tone that it sent a sudden thrill through Violet's heart.

Involuntarily she lifted her eyes, met his look, and something in it made the hot blood come surging up to her brow and lose itself amid the waves of golden hair that lay in such pretty confusion there.

"Don't you wish so, too, Miss Huntington?" Bertha questioned, turning to her, and all unconscious that she was treading upon delicate ground.

Violet's eyes drooped, and she turned to the window to hide the vivid color in her cheeks.

She hesitated a moment before replying to the child's question, then she said, in a low, quiet voice:

"I have been very happy since I came to stay with you, dear."

The further trials and experiences of Violet and how her future happiness was secured is told in the sequel to this story entitled "With Heart So True," and is published in handsome cloth binding uniform with this volume.

THE END.

Lightning Source UK Ltd.
Milton Keynes UK
UKHW010740150822
407319UK00001B/240